Praise for *Miss Invisible*

Every double-digit-jean-sized girl will love Laura Jensen Walker's latest fiction send-up! Walker's witty dialogue and tasty food references are thoroughly satisfying but it is her oh-so-believable Freddie, Miss Invisible herself, who triumphs in this entertaining read. Trust me, you'll read this in record time and recommend it to real women and real friends everywhere—even those single-digit chics in jeans!

—Julie Barnhill, author of *She's Gonna Blow!*,
Scandalous Grace, and *One Tough Mother*

Laura Jensen Walker can take an ordinary life and make it into an extraordinary story. Once you meet Freddie you won't want to say goodbye. *Miss Invisible* is captivating, emotionally moving, and outrageously funny.

—Rene Gutteridge, author of *Scoop* and *My Life as a Doormat*

Miss Invisible delivers a tale of life in the plus-sized girl's lane. At once witty and moving, readers will find this story appealing regardless of whether one's experience with being overweight is firsthand or second-hand by way of a friend or loved one. Bravo, Laura!

—Tamara Leigh, author of *Stealing Adda* and *Perfecting Kate*

Miss Invisible is anything but! Between the layers of this story of a wall-flower wedding cake baker is a truth every woman needs to hear—no one is invisible to God. Fredericka's struggles to be seen in her world of small-minded men (and small-waisted women) made me laugh and cry. This book is definitely some serious fun! Don't miss it.

—Marilynn Griffith, author of *If the Shoe Fits* and *Made of Honor*

miss invisible

Also by Laura Jensen Walker

miss invisible

• • • •

Laura Jensen Walker

Published by
THOMAS NELSON
Since 1798

www.thomasnelson.com

Published in Nashville, Tennessee, Thomas Nelson, Inc.

Thomas Nelson, Inc. titles may be purchased in bulk for educational, business, fundraising, or sales promotional use. For information, please e-mail SpecialMarkets@ThomasNelson.com.

The following scriptures are quoted in this book and are from the HOLY BIBLE, NEW INTERNATIONAL VERSION,. Copyright © 1973, 1978, 1984 by International Bible Society. Used by permission of Zondervan. All rights reserved:
Chapter 4: Psalm 34:8
Chapter 10: Psalm 37:8–9
Chapter 24: Matthew 12:48–49

Publisher's Note: This novel is a work of fiction. Names, characters, places, and incidents are either products of the author's imagination or used fictitiously. All characters are fictional, and any similarity to people living or dead is purely coincidental.

Library of Congress Cataloging-in-Publication Data

Walker, Laura Jensen.
  Miss Invisible / Laura Jensen Walker.
    p. cm.
  ISBN-13: 978-1-59554-068-3 (pbk.)
  ISBN-10: 1-59554-068-7 (pbk.)
  1. Overweight women—Fiction. 2. Bakers—Fiction. I. Title.
  PS3623.A3595M57 2007
  813'.54—dc22

                    2006029057

Printed in the United States of America
07 08 09 RRD 6 5 4 3 2 1

For Lonnie,
who took a chance on me when I was feeling invisible.

And for all those women who feel invisible—
whether by size, age, or circumstance . . .
The old hymn says, "His eye is on the sparrow."
His eye is on you.

*It is never too late to be what
you might have been.*

—George Eliot

:: *chapter one* ::

One size does *not* fit all.

   "Not women like me," I muttered as I tried to wriggle the cotton peasant skirt over my double-wide-trailer hips in the cramped dressing room.

   I don't know what possessed me even to set foot in that hot new mall boutique. I should have just continued on my normal way to Payne Tryon, the second home to big women everywhere. But the flowing boho-chic outfit on the larger-than-standard twig mannequin in the window caught my eye. Its flared and tiered fullness beckoned me with its ample waves of "one size fits all" material.

   Only the waves weren't ample enough, and the material in question didn't have one whit of rayon or spandex in it. A blend is forgiving and will stretch. One-hundred-percent cotton will not. And didn't.

   As I said, I should have known better. Places like that aren't for big women like me.

   Notice I didn't say "plus-sized." I hate that term and refuse to use it.

   My name is Freddie—short for Fredericka. Fredericka Heinz. Yes, like the ketchup. A sturdy German name, for a sturdy German girl descended from good, sturdy German peasant stock. *Jawohl!* My father, who'd never be confused for a peasant even on his worst day, longed for a son to carry on the family name but got me instead.

It's been downhill for me ever since.

At last I managed to free myself from the constricting skirt. Turning my back to the mirror, I quickly pulled on my big-girl uniform of black pants and black tunic, eager now to escape the claustrophobic cubicle. Hopefully, I wouldn't run into the Paris Hilton–lookalike salesclerk on my way out.

No such luck. She flicked her platinum hair and gave me a bright, lip-glossed smile. "Well?"

"Not really me," I mumbled, handing over the traitorous skirt draped over my arm.

We both knew I was lying, but at least she didn't suggest I'd be better off at Payne Tryon, like the last snippy salesgirl when I tried to shop in a regular store.

· · · ·

"About time you got back." My boss, Anya Jorgensen, folded her arms across her silicone-enhanced chest, tapped her stiletto mules on the tile floor, and glared from me to the bakery's wall clock, which showed I was seven minutes late from lunch.

I drop-kicked her skinny butt out the door, pausing only long enough to smash a banana-cream pie into her perfectly made-up face.

Well, I always did have a great fantasy life.

Pulling on my requisite white coat and shoving my hair up into the white hat Anya always insisted upon, I murmured, "Sorry. My errands took longer than I thought." No way was I going to let her know about the skirt debacle. Not Anya. Especially not Anya.

"Well, hurry up." She thrust a pink order form at me. "We got a rush for a birthday cake. They're picking it up at five."

I stared down at her precise black lettering. "But I still have another birthday cake for today, plus the Wallace wedding cake to decorate for tomorrow morning."

"So you'll have to work a little late. You could probably use the overtime . . ."

"Actually, I—"

The bell over the front door jangled.

I scooted toward the swinging double doors to the kitchen, where I set the order form down on the floury counter and released a heavy sigh as I drummed my French-manicured nails on the countertop. My nails are a little shorter than I'd like, but I learned early on you can't work in a kitchen and have gorgeous, long fingernails. So instead, I have gorgeous *short* fingernails, thanks to my weekly manicure indulgence. Hey, I may not be body beautiful, but a girl's got to play up her assets, right? And this manicure was fresh, because I actually did have someplace to go that night.

Any other Friday, Anya would be right about my plans. I usually picked up Chinese or pizza on my way home and settled in for the evening with a good book or my *Alias* DVDs. I love watching Sydney Bristow kick some serious bad-guy butt. Plus, that Vaughn is really easy on the eyes.

Tonight, however, I had other plans. That's why I'd dared to don the peasant skirt on my lunch hour. Drop-dead gorgeous Jared Brown from church had actually invited me to a party.

Okay, so he hadn't invited me specifically. He'd asked a whole group of us from church to come, and I'd happened to be on the outer fringe, getting ready to leave the nine-thirty service.

Jared pointed to me and said, "Hey, don't you work at Jorgensen's?" He smiled, revealing dimples so deep even a girl like me could fall into them and never come out. "Think you could bring one of their great cakes?"

It was the first time Jared had ever noticed me, and I wasn't about to pass up that chance. Even if my pass to the party was a cake—a cake I'd pay for, of course, but that I still had to bake and decorate. Along with this last-minute birthday cake and tomorrow's wedding cake.

I sighed again.

My fellow baker, Millie, who was boxing a standing Friday afternoon order of her fabulous oatmeal-raisin-chocolate-chip cookies, gave me a sharp look. "You need to start standing up to Anya. Learn to say no."

Shane, our intern, grunted. "Hah. In what universe?"

"Watch your mouth, young man," Millie said.

"Sorry." He shot a contrite look my way. "I wasn't trying to be mean."

"That's okay. You're right. It would have to be a parallel universe before I got the nerve to stand up to Anya."

Shane crossed the space between us in two eager strides. "I could do one of the cakes for you, Freddie. That way you wouldn't have to stay so late."

My eyes flicked to the double doors. "I don't know. Anya would have a cow. She hasn't decided if you're ready to graduate to cakes yet."

"She wouldn't even know. Come on," he pleaded. "You know she never comes back here in the afternoons."

"He's right," Millie harrumphed. "Wouldn't want to get her fancy designer shoes dirty." She peered through the face-sized window on one of the swinging doors. "Besides, she's busy yakking on her cell, like always. Give the boy a chance."

Jared Brown's deep dimples flashed before my eyes.

"Okay, you can do the carrot cake." I handed him the order form and Jorgensen recipe book. "And don't forget—when you make the cream cheese icing, add a couple drops of almond extract." The almond extract was my special touch—it set our cream-cheese icing apart from all the other carrot cakes in town.

I checked my supplies in the walk-in. Still plenty of lemon curd left over from the lemon-chiffon wedding cake I'd baked earlier in the week, plus half a flat of fresh raspberries. I decided to make a lemon raspberry cake for tonight's party. And while the lemon sponge cake was baking, I'd begin icing the wedding cake in the pretty garden-lattice design the bride requested. Tomorrow, before Anya arrived to transport that cake to the reception, I'd finish it off by applying the fresh daisies and yellow rosebuds to the base, crowning the top tier with the delicate rose nosegay topper the florist would deliver first thing in the morning.

I attached the beaters to my industrial-strength mixer, my face flushing as I thought how impressed Jared would be with my cake.

· · · ·

I've perfected the fine art of leaning.

Leaning is the secret of big girls everywhere, especially at outdoor activities involving food. Like tonight's party.

"No thanks," I smiled and said to Pastor Chuck when he offered me a seat in one of those flimsy white plastic outdoor chairs. "I need to stretch."

And stretch I did. Then leaned some more. Against the patio wall, a tree, or the back of the house. I'd gotten quite good at balancing a paper plate in one hand and eating with the other. This pretty much limited me to carrots, celery, grapes, and the occasional drumstick. But that was a good thing, because it preempted those knowing looks from everyone that translated into, "Well, no wonder she's so big. Look at what she's eating."

I'd just wait until I got home to dig into a burger, a little potato salad, and maybe just a sliver of the Sara Lee cheesecake I'd squirreled away in the farthest recesses of the freezer.

From my invisible corner, leaning against the far end of the patio wall in my second loose black skirt and top of the day—I'd changed into a fresh set I keep at work—I watched Barbie and Ken and all the giggling twenty-something girls, in their cute capris and tight camisoles, oohing over Barbie's ring.

Barbie and Ken were the guests of honor at the party, the former leaders of the singles group—now newly married. (He was the singles pastor; she was his right-hand woman and social director.) Their names weren't really Barbie and Ken, but they were so disgustingly perfect and adorable, with their tanned California hard bodies, bleached teeth, and perky, upbeat demeanors, that I'd christened them that in my head.

I nibbled on a baby carrot and let my eyes roam the yard.

Potlucks and barbecues are the only outdoor activities I do. I shun all the rest—camping, hiking, jogging, and especially any kind of water sport. I know better than to inflict my big, white, twenty-nine-year-old self in a bathing suit upon the unsuspecting world.

It's not a pretty thing.

Besides, even though I'm a born-and-bred California girl, I can't handle the heat. So when family or friends are frolicking at the pool in the blazing heat, I usually escape to my room with a good romance novel or go to a matinee. Invisible in the darkened coolness of the theater, I indulge in a large buttered popcorn, a Diet Coke, and a box of Junior Mints as I pretend I'm the girl on the silver screen who gets the guy.

Tonight, though, instead of the silver screen, I'm watching

Jared and all the girls clustering around him, wishing I were one of them.

But not just one of them.

The one.

I glance down at my big, sturdy calves and know it will never happen.

When I first arrived, I'd hoped to be able to present my to-die-for lemon raspberry layer cake to Jared, who'd be so overcome by the mouth-watering sight and scent of my culinary work of art that he'd overlook my overblown physique and fall head over heels.

Unfortunately, Jared was nowhere in sight when I pushed through the backyard gate, see-through Tupperware cake tote in hand.

"Ooh, is that the cake?" Shauna, the lean marathon runner whose metabolism allowed her to eat like a horse yet never gain weight, was practically drooling. "It looks yummy." She relieved me of my masterpiece. "Jared told me where he wants it. Thanks." She jogged away.

I considered tackling her and fighting her for the cake, but I knew I'd never be able to catch up with marathon girl.

Now, stomach rumbling, I crunched on another carrot and stared at the almost decimated cake on the table near Jared. One of his groupies giggled and reached her hand up to wipe a speck of frosting from the side of his very kissable mouth.

All at once, something loomed in my peripheral vision. I turned to see a tall, majestic African-American woman in a turban sweep across the backyard, her vivid, multicolored silk caftan billowing in her wake.

There was nothing invisible about that woman. She *owned* that room—I mean yard. I watched her as she moved from one cluster of people to another, talking and laughing and passing out business cards.

I just stood there with my mouth open. That gorgeous Amazon was bigger than me. A good size 22. Easy. Maybe even a 24. But she didn't let that stop her from filling her plate right in front of God and everyone.

"Mmm, I love ribs," she said, selecting a couple from the buffet table, along with a generous helping of green salad and a dollop of potato salad.

I looked longingly at the juicy, succulent ribs on her plate, then down at my little pile of carrots and grapes.

"Hey." She approached Jared, who was sitting on a durable metal patio chair, chatting with the gaggle of skinny, giggly girls. "You with your fine self—you mind giving up your seat for this big, beautiful woman?" She grinned and nodded at one of the flimsy plastic chairs nearby. "And sitting on that instead? There's no way that puny thing'd hold me, and I don't feel like wearing my ribs today."

My cheeks flame on her behalf. Didn't she know everyone was staring at her? And how could she admit that to Jared, of all people?

But he flashed his dimples and gave up his seat, executing a little bow to her in the process. Then, to my astonishment, he pulled up the plastic chair, scooted next to this bold Amazon, and struck up a conversation. Within moments he was roaring with laughter.

What I wanted to know is how come her fat looked so much better than my fat?

:: *chapter two* ::

Starving, I yanked open the fridge when I got home and pulled out the oversized orange plastic tub from my allocated shelf. I wrenched off the lid, grabbed the quart of potato salad sandwiched between the can of fudge frosting and the tapioca pudding, and dove in, thankful my roommate wasn't home.

With the eggy spoon clamped between my teeth, I removed another orange plastic container from the freezer and chipped off a hamburger patty from the frozen roll of individual patties inside. This I defrosted in the microwave so it would cook even faster on my George Foreman grill. As I closed the grill lid, I noticed a note on the fridge door:

Hey, Fred—

Got a late meeting at work—again! Could you feed Henry and Eliza? Please? Thanks a bunch—I owe ya.

Brooke

Henry must have read Brooke's note—or maybe he just smelled my burger. He rubbed back and forth against the back of my calves, releasing a plaintive meow.

"Poor baby." I flipped my burger, then reached down to stroke the old tomcat's fur. "You got the hungries? I know just how you feel." I popped open a can of cat food and transferred half of it to his bowl on the floor next to the fridge. Then I filled Eliza and Zsa Zsa's bowls as well—at opposite ends of the kitchen so they wouldn't eat each other's food—and whistled.

Zsa Zsa, my Bichon Frise–Pekinese-mix puppy, came caroming down the hall, sliding on the hardwood kitchen floor in her haste, while Eliza, a regal Siamese, followed at her more cool, cruise-along cat pace.

The cats belong to my feline-loving roommate Brooke, who runs a pet rescue group with two of her vegetarian friends. She's had Henry and Eliza for years—both had been abandoned—but Zsa Zsa is a recent addition. Because she'd been born without one eye, her owner was going to have her put down. But Brooke, who happened to be at the vet's that day, had asked if she could take the trembling pup instead and find a home for her. Now, six weeks and several chewed paperbacks later (Zsa Zsa's a very discerning dog; doesn't bother with books that haven't made the *New York Times* Best Seller List), Zsa Zsa's still here.

And that's more than fine with me. I was never allowed pets growing up, and Zsa Zsa and I have developed a special bond. I think it's that whole misfit connection.

I don't know how I ever got along without her.

Don't get me wrong—I love Henry and Eliza too. Actually, one of the best things about living with Brooke is the parade of animals always coming in and out. But Zsa Zsa gets a little jealous, so I have to be careful how much attention I pay to the kitty cats—or any other critter my roommate drags home.

Actually, though, Brooke and I aren't full roommates. I simply rent the master bedroom and bath from her, although I do have kitchen and family room privileges.

Hence, the single shelf in the fridge.

"All I ask is that if you're going to eat meat," Brooke said with a shudder when I answered her room-to-rent ad, "I don't want to see it or smell it, so please don't cook it when I'm in the house."

Worked for me.

I really didn't want her seeing—or commenting on—the types of food I ate anyway. So when I moved in two years ago, I bought two rectangular, non-see-through Tupperware-type food containers—one for the fridge, one for the freezer—where I store my stash of carnivore-and-other goodies. The rest of my shelf (visible to Brooke and her friends) holds nonfat yogurt, skim milk, fresh fruit and veggies, light margarine, low-carb sprouted wheat bread, and the occasional piece of salmon.

The remainder of the fridge—Brooke's space—usually holds Trader Joe's organic carrot juice, bottled water, packages of tofu, a lone apple or pear, to-go hot food containers from Whole Foods, and the occasional half-empty bottle of wine.

Brooke's rarely home—always busy saving the world, or at least animals from the cold, cruel world—and when she is home, she's almost never alone. Usually one of her Birkenstock-type pals is with her. But they're nice people, and we get along fine, just as long as I have my room to hide in.

My refuge—where I was headed now.

Shutting the door behind me, I set my hamburger, potato salad, and the last of the Sara Lee cheesecake on my nightstand while I shucked my clothes in favor of a comfy Tigger nightshirt. What can I say? I always loved Winnie the Pooh.

I shoved a stack of romance novels to one side and lifted the lid of the plastic bin next to my bed to pull out my bag of baked

tortilla chips. Then I popped in a disk from the third season of
Alias and chowed down.

*Sigh. Bet if I had Jennifer Garner's defined biceps, Jared would sit
up and notice me.*

I swallowed the last of my burger and hopped off my bed to
do one of Sydney's signature kicks facing the mirror—imagining
myself in one of her cool wig disguises—but I lost my balance
and went down. Luckily, the futon cushioned my fall, and the
only thing bruised was my ego.

Ready for a little less active pursuit, I picked up my current
romance novel. So far, the heroine—a spunky redhead from
Ireland (ever notice how heroines are always either "spunky,"
"plucky," or "feisty"?)—was still in the "I hate you" part of the
hate-love dance with the hero, who had taken ownership of her
family's ancestral home.

Just when I got to the good part—where she was fighting her
feelings for him after he'd surprised her with a passionate kiss—
Zsa Zsa scratched at the door and whined. Right on schedule. I
set my book upside down on the comforter so I wouldn't lose my
spot and got up to let her in. She made her usual beeline for the
bed—and my book.

Uh-oh.

"No, Zsa Zsa, no!" I'd left the poor defenseless paperback
right there in front of her.

But I needn't have worried. After pushing the novel over with
her nose and sniffing and circling it a couple of times, she gave
one final disdainful sniff and scampered to my pillow, where she
made herself at home.

"You're such a snob. So it's not Joan Didion. So what? A girl
needs a little escapism now and then."

She gave me a smug look.

"Well, don't get too comfortable." I picked up my paperback and slipped beneath the covers again. "I want to finish this chapter. But then you and me are going outside."

· · · ·

The next morning I awoke with a crick in my neck and a Zsa Zsa fur hat. Peering bleary-eyed at the luminous numbers on my alarm clock, I shrieked and bounded out of bed. No time for a shower. When I scrambled through my closet, I remembered I hadn't done laundry in a while and all my black pants were dirty. So I yanked on a pair of khakis and my Northwestern T-shirt, scraped my flyaway hair into a ponytail, let Zsa Zsa out into the fenced backyard, and flew to work in my trusty metal steed, my seven-year-old Honda Civic.

I've never overslept before. And on a wedding day, no less.

I glanced at the digital numbers on the dash. Still plenty of time to finish the decorating before the reception, so at least I didn't need to worry about ruining the bride and groom's big day. One of the things I loved most about making wedding cakes was the opportunity to have a small part in someone else's happily-ever-after. Especially since the chances of my having one are . . .

Okay, don't go there. Focus, Freddie, focus.

Would I beat Anya to the bakery? She always liked to deliver and set up the cakes a good hour or two before the reception begins. I looked at my watch again and groaned as I hit the home stretch of streets leading to Jorgensen's Bakery.

Jorgensen's had been a popular family-run business in Lantana, California, for generations. And Anya, the last of the Jorgensens, was now the face of the bakery. Aside from the sun damage and makeup-plastered laugh lines, it was a pretty good face.

Problem was, Anya couldn't bake a lick.

Still, she'd majored in marketing and used to work at a high-end PR firm, so she was great at that end of the business. When her parents died and left her Jorgensen's, Anya had installed a cappuccino maker and a few bistro tables out front so we could compete with Starbucks. When she was actually at the bakery, she spent all her time out front, schmoozing and chatting with customers.

I couldn't schmooze if my life depended on it.

That's why I was one of the two behind-the-scenes bakers. That and the fact that Anya thought my size would put people off. Okay, she'd never actually *said* it, but I knew what she thought. It didn't take a rocket scientist to read behind her shallow baby blues . . . which widened in horror as the restraints on the hospital bed pinned her skinny arms and legs down, and I, clad in my white baker/mad scientist coat, force-fed her cookie after chocolate-chip cookie until she swelled like a balloon and popped, deflating from view like the Wicked Witch of the West.

So glad I don't have anger issues.

Truth is, though, I don't really mind staying out of sight. I'm more a behind-the-scenes kind of person anyway. Now I was just hoping I could get my behind-the-scenes work finished in time. I was tired of having Anya fire me.

Just as Anya's silver BMW pulled into its reserved space out front, I ducked in the back door. Bracing myself for her any-minute-now tirade, I quickly pulled on my white coat and hat, then stopped short at the astonishing sight before my eyes.

The double doors pushed open, and her high heels click-clacked their way to me. "Good to go?" Anya's sage-shadowed eyes flicked over the fully decorated cake all packed and ready to go in its carrying box.

"All set," Shane said, winking at me behind her back. "I'll just load this in the van." He carefully lifted the box and carried it out the same door I'd raced through just moments before.

Anya, who wore a tight spring floral dress with a pale-green jacket from some high-end designer or other, grabbed a blueberry muffin off the cooling rack. "I won't be coming back today. After I deliver the wedding cake, I'm heading to San Francisco with a friend."

From the way she says *friend*, I can tell it's a guy. It's always a guy. Anya goes through men like *American Idol*'s Simon Cowell goes through tight black T-shirts. "Nicole will be here soon," she continued. "But if she gets slammed, have Shane help her out or just call in Millie." She click-clacked her way out the door.

Nicole was the cute, sweet college student who worked Saturdays and a few afternoons during the week. Millie worked Saturday mornings for years, but the pace was starting to get to her.

Millie Ames has worked at Jorgensen's for nearly four decades now. Anya's grandfather, old Mr. Jorgensen—long since passed away—hired her after her husband ran off and left her to raise two kids on her own. Millie, with a little help from our culinary-school intern, Shane Armstrong, makes most of the pies, cookies, muffins, breakfast breads, and coffeecakes. Jorgensen's is known far and wide for their melt-in-your-mouth crumb coffee cake.

And me? I help with the breakfast breads and cookies as needed, but mainly I'm in charge of the wedding and birthday cakes. Millie used to do cakes too, but her worsening arthritis made the delicate decorating difficult. Which is the only reason Anya hired me in the first place.

"Thanks for getting my back." I poured Shane some coffee and held up my mug of Earl Grey in salute. "Great job adding the flowers, by the way."

"Aw, shucks. 'Tweren't nothin'," he said, doing his Opie-from-Mayberry impression.

"Seriously. I really appreciate it. I owe you."

The back door opened. "Hi guys." Nicole, who could be Kate Hudson's twin and Goldie Hawn's long-lost other daughter, flashed us a pleading smile. "Any dented breads or broken cookies this morning? Didn't have time for breakfast, and I'm staaaarved."

Shane handed her the oatmeal-raisin cookie he was about to eat. "Here you go."

"Thanks. You're a doll." She took a big bite and closed her eyes in rapture. "Mmm."

He stared at her with naked longing. Shane's crush on Nicole was no secret, but he just couldn't work up the nerve to ask her out.

"Hey, Shane, why don't you help Nicole out front for a bit? I have a feeling we're going to have a lot of customers this morning, and besides, I need to concentrate on a special cake." I shooed them out, taking my turn at doing the wink-behind-her-back thing.

Shane mouthed *thank you* and followed the object of his desire while I pulled out cake pans.

Jorgensen's offers five wedding-cake flavors (which triples in number with the varied filling choices): traditional white, carrot, lemon chiffon, chocolate fudge, and our specialty, Danish layer cake.

The latter is the most work-intensive because this moist yellow cake is split into six layers. One layer is spread with custard, the next buttercream, and the next raspberry jam. Then the whole process is repeated, and the entire cake iced in thick buttercream.

This was the cake I planned to make for tonight. A special cake for a special occasion.

As if anyone would care.

. . . .

Candy gives me a headache—and I'm not talking about Reese's Pieces.

My stepmother, Candy, doesn't allow Reese's in their luxury custom home. Or any sweets, for that matter. She says she doesn't want to tempt me. But I know she's also terrified of gaining an ounce of fat herself. My father likes his women slim and beautiful.

And Candy is beautiful—in a polished and plastic way, with her severe cheekbones and Angelina Jolie lips. She's also a stick. A stick with big boobs, which, technically speaking, really belong to my father, since he paid for them. Her skinny legs—especially when she's just finished exercising in the workout room Dad had custom built—remind me of a couple of Red Vines.

Mine are the whole tub of Red Vines—one tub for each thigh. But those tubs were hidden tonight under a flowing black dress.

In honor of my father's sixtieth birthday, Candy had broken her no-sweets rule. After much pleading on my part and repeated assurances that my offering would rival that of any caterer she could hire, she had allowed me to make my dad's birthday cake.

It was a pretty big concession on her part, and a big risk on mine. When it comes to my dad, nothing less than perfection would do.

Frederick Wagner Heinz Jr. turns heads wherever he goes. Tall and imposing like a California redwood, he has granite-gray eyes that don't miss a thing and a leonine head of thick, silver hair, which makes him look a little like the first-season *Dancing with the Stars* winner, John O'Hurley.

Minus the humor.

Whenever people saw us together in public (which was seldom), they always stared. And I knew what they were thinking: *Who's that mousy fat girl with that gorgeous man?*

His secretary? No, she'd dress better.

Must be his housekeeper. No, why would he appear in public with her?

Has to be the nanny.

They were always shocked when they found out I actually sprang from the man's loins. I think it still shocks him.

To say my real-estate mogul father was formidable was like saying Donald Trump was having a bad hair day.

I've never been formidable—except in size. Far from it. I was the biggest wuss I knew. I shrank from conflict and preferred to blend into the background.

My mother, from what I've been able to glean, was also a bit of a wuss. She apparently wanted to name me Angelica, but Dad vetoed that out of hand.

He was proven right once he saw me in the hospital. Even then I was big for my age—ten pounds, thirteen ounces. I was so big that I broke my mother's pelvis.

At least that's what they told me.

Maybe that's why she left.

* * * *

"Fredericka, this is sinfully delicious." Shirley, the plump, diamond-ringed wife of my father's long-time partner moaned in sweet-toothed ecstasy. "Jim"—she turned to her husband—"isn't this cake absolutely luscious? I love the marriage of the custard and the raspberry."

James Weaver wiped his mouth with his monogrammed linen napkin. "Absolutely." He smiled at me across the elegantly laid table. "Best cake I've ever had. You've truly got a gift, Freddie."

I felt a happy flush suffuse my cheeks.

James turned to my father, and my hands twisted the linen napkin in my lap.

No, don't do it. Please. Don't do it.

"Frederick, you've got a talented daughter there. You should be really proud of her."

"Proud?" My father pushed his untouched cake plate away and drained his Chardonnay, slapping his empty wine glass down and motioning for a refill. "For this I sent her to that fancy university?"

Candy sent him a discreet warning look. Just in time.

My father released his hearty party laugh, the laugh I knew so well. He trotted it out for his friends and colleagues on a regular basis. "But hey, that's a parent's job, right? To provide for their kids and make sure they get a good education? And it's the kids' job to find themselves." He grinned at his business partner and deftly maneuvered the subject away from my shortcomings. "So how's Jim Junior's latest business venture going?"

I looked down at the napkin in my lap, twisting it even more.

This is *why* I went to college at that "fancy university" in Chicago. I couldn't wait to get away from my disapproving dad and the collagen-enhanced Candy, who had padlocked the refrigerator once I was old enough for my enquiring fingers to open it.

Growing up, I was always hungry. While Dad and Candy were having coq au vin, coquilles St. Jacques, or some other fancy French or Italian dish with potatoes and pasta, I'd get a broiled piece of fish or chicken and a green salad or huge bowl of steamed Brussels sprouts.

To this day, I can't eat Brussels sprouts.

On weekends, I was allowed a serving of rice or a plain baked potato with my dinner. The first time I had a baked potato with butter and sour cream at a friend's house, I nearly swooned with pleasure.

We had a series of live-in cooks who were given strict instructions that the only food I was allowed in my parents' frequent absences was broiled, grilled, or boiled meat with steamed vegetables. Nothing fried, no sauces, minimal starches, and never *ever* candy, cake, or cookies.

Martha, one of the earliest cooks I can remember, made me Christmas sugar-cookie cutouts the year I was four. She let me help decorate them—the most fun I'd ever had in a kitchen. But Dad and Candy found out, and Martha was sent packing before the New Year.

Priscilla was more discreet. Trim, reserved—at least around my parents—and in her fifties, she found ways around my parents' strict food edicts and let me help her out in the kitchen whenever they were out of town—cranking up her favorite music on her portable blaster and letting her hair down. She didn't go so far as to make cake and cookies—she, too, thought sugar wasn't good for kids—but she did treat me to some great spaghetti and meatballs on occasion and the most amazing macaroni and cheese. And oh my goodness . . . fried okra. Absolutely to die for.

To get my sugar fix, I'd hoard Twinkies and Kit-Kats—bought from other kids at school. But Candy almost always discovered them. And when she did, I paid for it.

Straight to bed without dinner.

Most days, I felt *muy simpatico* with Oliver Twist, whom I'd read about by flashlight under the covers, longing for the day when my kind, older gentleman (who turned out to be my grandfather) would come along and rescue me too.

But no rescue came, at least not when I was a kid. I had to rescue myself and get out of Dodge.

Or at least out of California.

Men were another reason I chose the Midwest for school. I figured the boys there might appreciate my German and Polish (Polish on my mom's side) sturdiness more than the Golden State boys.

One did. Greg Wysocki, the love of my life.

Greg was in several of my English classes. (At that point I thought I wanted to become a teacher.) An intense, pale, wannabe writer with John Lennon glasses, he was planning to pen the Great American Novel. Greg minored in art and had a fondness for Renoir, Rembrandt, and Rubens, which worked in my favor. He also loved food, which fascinated me. I'd never known a man who seemed to think food was a good thing.

I gave my heart, soul, and body to Greg. He made me feel beautiful and desirable for the first time in my life. The night he proposed, I thought I'd died and gone to fat, lonely-girl heaven. His all-American (mostly German and Polish, but with a little Italian) family embraced me, and his mother taught me how to cook her son's favorite foods: pot roast, bratwurst, meatloaf, chicken parmesan, and a carb-laden array of potato choices.

Living in Chicago was food paradise—and so much more than just deep-dish pizza, hot dogs, and thick, juicy steaks. Greg and I loved trying Greek, Japanese, Thai, German, and, of course, countless Italian restaurants. I subscribed to *Gourmet* magazine and tried out exotic recipes on Greg every week. He loved it—especially since the only two things he could cook were grilled cheese sandwiches and lasagna. (He claimed to make the world's best lasagna.) Greg even proposed to me over rack of lamb in the Signature Room atop the John Hancock building.

I couldn't wait to begin our white-picket-fence happily-ever-after. But a week before our wedding, I found Greg in bed with his best man's sister—a tiny redhead whose two thighs pressed together didn't equal even one of mine.

Guess I should have caught a clue when his art tastes changed from Rubens to El Greco.

Not wanting to return home with my tail between my thunder thighs, I stayed in Chicago but dropped out of my master's-degree program—which Dad had insisted upon, so I could "at least teach at a community college." That way I wouldn't have to see Greg-the-wedding-killer. I got a job in a bakery to pay the rent on a studio apartment and, having discovered my innate knack for cooking, even took some culinary classes. Those in turn led to an intensive cake decorating class and an apprenticeship at the bakery.

I've been making wedding cakes—and specialty cakes like this one for Dad tonight—ever since.

You're probably wondering why I ever came back home. Well, as I worked to put my life back together after Greg, I kept having this recurring fantasy that Dad and I might one day have a good father-daughter relationship. Hah!

Looking up from my bittersweet trip down memory lane, I caught Shirley's pitying glance and saw that my cake offering had been cleared away.

On the way home, I drove through McDonald's and ordered a Happy Meal and a hot-fudge sundae.

:: *chapter three* ::

"Sistah, that is one gorgeous cake," an admiring voice with a Southern accent said behind me in the reception hall the next Saturday.

Uh-oh. Anya didn't usually like me to be seen by the public.

All right—she would never actually *say* that. She didn't want to get sued for size discrimination. (Like *I'd* ever sue anyone.) But she always made sure that she was the one to deliver and set up the wedding cakes. Today, though, we had booked two receptions at the same time. So Anya had chosen the country club and sent me to the less posh reception at a local parks-and-recreation hall. "Just get in, set up, and get out," she'd instructed.

"Mmm, mmm," the honeyed drawl continued. "Does it taste as good as it looks?"

"Absolutely." Still facing the three-tiered cake with icing the palest whisper of blush and a fine network of white piping resembling a lacy veil around each layer, I adjusted the purple and lavender pansies at the base and recited the company line. "All Jorgensen's cakes are made with only the finest and freshest ingredients and lovingly decorated by hand by our master cake decorators."

Finished, I turned around with my professional smile plastered in place.

Only to find myself face-to-face with the larger-than-life Amazon I'd seen at the going-away party last week. Today she was dressed head to toe in purple, complete with a purple silk scarf wrapped turban-style around her head. Before I could get over my surprise, she enfolded me in a massive hug. "Hey, girl. Saw you at that outdoor party last week. Guess we go to the same church."

"Awmpht," I mumbled, squashed up as I was against her ample bosom.

She released me and let loose a booming laugh. "Sorry. Didn't mean to suffocate you." She held out her hand. "I'm Deborah. Not Debbie. Although I don't mind a Little Debbie treat every now and then. And you are?"

I ducked my head. "Freddie."

Her left eyebrow rose over a two-toned purple-shadowed eye. "Short for Fredericka."

"No wonder you go by Freddie." Her cocoa-brown eyes lit up. "Hey, you ever think about 'Reeka' instead? That's pretty."

Clearly I wasn't the only one who hated my name. I stiffened and said politely, "I'm afraid you're really early. The reception doesn't begin for another hour."

She boomed out another laugh. "Good thing too. I got lots to get done in that time." She smiled at my confused look and handed me a yellow business card. "I'm the caterer." Deborah pulled a fistful of cards out of her pocket. "And feel free to pass these out to all your friends—we need to build our business."

Just then a tall, slender man with the regal bearing and salt-and-pepper hair of a Morgan Freeman carried in a stack of metal food-warming trays.

"Samuel, can you come here, please? Someone I want you to meet."

He set the fragrant containers on one of the banquet tables, removed his oven mitts, and reached us in four long-legged strides, his face creased into a welcoming smile.

"Samuel, this is Freddie, from our church. She's the creator of this beautiful cake. And this fine-looking man"—she linked her arm through his and gazed up at him with adoration—"is my husband, Samuel Truedell."

Husband? For the first time I noticed the simple gold band on her left ring finger.

Samuel gave her a squeeze before extending his hand to me. "Pleased to meet you, Miss Freddie." He looked beyond my shoulder. "And *that* is one fine-looking cake. What flavor?"

"Chocolate fudge with orange-cream filling."

"Oh honey, hush." Deborah leaned toward the cake and sniffed the way Zsa Zsa does before she marks her territory on her walks. "I just *love* the combination of chocolate and orange. And chocolate and raspberry—"

"And chocolate and chocolate," Samuel said with a devilish grin.

"That's my man." She gave him a lingering smile. "He knows what I like."

"Well, I'd better be going." I backed away from the private tableau. "Nice to meet you."

"Oh, don't go," Deborah said. "I'm sorry. We'll be good. Besides, we got to get to work." She turned to her husband. "Baby, can you finish unloading the trays? I'll set up the Sternos under the chafing dishes after I put the tablecloths on the buffet tables." She swung back to me. "Freddie, why don't you keep me company while I work, and we can get to know each other. That is, if you have time."

The heavenly smells wafting from the food containers tempted me, but I knew Anya wouldn't want me hanging around. So, feeling like Cinderella at the ball, I made my excuses and hurried away before I turned into a pumpkin.

That extra roundness I didn't need.

"See you in church, honey," Deborah's voice thundered after me.

I looked back over my shoulder to see Samuel nuzzle her neck from behind as she tied her yellow apron.

She swatted at him. "Quit that, now. We need to get this food laid out." But she smiled as she said it.

As I pulled out of the parking lot, I noticed a bold yellow van with black trim and "A Taste of Honey Catering" emblazoned on the side—a fat, happy bumblebee buzzing above the word *honey*.

I had to smile. It was all just too perfect.

. . . .

Before returning to work, I made a detour. Twice a month I allowed myself this midmorning luxury—a new paperback novel (romance or mystery), hot chocolate, and a lemon bar at Bramwell's Books. The café in the back of the bookstore was renowned for its lattes, mochas, and cappuccinos, but . . . how can I put this gently?

I always hated coffee. The taste and the smell. And anything coffee related.

This obviously set me apart from the rest of the Starbucks-swigging, latte-loving world. But hey, I already stood out from the crowd—might as well go for broke. At home and at work, I usually drank tea, but Bramwell's made the best hot chocolate anywhere, so I liked to treat myself to it now and then. I'd sit at my favorite corner table, tucked away from the main traffic flow and coffee smells, sip my hot chocolate, and read in peace. The only problem about sitting in the corner was that the servers tended to overlook that out-of-the-way spot, so I always wound up having to go up to the counter to place my order.

Before heading for the café, I scanned the new-release table at the front of the store. I read the back covers of two paperbacks by my two preferred historical-romance authors; both sounded equally appealing. Sighing, I discovered with delight that my favorite wisecracking female sleuth had a new adventure out.

Only it was in hardcover.

I deliberated for a second, then set the paperbacks down. After shelling out three times more than I'd intended to spend on a book, I was tempted to skip the café altogether, but the hot chocolate kept calling my name. I decided to forgo the lemon bar to set my guilty conscience at ease.

When I got to the café, however, I saw that my corner table was occupied by a size 2 bleached blonde who obviously had just sat down. I hung back, hoping she'd get tired of the wait and leave so I could reclaim my spot.

No such luck. The teenaged waiter with the small silver earring whom I'd ordered from several times before—always at the counter—made a beeline for her table.

I sighed and trudged over to a table closer to the front. There I waited. And waited. And waited. As the waiter passed me on his return from delivering the blonde's skinny latte (no foam), I finally cleared my throat and managed an "Excuse me, could I order, please?"

"Oh, sorry. Didn't see you there."

Do you realize how clueless that answer is? He didn't see . . . me?

But I've heard it before. In fact, the same thing happened almost every time I went to a store or restaurant. Especially a restaurant. I guess big people aren't supposed to eat out. Maybe that's why so many of us stick to drive-throughs.

I'll bet this never happens to Deborah. No way could that woman ever be invisible. I sipped my hot chocolate, thinking about her and her husband. I'd never thought I'd be jealous of a woman larger than me, but I was. That good-looking Samuel was clearly head over heels. And her size didn't seem to bother him one bit. In fact, quite the opposite.

Must be the black factor.

I'd always heard that black men like their women to have curves. I once heard an up-and-coming African-American comedian on a talk show state that the thing he didn't like about Hollywood was that—especially from the back—most of the women looked like twelve-year-old boys.

Once they turned around, of course, I'm sure they almost knocked him out with their inflated chests.

I shifted in the uncomfortable chair. Wonder if Deborah and Samuel have any sons? Wouldn't my dad just love that?

Yeah, right. Like you'd ever have the nerve.

•　•　•　•

When I got home from work that evening, several cars were parked out front. Laughter and impassioned voices filtered into the night air. Probably another one of Brooke's animal-rescue meetings.

There went the chicken-parmesan dinner I'd planned to make.

My stomach growled. Hopefully I could just get to my room without anyone noticing I was there. Shouldn't be too hard. I was invisible, after all.

I took off my shoes and opened and closed the front door softly before starting to tiptoe down the hall. But a ball of white fur streaked from the living room and hurled itself at me, yapping happily.

Kind of hard to be invisible when you've got a hyper one-eyed dog clinging to your leg.

"Hey Freddie, I went ahead and fed Zsa—" Brooke poked her head around a corner, then shot me a puzzled glance. "What's with the no shoes?"

"Um, I—I stepped in mud and didn't want to track it in." I shifted from one foot to the other, hoping I could make it to my room without having to talk to anybody.

Too late. "Hey, I want you to meet someone." Brooke dragged a shaggy giant of a man in ripped jeans and a dove gray, bleach-spotted T-shirt around the corner. "This is the new vet in town—Hal Baxter. He just moved here from Oregon."

That would explain the grizzly-bear resemblance.

A massive hand with fingers like biscotti engulfed my Pillsbury Doughboy one. Thank goodness I had a nice manicure.

"Hey, excuse my clothes." He looked down ruefully. "I was doing a little cleanup at my office and didn't have time to change." He glanced down at Zsa Zsa, who had now plopped atop my bare feet and was busy licking my toes. "I like your footwear. Better than Uggs."

"Softer, too. And I especially like the built-in-shower feature."

He laughed, and I thought I saw a spark of interest flare in his caramel eyes. Then decided I must be imagining it. The man just liked dogs.

"I'm Freddie," I mumbled, noticing upon closer inspection that his beard and mustache were neatly trimmed and not as Grizzly Adams-ish as I'd first thought.

"Glad to meet you," he said. "Care to join us?"

"Yeah." Brooke gestured to the coffee table full of half-empty takeout containers. "We've got lots of quinoa and tabouli left and some great tofu chili."

"If it weren't for you, Whole Foods would go out of business," Jon, Brooke's on-again, off-again, now on-again boyfriend teased her. "Wouldn't it be cheaper if you just learned to cook?"

"Not interested. But there's nothing stopping you from becoming the next Wolfgang Puck." She batted her lashes at him before holding up a container to me. "Chili?"

"No thanks." I managed a smile. "I'm kind of tired. Long day. Think I'll just head to my room. Nice to meet you, Doc." I waved and hurried away, Zsa Zsa close on my heels, before anyone could hear my growling stomach.

The minute my door shut behind me, I undid my torture-chamber bra and dropped it on my white wicker chair. I shucked off the rest of my clothes and donned my plaid flannel pants and nightshirt. All the while, Zsa Zsa eyeballed me with her lone eye.

"Just a minute and I'll give you a treat. I'm hungry too." I leaned toward her and said in a stage whisper. "You know, if we'd played our cards right, we could have both had a little tofu."

I popped open the plastic container holding Zsa Zsa's jerky strips and broke one in half, extending it to her. She inhaled it and sat back on her haunches, her single eye fixed unwaveringly on me.

"Don't look at me that way. I happen to know you've already had your dinner."

She tilted her head at me, and I gave in.

"All right. But just one more."

She went into her happy Snoopy dance.

I washed my hands in my master bath, wondering what I might have in my food stash that would be a good dinner substitute. I opened my plastic tub to reveal a bag of barbecued potato chips, half a bag of miniature Reese's Peanut Butter Cups, and some lowfat microwave popcorn. The popcorn sounded the most filling, but fixing it would entail going to the kitchen.

Sighing, I munched on potato chips and popped in one of my *Gilmore Girls* DVDs. I just loved the relationship between Rory and Lorelai. She was such a cool mother. I thought they must have the best mother-daughter relationship on the planet.

Mom and daughter were in the middle of stocking up on junk food at the Stars Hollow grocery store for one of their marathon movie nights when I heard a soft rap on my door. I muted the TV and padded to the door, wondering what Brooke wanted.

Only it wasn't Brooke.

Dr. Baxter—Hal—stood there smiling, his hands behind his T-shirted back. An unmistakable, much-loved scent sucker-punched my stomach and nostrils.

He whipped out a bucket of KFC with one hand and grinned. "You looked hungry, and there are times when nothing but the Colonel will suffice—especially in a house full of tofu. Whaddya say?"

I say grab the bucket and slam the door. "Um . . ."

"Okay if I come in?"

In my bedroom? Conscious all at once of my Tigger nightshirt, I used the door as a shield. "Uh, I don't really think—"

"Hey, it's just a little chicken and conversation. Nothing more. We carnivores have to stick together." He leaned forward and whispered, "Besides, they'd eat me alive in the living room if I took the Colonel in there. I slipped out when they weren't looking and did the drive-through."

I hesitated.

He produced a KFC bag in his other hand. "There's mashed potatoes and biscuits and honey, too."

My stomach released an embarrassingly loud growl, and Zsa Zsa let loose an excited yip.

"Shall I take that as a yes?"

Heat flamed my face, and I just knew it was stop-sign red.

"Come on," he coaxed. "Even your little foot warmer knows I'm harmless—and dogs are great judges of character." He adopted a mock-official air. "That's a professional opinion."

Zsa Zsa wagged her tail, propellerlike.

"Just a sec."

Sometimes a woman's gotta do what a woman's gotta do.

I shut the door, pulled on my bra, and exchanged my night-shirt for a baggy gray T-shirt. I scooped the dirty clothes off the chair and tossed them into the closet, cleared off my nightstand, shoved three romance novels beneath the bedsheets, and smoothed out my comforter.

At last I ushered in the man with the food—careful to leave the door open a couple of inches.

"Um, have a seat." I pointed to the wicker chair and pulled my nightstand over between the chair and the bed.

Hal spread napkins on the nightstand and began removing food and drink containers from the bag while I perched on the edge of the bed, trying to get comfortable. But something kept poking me. I shifted and felt that same something start to slide. Realizing what it was, I tried to block its downward spiral first with my thighs, then with my calves. Finally I stood up and pressed my legs tightly against the side of the futon.

"You okay?" The vet paused in his food ministrations to give me a quizzical look.

"Fine. Just hungry." I grabbed a drumstick from the bucket and tried to distract him from the soft plop of one of my paperbacks falling to the carpet. "Thanks for coming to the rescue. I mean, with the food and all. This is really nice."

"No problem." He drizzled honey from a plastic packet onto one of the biscuits and took a bite. As he chewed, he nodded toward the novel at my feet. "*Love in the Highlands*? I'm more a Louis L'Amour fan myself, although I have read a couple Barbara Cartlands in my time."

I sprayed out my soda.

"What?" He handed me a napkin. "I have four sisters, and they devoured those things, so I picked up a couple to gain a little insight into the female mind."

"And did you?" I bit into my Dr Pepper–drenched chicken. "Gain insight, I mean."

He gave me a slow wink. "No complaints yet."

My face grew hot again.

Thankfully, Zsa Zsa diverted his attention by attacking the fallen romance novel and shaking it back and forth, which set Hal to laughing.

"Hey, what are you two doing in here?" Brooke pushed open the door. "You'd better not be taking advantage of my roomie, Hal," she teased. Then she saw the chicken.

"You guys are so busted."

:: *chapter four* ::

When I was growing up, we only went to church on Christmas and Easter—and then just for appearance's sake. My dad always thought religion was a crutch for the weak.

Which made it perfect for me.

After catching Greg in bed with his best man's sister, I sought sanctuary in church. The music soothed me, and the messages brought healing to my hurting heart. But I rarely went to the same church more than a couple of times. I didn't want to have to make small talk with strangers or get caught up in the whole brotherly-love hugging thing. So I always arrived late—slipping into the back pew—and left early.

When I returned home to Lantana, a bustling bedroom community full of high-tech firms outside of the state capital of California, I again sought out church. And church singles groups.

Although that wasn't my idea, but my friend Susan's.

Susan Black and I met at a new weight-loss program I was attending in hopes of losing more than the same twenty-two pounds I always lost and gained. This program had a rah-rah leader who wore bicycle shorts and a sports bra on her hard body as she spouted the company's self-help speak: "Say it with me, ladies: Chocolate is not my friend."

"Chocolate is not my friend," we repeated, although I was lying. Chocolate was one of my best friends.

"Everybody all together now," she urged as she had us stand up and jog in place at the end of the meeting. "Just say no to pizza!"

"Just say no," we chanted, all except for one roundish short woman with curly brown hair across the room, who rolled her eyes. As we filed out of the room, I heard this same curly-haired woman say, "Oh, the heck with it. I'm going for pizza. Anybody game?"

"Just say no," one of the women scolded her.

"*You* say no," she shot back. "I'm hungry." She caught my eye, and I recognized a kindred starving spirit.

Susan was my age and about the same size as me. But whereas I had large, strapping wrists and ankles, hers were slim. It was just the rest of her body that was round. Like an apple. She used to say she was fluffy, not fat, and that made me smile, although I could never think of myself as fluffy. I was more solid and sturdy.

We clicked right away, though, and over a combination pizza at my favorite chain, we compared notes about favorite foods, diet plans, and our social lives—or lack thereof. I learned she was a Christian just like me. That's when she suggested we check out a church singles group. "Come on. What've we got to lose? We might meet some cute guys." She grinned. "And Christians are supposed to look at the inward, not the outward. So we'd have a better chance there than in a bar. Right?"

The first singles group we visited had seventeen women and three men. One guy was in the middle of a contentious divorce—his third. Another had never heard of oral hygiene and was in-between jobs "at the moment." And although the last had a job and appeared to bathe regularly, all seventeen Presbyterian women had already staked their claim to him.

Susan said we needed better odds, so the next group we tried met at a Pentecostal megachurch. This singles group was well stocked with men—nice, godly men who raised their hands during worship and marked important passages of Scripture with yellow highlighters. But the women still outnumbered them five to one, so the guys could afford to be choosy.

And, of course, not one of them chose us.

That was enough for me. But Susan convinced me to try one more singles group—at a midsize, nondenominational church called Daystar Fellowship, where the odds were only three to one. Here the good-looking singles pastor had us break off into small groups of three or four to share and pray. One plain but eager (and thin) thirty-something woman in a brown polyester pantsuit barreled over to us that first night. "Hi. I'm Linda. You're new, aren't you?"

We nodded.

"Welcome." She grabbed both our hands. "I'll start." She leaned in toward us and shared in a stage whisper, "God told me I'm going to marry the singles pastor."

"He did?"

She gave an emphatic nod.

"So have you two been dating long?" I asked.

"Well, dating's not really biblical, you know. That's more a twentieth-century thing. It's better—and safer—just to get to know each other in a group situation."

"And that's how the two of you have gotten to know each other?" Susan raised a disbelieving eyebrow.

"Oh yes. We've been at all the potlucks and the same social events, and he's prayed with me a few times in a small group."

She sighed. "He's so kind and understanding. And he really listens to you when you talk."

"So have you set a date yet?"

"Not exactly." Linda scooted in closer and said in a confiding tone, "But I have a feeling it might be sometime this fall. I keep getting visions of autumn leaves, apples, and schoolbooks."

Linda's vision, it turned out, was a little off.

The wedding was in the spring. And the singles pastor, the one who looked like a Ken doll, married a spiritual Barbie named Chloe, whom he'd been dating for three months. They were the ones Jared threw the going-away party for—the one where I supplied the lemon raspberry cake. Linda missed both the wedding and the party. And so did Susan, who'd been transferred to Denver a month after we first discovered the Daystar singles group.

I'd stayed at Daystar after Susan left and had even begun attending Sunday services, though I still tried to slip out early. This morning as I got up to leave, a now-familiar Southern voice stopped me in my tracks. "Freddie! I hoped I'd see you."

Slowly I turned around. Today Deborah wore a bright orange pantsuit and an orange scarf that billowed in her wake as she sped my way with her husband and a beautiful girl who looked about sixteen—both in age and size. Although her size didn't hide the fact that she was obviously pregnant.

Deborah hugged me and turned with pride to the girl next to Samuel. "And this is my baby, Lydia. Lydia, this is Freddie. She's the one I told you about."

"Pleased to meet you." Lydia gave me a wide smile that revealed a slightly crooked front tooth. "Mama said you made the most delicious cake she's ever had."

I stared at Deborah, who gave me an innocent look.

"Can I help it that some skinny white girl didn't want her cake? Pushed it away like it was going to bite her or something and then went to dance. I didn't want the poor girl to stumble, so I just cleared her plate for her."

"Cleared it all the way back to the kitchen." Samuel crinkled his acorn-colored eyes. "But at least my lovely wife saved me two bites." He put his hand to his heart and smiled at me. "And may I just say those two bites were heavenly?"

"Girl, you can *bake*." Deborah linked her arm with mine as we walked to the exit. "And to thank you for that little taste of heaven yesterday, you're going to join us for lunch today."

"Mama, don't push. She might have other plans." Lydia turned to me. "We'd love you to join us if you're free."

I hesitated. I'd heard Jared and some of the others say they were going to lunch at Mimi's Café, and I'd hoped for the chance to maybe sit near him. I scanned the sanctuary and noticed him leaving out a side exit, his head bent to hear what the tiny girl clutching his arm was saying.

Deborah followed my glance and gave me a knowing look. "Honey, do I sense potential boyfriend material?"

Yeah. In my dreams . . .

"You'd best go get that Delilah away from him," she continued a little too loudly.

Praying no one had heard, I urged her to the nearest exit. "I'd love to come to lunch. Thank you."

"Well, good." She beamed. "Now I can return the favor. We live just a few blocks over. You can follow us. We're in a yell—"

"Yellow van with black trim," I finished as we stepped outside to the parking lot. "Hard to miss."

The house was the same. The minute I turned into their street I could tell which one was Deborah's. With its glossy, fire-engine red front door and matching window boxes, it was the only spot of color in a sea of beige stucco cookie-cutter boxes. A riot of colorful flowers cascaded from the window boxes and erupted from the flowerpots on the front porch. As I approached the door, I noticed a discreet black-and-yellow plaque off to the side that quoted Psalm 34:8: "Taste and see that the Lord is good."

Once inside, I lusted over the baseball-field-sized kitchen. Outfitted with two sinks, two ovens, and walk-in refrigerator, it also boasted stainless-steel appliances, a granite-topped island, cherry-red walls with yellow crown molding, and an industrial-sized pot rack with stainless steel cookware and accessories.

"Wow. This is some setup."

"I know!" Deborah said. "Definitely the Lord's provision to find a professionally outfitted kitchen. Another caterer owned this house before us, so it was clearly God's hand working it all out for us. We just had to do a little painting—it was pretty boring when we first saw it." She pulled one of her pale yellow catering aprons off a hook on the pantry door and shuddered. "All white with just this black countertop. I need some color around me."

"No." Lydia made her eyes all wide and surprised. "Really, Mama?"

"All right, now, baby girl." Deborah playfully swatted her daughter's backside with a towel. "Don't think 'cause you're about to be a mama yourself that you can make fun of yours."

"Somebody's got to do it." Lydia stuck out her tongue. "Besides, you know you love it."

"Y'all be good, now, in front of our guest." Samuel headed toward the patio door. "I'll fire up the grill for the salmon."

I perched on the yellow Windsor-style stool where Deborah indicated I should sit.

"Hope you like fish." She pulled out some baby red potatoes and began peeling a thick center strip on each one.

"Love it." My stomach growled in anticipation, and my cheeks flooded with color.

"Aw, isn't that cute? Now, don't you be embarrassed." Deborah turned to her daughter. "Get out some of those leftover hors d'oeuvres so this poor girl can have something to eat."

"Yes ma'am." Lydia pulled a couple of containers from the fridge and transferred their contents to serving plates. She stuck some stuffed mushrooms in the microwave to nuke and slid a plate of deviled eggs my way, but not before popping one into her mouth. "Here you go," she mumbled around the egg.

I followed her lead before my stomach could betray me again.

Deborah placed the potatoes in a steamer, flicking a curious glance my way. "Why you wear black all the time, girl? You need some color. Got to let your light shine."

My face flamed once more.

'Mama, you're doing it again."

"I'm sorry." Deborah looked at my red face, contrite. "My daughter tells me I'm way too blunt most of the time. Been that way all my life. But if I offend you, don't be shy—you just go 'head and tell me." She opened the refrigerator and pulled out a package of dinner rolls, which she transferred to a cookie sheet and slid into the oven "just to warm."

"Now, tell us all about yourself. How old are you? You got people here?"

I gulped down another deviled egg while she was still bent over and Lydia had gone to the fridge to get drinks. When Deborah lifted her head with a quizzical look in my direction, I pointed to my chewing mouth.

"Well, at least you were raised right." She gave her daughter a mock-stern look. "We mamas do the best we can, but some-times our children still forget their manners."

Lydia bussed her on the cheek with a loud smack. "I'm sorry, Mama, but you know you still love me."

"Ain't that the truth."

I sipped the glass of water Lydia had set before me and turned to face Deborah. "How old are *you*, if you don't mind my asking?"

"Don't mind at all. I'll be thirty-eight the end of this month."

"Really?" My head swiveled to Lydia. "How old are you, then?"

"Nineteen." Lydia popped another deviled egg in her mouth.

"Nineteen?"

She nodded but kept her mouth shut this time as she chewed.

Deborah grinned. "Lydia's the youngest. We had twin boys first—Sam Junior and Isaiah—and a year and a half later the Lord answered our prayers with this precious baby girl." She squeezed her daughter's thickened waist.

I stared again—this time at Deborah. "You have sons who are twenty-one?"

A shadow crossed Deborah's face. "Isaiah's back in Georgia. He's a junior in college. And Sam Junior—he's in heaven."

Lydia put her arm around her mother, whose eyes had filled, and told me softly, "Sam died three years ago. He was killed by a drunk driver."

Fat tears plopped onto Deborah's full cheeks.

"I'm so sorry," I stammered. "I had no idea."

She brushed the tears away. "Of course you didn't. Don't fret yourself." She glanced heavenward, and her tearstained face broke into a radiant smile. "I know my sweet baby's home with Jesus, and I'll see him again. But that don't mean I don't miss him every day."

"Me too," Lydia said, hugging her mother hard.

Deborah sniffed the air. "My rolls!" She yanked the oven door open as the smoke alarm screeched.

Samuel rushed in from the patio, broom in hand, and jabbed at the screaming smoke alarm until it stopped. His mouth twitched as he glanced at the hard, brown dinner rolls Deborah had set on the countertop. "Guess it's a good thing I froze that last loaf of rosemary-herb bread yesterday."

Deborah flung her arms around his neck and planted a huge kiss on his lips. "You're the best husband ever. Thanks for havin' my back, baby."

"Always, sug'." He returned her kiss. And held it for awhile.

That kiss. What a kiss. I hadn't been kissed like that in forever. Not since Greg. Although . . . had Greg ever really kissed me like that? Maybe not. But I was willing to bet that cute Jared Brown would be a good kisser . . .

"Okay you two, break it up." Lydia put her hands on her hips. "We've got company, remember? And if she's even half as hungry as me, then she's starving."

"I'm sorry." Deborah disentangled herself from Samuel with an apologetic smile and pulled a covered bowl from the fridge. "Could you put this on the table for me, please?"

Lunch was a mouthwatering affair of grilled salmon with dill sauce, steamed baby red potatoes with olive oil and parsley, cold three-bean salad, and homemade rosemary-herb bread with butter. Not diet margarine or that fake, no-fat imitation spray butter stuff Candy always used, but real butter.

"More potatoes?" Lydia passed me the bowl and, as she did, I noticed for the first time a silver band on her left ring finger.

"You're *married*?"

Stereotype much, W.A.S.P. girl? I rushed on to cover my faux pas. "Will your husband be joining us later?"

"Hah." Samuel grunted. "Wish he was. Plenty of things I'd like to say to that boy."

"Please, Daddy."

Samuel scowled.

"You and Mama raised me in the church and taught me that wedding vows are sacred."

"I know, baby girl, but—"

"But nothing." Lydia lifted her chin. "I'm still married to Donnie. For better or worse."

Samuel started to say something, but Deborah cut him off with a warning look.

Lydia turned to me with a tremulous smile. "Donnie and I got married back home in Decatur—that's right outside Atlanta. But we moved out here when his job transferred him. I got a good job at a credit union, and things were going real well." A shadow crossed her face. "At least I thought they were. But Donnie started having second thoughts—wondering if maybe he'd gotten married too young and wasn't quite ready to settle down yet, and—"

"And then that no-'count boy run off and left my daughter." Samuel glowered.

Lydia shoved her chair back, eyes snapping. "I told you I'm not going to listen to you run down my husband. Excuse me, Freddie. Mama." She bolted from the room as fast as a pregnant woman could bolt.

"Uh-huh. You'd *better* get up." Deborah snapped, eyes flashing at her husband as he stood.

"I'm sorry." Samuel sent me an apologetic look. "I had no call to behave that way, especially in front of a guest. Please forgive me." He squeezed his wife's shoulder. "And now, if you'll excuse me, I'll go make things right with my baby girl."

Deborah released a heavy sigh as Samuel disappeared down the hall. "If that boy ever does come back, he'll have a world of making up to do. And not just to Lydia. The last thing you want to do is hurt Daddy's little girl."

Unless, of course, you are Daddy. And then you have carte blanche to do so.

I shook my head to clear away the bitter thoughts. "Is Lydia the reason you moved here?"

She nodded. "After Donnie ran off, we wanted her to come back home, but she was sure he'd be back any day and didn't want to leave. Then the days turned into weeks, and Lydia found out she was pregnant. And my baby, who takes after me"—Deborah gave a rueful smile—"dug in her heels and said she had a good job out here with full medical benefits that she'd need. She just wouldn't come back home. So since she wouldn't come to us, we came to her. We weren't about to leave our baby all alone in a strange city when she was about to have her own baby—and our first grandchild, no less."

Deborah began clearing the table. "We prayed and started doing some investigating online and found this catering business for sale, so we sold our house and our catering company back home to some church friends and moved out here."

"So you've only been here a little while."

"'Bout six months. The miracle is, we were able to sell back home and buy out here so fast and keep on working." She smiled and nodded. "That's the Lord at work. And I just love to see him do his stuff."

I had to smile too. It was contagious. "How do you like California so far?"

"Love it. Great weather, and there's so much to see—though we haven't had time to see much. But Lydia drove us up to Lake

Tahoe, which must be what heaven's going to look like. Took my breath away." She flapped her hands before her face and opened the window over the sink. "Is it hot in here, or am I just having another hot flash?"

"It's not hot." I gave her a puzzled look. "Aren't you a little—"

"I went into early menopause 'cause of my hysterectomy last year. Fibroids," she explained. "Wish I was in San Francisco right now. It's cooler. We went to Fisherman's Wharf when we first came, and we had clam chowder in those sourdough bread bowls. Mmm, nothing like it! I surely do like everything about California." Deborah looked around her state-of-the-art catering kitchen and sighed. "Except the real-estate prices. Sure a lot higher than back home. But the Lord will provide. He hasn't let us down yet."

She began loading the dishwasher. "But enough about us. I want to know more about you." She winked. "I saw how you looked at that fine-looking Jared . . . something going on there?"

I handed her a plate. "No. I barely know him. Besides, he'd never look at me. I'm not his type."

"So what's his type?"

"Skinny and gorgeous. Fat girls just aren't his thing."

"But you're not fat." Deborah gave me a measuring glance. "Shoot. I'm bigger'n you. What do you weigh? I'll bet you're not even two hundred."

"I'm not sure. I don't like to get on the scale."

I was lying through my teeth. I knew exactly what I weighed, thanks to a recent doctor's visit when I had the flu. I flushed at the memory.

"Well, I'm two hundred and thirty-six pounds of voluptuous woman," Deborah said. "*And* I'm the same height as Tyra Banks— five foot nine. Of course, Tyra's only one hundred and fifty, but at least my girl has some curves, and they're all hers. Not like most of them Hollywood types." She gave me a wicked grin. "You know that scrawny Willow girl who used to be on that one TV show and is now making movies?"

Of course. Who didn't know Willow Reed, the slim, golden-haired beauty with the big chest, pillow lips, and gorgeous blue eyes? Men wanted her. Women wanted to *be* her.

"Well, she came to town to shoot a movie, and we were hired as the on-set caterers." Deborah giggled. "I want to tell you, Miss Thang has no booty at all."

"Are you serious? But I remember her wearing jeans on the show, and she definitely had curves—top and bottom."

"The magic of television." Deborah shook her head. "I saw that girl on the movie set, and I'm tellin' you, ain't nothin' there. Her behind is flatter than a pancake. Or at least it was before she went into the wardrobe and makeup trailer. She came out a lot more bootylicious than she went in." She winked. "And those famous blue eyes that turn grown men to Jell-O? They're really brown."

"I wonder who else in Tinseltown is totally fake?"

But Deborah was bored with Hollywood. She turned her all-natural brown eyes on me. "You never said if you've got people here. Any brothers and sisters?"

I shook my head. "I'm an only child."

"Parents?"

In name only. "My dad and stepmom."

"I'm sorry, honey. Did your mama die?"

"Worse. She left. Took one look at me and took off."

Deborah gave me a look of naked sympathy that left my cheeks burning. I nodded my head toward the hall and changed the subject. "So, do you think Samuel and Lydia are okay?"

"Uh-huh. They can't stay mad at each other long." Deborah leaned over the dishwasher again and, as she did, the silk scarf that had been wrapped around her head came loose and fell to her shoulders.

I gasped. "I—I'm sorry. I didn't know you had cancer."

She straightened, cupped her nearly bald head, and gave me a reassuring smile. "I don't. This is alopecia."

"Alopecia?"

"Hair loss." She shrugged her orange-clad shoulders. "Sometimes it's hereditary. Sometimes it's a vitamin deficiency. And sometimes the doctors can't figure out what causes it. Like my case—I've tried Rogaine and all those other expensive regrowth treatments, but none of them works for me."

"What about a wig?" I tried not to stare.

Behind me, Lydia giggled. "Mama says she's not Dolly Parton." She giggled again. "Which I'd say is pretty obvious."

Samuel kissed his wife's head. "That's right. My sugar stands above the rest. She's so fine she don't need hair." He caressed her almost-bald pate with exquisite tenderness. "Have you ever seen a more regal head? Like an Ethiopian queen."

"You must be blind, man. All those bald women we knew in Ethiopia when we lived there were like sticks."

"Twigs." Lydia munched on a carrot stick. "Starving tends to do that to you."

"You lived in Ethiopia?" My head swiveled from one to the other. "For how long?"

"We were missionaries there for a few years when the children were young." Samuel squeezed Deborah's shoulder. "We only came home to Georgia 'cause our boys had health issues that needed tending to."

"Which cleared up after we got home," Samuel added.

"Thank you, Jesus." Deborah raised her hands heavenward. Then she turned to me. "So how long you known the Lord, honey?"

. . . .

How long have I known the Lord? I mused as I drove home.

I'd been introduced to him in Chicago at one of the churches I attended after my break-up with Greg. I'd walked the aisle and prayed the prayer and everything. Lots of time, my faith was the only thing that got me through the day.

But as far as really *knowing* him . . . did I?

Did anyone?

:: *chapter five* ::

'll swap you two in my Love Labors Not series for the latest in the O'Hara Chronicles." Millie slid her two PG-rated bodice rippers across the counter between the cooling racks of oatmeal-raisin, peanut-butter, sugar, and chocolate-chip cookies.

"Deal." I handed her my bedraggled paperback with the spunky Irish redhead on the cover.

She looked askance at the bloated pages. "Let me guess. You were reading in the tub and fell asleep again."

"Guilty."

"Better be careful you don't drown."

"With this body? Fat chance."

Millie had gotten me hooked on romance novels within two weeks of my starting work at the bakery. She'd begun reading them after her husband left. "It's nice to have something to curl up with when you go to bed."

I hear that.

But she kept it strictly PG. No heaving bosoms and ripping off of clothes in a lustful frenzy for her—or me. That was the last thing either one of us needed. No way did I want to be reminded of all of those intimate nights with Greg. Intimate nights I'd probably never again know. Not as a good, single, now-Christian woman.

"So how was your weekend?" Millie pulled a pan of honey-bran muffins from the oven while I began slicing some breakfast breads—banana-nut, chocolate, lemon, and our most popular, butterscotch—to be slipped into the display case out front.

"Nice. I had lunch with this new family from church, who moved here from Georgia."

"Mmm." She gave me a knowing look. "They have any Southern-gentleman sons of marriageable age, by chance?"

"Not in town, Yenta." Finished slicing, I cracked an egg in a mixing bowl for the raisin scones. "They had twin sons—one's still in college, but the other one died a few years ago."

"How sad." Millie's eyes glistened. "I can't imagine losing a child." She added the honey-bran muffins next to the blueberry ones on the cooling rack. "So what brought them out here?"

"Their daughter. She's a sweetheart, but pregnant and only nineteen, and her jerk husband ran off and left her."

"Some things never change."

"Why are men such pigs?" I whisked the egg in a frenzy.

"Hey, hey. Watch it there." Shane, who'd just arrived, dumped his backpack inside the door in our little employees' corner.

"Sorry. Present company excepted, of course." Deciding a neutral subject was in order, I addressed Millie. "What'd you do this weekend?"

"Cleaned house and watched *The Best Years of Our Lives*." She sighed. "They just don't make movies like that anymore."

"Hmm," I said. "Don't think I've ever seen that one."

"You've *never* seen *The Best Years of Our Lives*?" Film geek Shane sent me an incredulous look as he began transferring cooled cookies to one of the display trays. "Great movie. A classic. It's about soldiers returning home from World War II and the difficult adjustments they face. One of the guys in the movie was a real soldier who'd lost both his hands in a training accident and had to wear artificial limbs with hooks for hands."

"That scene with his fiancée helping remove his harness and prosthetic arms makes me tear up every time." Millie's eyes grew wet again.

"I know. She was so cool." Shane blinked. "That's the kind of girl every guy wants."

"What kind of girl is that?" Nicole asked, striding through the back door. "Are you talking about Reese Witherspoon again?" She sent Shane a teasing smile. "Or is it Scarlett Johansson this week?"

Shane's neck turned blood-red as he bent his head over the cookie tray.

"We were just talking about a sweet scene in an old movie I watched this weekend." Millie rushed to fill the silence. "I couldn't even tell you the actress's name—I'm not sure if she made any other pictures. Don't remember seeing her in anything else."

"How old was the movie?" Nicole filched a chocolate-chip cookie from Shane's tray.

"Not sure." Millie frowned. "Late 1940s, I think."

"Nineteen forty-six." Shane had at last regained his voice. "Right after the war."

"Eew." Nicole scrunched up her nose. "Is it one of those black-and-white ones? Those are always so boring. I don't like movies without color."

"This movie is far from boring." Millie gingerly lifted the crumb coffee cake onto the doily-topped glass cake stand. "Tell you what. Since neither you or Freddie has seen it, why don't we have a special movie night at my house sometime soon and all watch it together?"

Millie and I had a standing twice-a-month dinner-and-movie date at her home. We'd been doing it for the past year—ever since the day I happened to mention I'd never seen *Gone with the Wind*. Appalled, Millie had made it her personal mission to introduce me to classic movie culture. We'd take turns making dinner, and Millie supplied the film.

Once Shane started working at the bakery, he'd readily and happily joined us for our movie nights. He'd originally wanted to go to film school and knew way more about old movies than your average twenty-year-old. So when he and Millie got going on an old movie roll, there was no stopping them.

To be honest, I wasn't quite as enthusiastic about the movies as they were. Some I liked, but some were pretty boring. *Citizen Kane*? Hello. So Rosebud was his sled. Big deal. But it was nice spending time with Shane and Millie, and it was the one time I got to cook for other people. Since Greg and Chicago, I hadn't cooked much, so I liked the opportunity to keep my hand in— even if it was just once a month.

But how would Nicole fit into the mix?

Popular and pretty, Nicole drew a lot of young male customers from the nearby community college to the bakery the afternoons she worked. I liked her, but she didn't really fit in with our merry little band of misfits.

I could tell exactly what she was thinking as she looked from one of us to the other. An old lady, a fat chick, and a geeky guy who's got the hots for me . . . How much more loser can you get?

Nicole surprised me by smiling shyly. "I'd like that—as long as it's not on one of my study group nights. And I'll bring the popcorn. It'll be fun."

"Really?" Shane asked. I saw the dismay flicker over his face as he realized he'd sounded too eager. He feigned indifference. "Cool."

"You do understand that it's just me, Millie, and Shane. Right?" Nicole sent me a puzzled and slightly hurt look. "Of course." Open mouth, insert foot.

"What's going on back here?" Anya banged through the double doors to the kitchen. "Why isn't anybody out front? We open in less than fifteen minutes, and the display case is empty."

It was Nicole's turn to flush. "Sorry." She grabbed a tray of muffins and scuttled through the doors, Shane fast on her heels with the coffee cake and a tray of cookies.

"Are we running a social club or a bakery?" Anya glared at us. "Recess is over."

As the doors slammed shut behind her, Millie whispered, "Guess this month's boyfriend bit the dust."

Half an hour later, as I was covering a cake board with pink foil, the double doors swung open again. "Freddie, you have a visitor," Anya said through clenched teeth.

"What?" No one ever came to see me at the bakery. "Are you sure?"

"Last time I checked, you were the only Freddie here." She tapped her foot on the tile floor. "Hurry up. Don't keep him waiting."

"*Him*"? Oh no. *It couldn't be Dad, could it? Why would he be here?*

I wiped my now-sweating hands on a towel, pushed a stray wisp of hair beneath my hat, and followed Anya, who had spun on her high heels, out to the front.

There, drooling over the bakery case, was my KFC veterinarian friend.

• ∘ • ∘

"Hal?"

"Freddie." He rolled his stuck-to-the-display-case tongue

back into his mouth and straightened up. He looked less scruffy today, in unpressed twill shorts and a navy T-shirt without bleach spots. "How's it going?"

"Fine. Uh, what are you doing here?" My eyes flicked to Anya. She wore her happy, hypocritical customer face, but I glimpsed the daggers behind her eyes.

"I want to order a cake." His teeth gleamed through his dark forest of beard. "I'm having an open house next Friday to introduce my practice to potential clients in the community, and Brooke said Jorgensen's has the best cakes in town. When I heard you worked here, I figured I couldn't go wrong."

Anya's eyes glittered at the words *my practice* and *clients*. She smiled and stuck out her hand to Hal. "Jorgensen's does have the best cakes in town, Doctor. Hello. I'm Anya Jorgensen, the owner. What kind of cake are you interested in?"

I could tell she was discreetly trying to scope out whether he was wearing a wedding ring on his other hand.

"I—I'm not sure," he stammered, looking over at me.

"We have several flavors to choose from—carrot, chocolate fudge, lemon chiffon . . ." She handed him the laminated list she'd made up for customers. "Although not everyone likes lemon and some people are allergic to chocolate. Do you have an idea of your clients' tastes?"

"Liver. Tuna. Steak." His mouth turned up. "My patients are more of the four-footed variety." He turned to me. "What do you think, Freddie? What's your favorite?"

Anya, who'd never be considered an animal lover even on her best day—"they smell and shed, eew"—stiffened.

"Um, it's really hard to pick one," I mumbled. "All our cakes are delicious. It just depends on what you like."

"Well, carrot cake's my favorite, but I know most women are chocoholics. And I definitely want to keep the women happy."

Nicole, who'd been discreetly observing this entire exchange from her position at the cappuccino maker, giggled. Anya shot her a dirty look, but when the front door opened to admit one of our regular corporate customers, her lips slid over her barracuda teeth in what resembled a smile. While she made small talk with her silk-suited client, Nicole filled the client's standing Monday morning muffins-and-scones office order.

"How many people are you expecting?" I asked Hal.

"Fifty or sixty—I hope."

"You could do two cakes." I chewed on my pencil. "A half sheet of carrot with cream cheese icing and another half sheet of chocolate fudge with custard or raspberry filling." I flipped open the cake binder to show him potential decorating options.

"Could you write 'Happy Paws Welcomes You' and add some of this confetti-looking stuff?" He grinned at me. "Happy Paws is the name of my clinic."

"Sure. And I think it might be nice if we added a few dogs and cats too."

"Perfect!" He beamed. "I knew you wouldn't let me down. Not after the other night."

A spoon clattered to the floor at Anya's feet. Out of the corner of my eye, I saw Nicole grin and flash me a thumbs-up.

Thankfully, Hal didn't notice. His head was bent over a pocket-size notebook, where he was checking items off a list. "Got the cake taken care of, the drinks, and the decorations. Now, I just need to find a caterer for the hors d'oeuvres."

Anya smoothed back her hair and opened her mouth to recommend one of her friends, but I rushed in before she could form the words. "I know a great caterer. She's new in town and has fabulous food." I pulled one of Deborah's cards out of my pocket and handed it to Hal.

"A Taste of Honey, huh? Sounds great. Thanks, and I'll look forward to seeing you again next Friday." He nodded his good-byes to Anya and Nicole.

Anya whirled on me as soon as the door shut behind Hal. "Just what do you think you're doing?"

.   .   .   .

The loud music coming from behind the door drowned out my knock, so I rang the doorbell. Still nothing. I shifted the box in my hand and gave another tentative ring.

Finally the door swung open to a laughing Deborah in a red head scarf, oversized white T-shirt, and red shorts, revealing more naked leg than I'd ever seen on a big woman. Once again I was struck by the iniquity of brown fat versus white fat. Brown fat looks so much better—not all pale and veiny.

Maybe it was time to start using that tan in a bottle.

"Girl, I was going to call you! Thanks for that referral." Deborah moved to hug me, but the bakery box got in the way. "What you got there?"

"Just a little thank-you for that wonderful lunch on Sunday." I presented it to her shyly.

"You didn't have to do that." She snatched the box from my outstretched hands with a grin. "But, I'm glad you did. Mmm. Smells like chocolate."

"Chocolate raspberry torte."

Deborah put her hand over her heart and expelled a blissful sigh.

"Come on in. I was just getting down to a little Kirk Franklin."

She danced her way over to the stereo, cake box held high, and lowered the volume, then signaled me to follow her into the kitchen. "Set yourself down, and let's have a piece of this luscious concoction."

"Uh, I really wasn't planning to stay." I shifted from one foot to the other.

"What? You got somewhere else to be?"

Yeah. I'm really in demand these days. First I've got a hot dinner date with Hal the vet, and afterwards it's dessert with dimple-man Jared.

"No," I told her regretfully.

"Then take a seat." Deborah rummaged in a drawer while I lifted the chocolate torte out of its pink cardboard enclosure. As I set it on the counter, I cocked my head to one side. "Where is everyone?"

"Samuel's at his Wednesday night men's Bible study, and Lydia's at her accounting class. So it's just us. You want some coffee with your cake?"

"Got any tea?"

"Lipton."

I tried not to grimace, but Deborah caught me out.

"Are you one of those caffeine snobs like Lydia? She can't have regular coffee—always has to be cappuccino, mocha, or latte-something-or-other."

Heat rushed up my neck. "I'm sorry. I didn't mean—"

"Chill. I'm jus' playin' with you. How does a glass of milk sound?"

I nodded.

Deborah poured two glasses of one-percent, then grabbed my hand and bowed her head. "Lord, thank you for new friends. And for chocolate. Please bless this food and our conversation. Amen."

"Amen."

I started to cut the cake, but Deborah stayed my hand. "Did I say I wanted a sliver? Go ahead and cut us both a nice healthy slice so we can savor the full essence of this gorgeous cake."

"But—"

"But nothin'. Go on, now."

So I did. But I made sure the piece I pushed toward Deborah was thicker than mine.

"Mmm." She closed her eyes. "Is there anything better than chocolate?"

I shook my head.

"Although . . . a warm oatmeal-raisin cookie fresh from the oven is pretty great too." She gestured with her chocolate-covered fork. "And nothin' beats my grandma's peach cobbler with homemade ice cream."

"Homemade ice cream? I've never had any."

"Girl, you don't know what you're missing! All us kids loved it and fought over who got to turn the crank. Store-bought can't hold a candle to homemade." Deborah sighed. "What was your favorite flavor of ice cream growing up?"

"Chocolate, I guess. But actually, ice cream wasn't allowed in our house."

"Say what?"

"No ice cream, no cookies, no sweets of any kind."

"Why? Your Daddy diabetic or something?"

"No. Just making sure his darling daughter didn't get any fatter than she already was."

Deborah sucked air between her teeth. "Tell me about your daddy," she said gently. "And your life."

:: *chapter six* ::

There's not much to tell."

"Sure, there is. Everybody's got a story. I'd love to hear yours."

"It's pretty boring."

"Quit that. No one's life is boring. The good Lord made us all individual, with a personal story all our own."

Sometimes the way she talked, Deborah sounded sixty-eight rather than thirty-eight. Must be that down-home Southern style.

"Maybe, but I'd rather not talk about it right now." I smiled to soften my refusal. "I'd rather hear about you and Samuel. How did you two meet?"

"It was in high school. He was a senior, and I was a junior." Deborah put her hand over her heart and sighed. "I'd seen him around and thought he was pretty fine, but so did a lot of the other girls—and I wasn't about to be no groupie. We were both in drama class, and he did an oral interp that made me go weak in the knees." Her eyes got all melty at the memory. "He didn't have me at hello. But he sure had me at 'But, soft! What light through yonder window breaks? It is the east, and Juliet is the sun.'"

"I'd go weak in the knees at that too."

"My Sam had that effect on all the girls." Deborah gave a

proud nod. "But then I did a section from *A Raisin in the Sun*. He came up to me afterward and told me he liked my sassy spirit and asked could he drive me home. From then on, there was never anyone else for either of us."

"Did you get married right after high school?"

"Oh no. We wanted to wait 'til after we'd both graduated from college." She laughed. "At least that was the plan. But he went to school in Atlanta, and I was at the University of North Carolina in Charlotte. After two semesters apart and just seeing each other on weekends, we couldn't stand it anymore." She shrugged. "So on spring break we got married, and I moved to Atlanta to be with him."

"And did you go to school there?"

"That's how it started out. I transferred to Georgia State, but I didn't even make it through a full semester before getting pregnant." Deborah chuckled. "God's timing is always different than man's. We found out we were having twins. From no babies to two—that took some adjusting. But I'd helped raise my younger sisters and brothers after my daddy died and my mother ran off, so we weren't too worried."

"Wait! Your dad died and your mom left?" Talk about familiar, except for the dad dying part. "How old were you?"

"Eleven. We moved in with my Granny Marsh, and she raised us."

"And did you ever see your mother again?"

"Once. She came back to try and get money from her mama—my granny. But she was all strung out on smack and living with a drug dealer. And Granny told her she loved her, but she wasn't going to give her money just to put that junk in her veins." Deborah gave a sad smile. "I remember it like it was yesterday. My mama was all strung out and begging for money, but Granny held firm. She told Mama she was welcome to come live with all of us, but she had to choose—us or the drugs."

Deborah lifted her shoulders in a helpless shrug. "And she chose the drugs. That night when we were all sleeping, she stole Granny's grocery money from its baking-powder can on the top shelf. She left, and we never saw her again. Four months later, she was dead of an overdose."

"How awful." I squeezed her hand. "I'm sorry."

"Church was my escape," Deborah said. "My sanctuary from all the ugliness."

"I hear that."

"That's why when Samuel and I got married, we made up our minds we'd protect our children from that kind of ugliness. I wanted to stay home and raise those children right." She sighed. "That meant we went without a lot of things in the beginning. But as the kids started getting older, I discovered I could make money from my cooking. Just simple, down-home stuff, but folks at church were always after me for my recipes, so I started catering a little bit here and there on Saturdays. Word spread, and pretty soon I had more business than I could handle on my own, so Samuel started helping me on the weekends. Not Sundays, though." She gave an emphatic shake of her head. "That's the Lord's day. Besides, Samuel sang in the church choir.

"My Sam's got a beautiful voice, but I'm terrible." She clicked her long red nails on the granite countertop. "I can dance, but I can't sing. Sounds like a bullfrog when I open my mouth."

"Well, I can sing a little, but I definitely can't dance."

Deborah pushed off her stool and grabbed my hand. "Let's go."

"Where?"

"To the living room."

"What for?"

"To shake your groove thing."

"But I just told you I can't dance."

"Girl, everyone dances. Unless you were raised in one of those strict churches that thinks dancing's a sin." She tugged on my hand. "Come on."

"I mean it. I'm really awful."

I'd never gone to any high-school dances. No homecoming or prom for this big girl. But once, at a college mixer, I'd tried a turn on the dance floor with a pockmarked boy with slippery hands—moving my feet from left to right and shuffling around in a circle. That "slow dance" was the extent of my experience.

Greg had never been into dancing. He'd preferred smoky jazz joints and poetry readings. And I'd gone right along with him. Happily.

"You can't be that bad," Deborah told me. "Besides, it's a great workout. And I'm bigger than you, so you have to do what I say." She gave me an impish grin. "Don't worry. There's no men here. Just us sistahs."

"I never thought of myself as a sistah."

"I'm making you an honorary one." Deborah riffled through her CDs. "Uh-huh. Here's my dance mix—Lydia made it for me." Pumping up the volume, she began mouthing the words to "I'm Every Woman" along with Chaka Khan. She swirled around me, her red scarf flapping against her shoulders. "Shake it, girl, shake it. You got to move those hips of yours. That's why God made 'em." She winked. "That and for havin' babies."

I slid my left foot to the right and back again, repeating the movement in a valiant attempt to copy Deborah's moves, but the rhythm gene had clearly skipped my family. Maybe my entire ethnic mix.

Deborah tried to keep a straight face, but failed.

"See. I told you I couldn't dance."

"Girl, you got to do more than just stand in that one spot.

Don't be so stiff. Move the rest of your body. Just close your eyes, feel the music, and let yourself go."

I closed my eyes and added a couple of tentative turns to my dance-fever routine.

"Uh-huh. Yeah. Now, that's what I'm talkin' about."

Encouraged, I let myself go. I waggled my arms and threw in a little jump and some funky-chicken action. Then I struck a pose. Take that, Madonna.

Pretty soon Deborah and I were both sweating up a storm.

"You're right. Dancing is a good workout," I puffed. "It's getting hot in here."

"Uh-huh." Deborah pulled off her scarf and fanned herself with it while I tried not to stare at her bald spots. "I'll be right back."

While she was gone, I sneaked into the kitchen, splashed a little cold water on my face, and grabbed a paper towel to wipe off my wet forehead.

"Here you go." Deborah returned and thrust a yellow tank top at me. "This will be cooler than that black, long-sleeved thing."

I looked down at the shirt in my hands. "This is sleeveless."

"Uh-huh."

"I don't do sleeveless. Not with these arms."

"You're not even thirty yet—what you worryin' about your arms for? That's a middle-aged thing. And no one's going to see but me." Deborah held out one of her arms and jiggled the flesh beneath it. "'Sides, girl, I got you beat. I got bat wings." She laughed. "Better stand back or I'll take you out. Grown men have sailed across the room after being whacked with one of these puppies."

"All right. I give." I slipped around the corner, slipped into the tank, and resumed my dancing. In fact, I was really getting into it.

· · · ·

"Ladies and gentlemen, welcome to *Dancing with the Stars, Hometown Edition*. The show where one ordinary woman and man from across America get the chance to mix it up with the dancing best from Broadway, Las Vegas, Hollywood, and beyond. That's right, ladies and gentlemen—this is how America dances. And our first contestant, selected from thousands of entries, hails from Lantana, California. Having stunned all the judges with her colorful moves, she'll now be partnering with Enrico Natale, winner of last year's professional ballroom competition."

The live crowd gasped as I entered with Enrico—Enrico of the smoldering eyes and jet-black hair skimming his shoulders. But the crowd fell silent as the two of us quick-stepped and tangoed our way to first place, knocking out the rest of the dancers like so many dominoes. We scored perfect 10s across the board, and the crowd went wild, throwing roses on the dance floor. Enrico gathered them into a bouquet and presented it to me in all my red-spangled glory, kissing my hand and gazing at me in mute adoration as the crowd gave us a standing ovation.

I smiled and twirled in grateful appreciation.

And bumped smack into Lydia.

"What is this?" she giggled, hands on hips. "*Soul Train?*"

· · · ·

Flushed from my dancing-queen workout, I treated myself to a visit to Bramwell's on the way home. I was tempted by a new romance novel with a dark, brooding hero on the cover who looked a lot like the dancing Enrico. But since I had yet to finish the two Millie had given me, I made my way to the music section instead.

My musical tastes have always varied according to my mood: Coldplay and Third Day, Etta James and Frank Sinatra, Edith Piaf and, of course, Eva Cassidy. As a huge *Wizard of Oz* fan, for years

I thought it a sacrilege for anyone but Judy to sing "Over the Rainbow." Then I heard Eva Cassidy. Her haunting rendition—especially poignant because she died of cancer in her thirties—spoke to a deep hidden place inside me. I played Eva's CDs over and over again. They were perfect for those quiet, introspective times. But for less quiet times, nothing but vintage Motown would do.

Priscilla, my favorite cook and mother figure, who introduced me to fried okra and peanut-butter-and-banana sandwiches—talk about comfort food and *not* on my diet—would always crank up her Diana Ross and the Supremes when my parents were out of town. When *Dreamgirls*, the behind-the-scenes tale of three girl singers (rumored to be based on The Supremes) opened on Broadway, 'Cilla was first in line to buy the soundtrack. Which, of course, she played for me, over and over.

"And I Am Tellin' You I'm Not Going" is still one of my all-time favorite songs. I have both the Broadway version and the movie soundtrack featuring Beyoncé and Jennifer Hudson, my favorite *American Idol* contestant of all time. When Brooke's not home, I'll crank up my stereo and sing along in front of the mirror with my hairbrush microphone.

Tonight, though, I was in the mood for a little dance music, so I snagged some discounted copies of disco-era Donna Summer and a *Dance Party* compilation.

As I started to leave, my stomach reminded me that all I'd had for dinner was that sliver of chocolate torte at Deborah's, so I detoured to the café section in hopes that they still had a little food left. In addition to pastries such as my favorite lemon bars, Bramwell's usually offered a few simple lunch and dinner choices—generally quiche, a Mexican egg strata, and sometimes a great spinach-and-turkey wrap.

Checking out the food display case on the way to my usual

table, I spotted two pieces of quiche Lorraine remaining. I settled my packages on the chair opposite and waited to be served.

And waited. And waited.

I tapped my foot and waited some more.

Then I watched as the waiter carried the last two pieces of quiche over to a slender, well-dressed, middle-aged couple who'd arrived after me.

You know, I might be fat. And I might be a wuss. But that didn't mean I didn't have feelings.

. . . .

Once home, I nuked a Lean Cuisine spaghetti, powered up my laptop, and browsed some favorite sites and blogs. And realized I was still mad. Then I had an idea.

Pulling out the scribbled instructions my friend Susan, a computer geek, had left with me, I steered through several screens to set up an anonymous blog. I'd toyed with the notion of blogging before but had never quite gotten around to it. Now my fingers flew furiously over the keyboard as I churned out *The Rantings of Betty Bigg*.

Wednesday

I've just returned from my favorite independent bookstore, where I was ignored yet again by the teenaged clerk-slash-waiter in the cafe, who was supposed to take my order. This isn't a one-time thing. I've been going to this store on a regular basis for a couple of years now, and it's always the same. For a while, I thought it was just because my preferred table is off in a corner and harder to see. You know; that whole out of sight, out of mind thing? So I never made a fuss. I just got up and went to the counter to place my order instead.

But then, a couple of weeks ago, I spotted another woman sitting at "my" table when I arrived. A skinny bimbo. You know the type. All boobs and teeth and bottle-blonde hair. And the bimbo was getting great service. That's when I realized the situation had nothing to do with the table's location and everything to do with me. My size.

I'm a big woman. Some would call me fat (and have, both subtly and not-so-subtly). And as any woman size 14 and over will tell you, that makes me the invisible woman. To everyone: waiters, salesclerks, the man on the street.

Especially the man on the street. Or men anywhere, for that matter.

When men aren't acting like I don't even exist, then they're making fun of me behind my back (yes, I do see them!) or giving me disapproving stares if they ever catch me eating dessert. But that's not just men, of course. Women do it too. All the time.

You see, I don't lie, cheat, steal, smoke, curse, gossip (much), or commit adultery or murder. Yet I'm guilty of the greatest sin of all: being overweight in a looks-obsessed society. And I pay for that crime every day of the week.

I don't know about you, but this big California girl is getting pretty fed up with such treatment! Where can a big girl go to get a little respect? Besides an Old Masters painting, that is.

Invisible in Northern California

I slapped my laptop shut with a vengeance and only then noticed Zsa Zsa cowering in the corner. She whimpered and flattened her ears.

"I'm sorry, baby," I cooed, cradling her in my arms. "I'm not mad at you. You don't ignore me, do you?"

She gazed up at me soulfully with her one eye—now I know why they call it puppy-dog eyes—and licked my hand.

"That's 'cause you're not a male dog." I scratched her tummy.

:: *chapter seven* ::

The next few days passed uneventfully. It was Thursday, a week later, when Deborah called.

"You going to Dr. Hal's open house tomorrow night?"

"Well, I'm delivering the cakes . . ."

"You're doing more than just that. My new client tells me you were invited to attend."

True. The cute vet had sent me an invitation with a personal note scrawled at the bottom of the blue vellum, saying he looked forward to seeing me. But I knew Anya didn't like me to mix with the customers, so I'd planned to just drop off the cakes and leave.

"You're going." Deborah's tone brooked no refusal. "You need to show your support for the man's business. It's the hospitable thing to do."

"All right, all right, I'll go. Cut me some slack."

"Good." Her pleasure resonated in my ear. "But you are not wearing black. What time do you get off work?"

"Today? Around three."

"Do you want me to pick you up, or should we just meet at the mall?"

"For what?"

"Shopping. We need to add a little color to your wardrobe."

"My wardrobe's fine."

"Yeah, right." She snorted. "If you're going to a bunch of funerals or you're a poet living in New York. But this is the Golden State, girlfriend. You need to add a little sunshine to your life." She began to sing "Let the Sun Shine," only in her voice it came across more as a croak.

"You really can't sing, can you?"

"Not a bit."

"And I suppose you're going to keep on singing until I agree."

"You got it."

"Okay. But I'm not going to Payne Tryon. Let's meet at Macy's."

. . . .

"What about this?" Four hours later, Deborah, who was wearing a sunny yellow caftan with African safari images at the hem, held up a tiered crinkle skirt in a vivid pink and purple print with an embroidered and beaded purple tee from Macy Woman.

I shook my head. "I don't like prints. And purple reminds me of that poem where the woman says when she's old, that's what she's going to wear. I may be big, but I'm not old."

Deborah draped it over her left arm.

"But—"

"This ain't for you, Miss Thang. I happen to look great in purple."

My face flamed. "I'm sorry. I—"

She waved it off. "No need. You're entitled to your opinion. Besides, purple doesn't make me feel the least bit old." She held the outfit beneath her neck and smacked her lips in front of the mirror. "And Samuel really likes it on me. But we're here to find *you* something."

She returned to the rack of skirts and began riffling through them, finally pulling out another tiered skirt—this one a rich, solid coral with a matching tee on the hanger with it.

"No prints and no purple." Deborah handed it to me, triumphant. "And it's a set, so you get two-for-one."

"Uh, isn't it kind of bright?"

"That's the point."

"I'll look like a pumpkin. Or a giant Creamsicle. Children will run after me, wanting a bite." I grabbed the same outfit in olive. "What about this?"

"You in the Army now?"

"It's a little more my style. Subdued."

"I know." She rolled her eyes. "That's what we're trying to change." Deborah released a heavy sigh. "Guess you might as well try them both on."

Behind her back I snagged a black T-shirt as I followed her to the dressing room, discreetly slipping the tee between the two outfits.

I was learning that Deborah broke every rule in the big girl's book. She wore sleeveless tank tops and horizontal stripes and white pants. She ate what she wanted. She talked comfortably about her size in public. And, horror of horrors, she didn't mind sharing her weight: "Two-hundred thirty-six pounds of big, black, beautiful woman."

I wasn't ready to share my weight. There's something called mystery.

Deborah followed me into the third curtained cubicle. "That coral is going to look beaut—"

"Um, you don't need to come in."

"I'm sorry. You one of those shy ones, huh? No problem. I'll respect your privacy." She grinned and left.

Making sure the curtains were closed, I removed my black big-girl uniform and hung it on the hook, careful to avoid looking in the mirror until the entire outfit was on.

Then I slowly turned around and faced the music. Just as I thought. A giant Creamsicle.

I poked my head out the curtain. "Deborah?"

But she was gone.

Pulling the curtains shut again, I started to lift the T-shirt over my head.

"Freddie?" Her distinctive voice rumbled through the dressing rooms. "Which one you in again?"

I pulled the T-shirt back down and poked my head out of the curtain once more, unwilling to reveal my big orange self to all the skinny girls trying on their size 6 jeans.

"Over here."

"Decided you needed a scarf or a belt, so I brought you a few that—"

Deborah stopped short when she saw me. "Maybe it is a little too much coral all at once."

"Ya think?"

She handed me a long black scarf with fringe at the ends. "This might help."

"Black? You brought me something black?" I backed up in mock horror. "I thought black was *verboten.*"

"Not as an accessory or accent piece." She tied it loosely around my waist, dangling the fringed ends to the side. "There." Deborah stood back, surveyed the result, and frowned.

"Now I look like a Creamsicle with a black belt." I shooed her out. "Give me a minute. I have an idea."

When the curtains shut behind her, I yanked off the coral T-shirt, replacing it with the black one. Then I pored through the scarves and belts Deborah had gathered until I found a long, multicolored scarf of coral, jade, gold, and black with black fringe. I knotted this around my waist, with the ends dangling against the coral skirt, and studied the results in the mirror.

Not bad. Not bad at all. I opened the curtains and stepped out.

"Now, *that's* what I'm talkin' about! Even though you tricked me with that black shirt, the scarf gives it a splash of color. With the right shoes, earrings, and makeup, you'll be lookin' good, girl."

"Shoes?" I looked down at my black, serviceable Clarks clogs. "What's wrong with these?"

"You don't want me to even go there."

Anya's fancy feet flashed before my eyes. "I'm so not wearing stilettos. I'd fall off."

By the time we left the store, I'd bought three pairs of pretty, low-heeled sandals (Macy's was having a 30-percent-off sale). A summery tan, a white, and a kicky coral pair that exactly matched the new outfit.

I'd balked at the latter. "Coral sandals? That's a waste of money to buy a pair of shoes I can only wear with one outfit."

"I count at least three outfits right here those shoes will go with."

"Three?"

"The new skirt and black top that you're wearing tomorrow with the scarf. The coral T-shirt you can wear with one of your many pairs of black pants. And this cute pair of white capris I'm buying for you that will go great with your new T-shirt and the scarf."

"*White* pants? Are you kidding? Big girls can't wear white pants."

"Says who?"

"Everyone. It's a known fact."

"From where? The Bible?"

"Of course not. From etiquette books and fashion magazines."

And skinny stepmothers.

"And you think I pay attention to those things?" Deborah drew herself up to her full, fabulous height, her oversize gold hoop earrings flashing. "Those girls in those magazines aren't real. They're all touched up and airbrushed and starving to death. No wonder so many young girls have eating disorders, trying to live up to a false image of beauty. You won't catch me followin' those things. Or my daughter." She wagged her finger at me. "And you shouldn't either. God made you who you are in all your big, beautiful womanness, and God don't make no mistakes."

"But he didn't make me this big to start with."

"If he did, I pity your poor mama." Her eyes danced. "Mmm-hmm. That would have been one painful birth."

I sucked air through my teeth and sat down hard on the chair I'd just vacated.

Deborah gazed at me, stricken, and shook her head at the approaching shoe salesman. "I'm sorry. I'm always putting my big foot in my big mouth."

"That's okay. It's not a big deal. I don't know why I'm reacting this way."

She put her hand on my knee. "Was yours a difficult child-birth for your mama?"

I nodded and lowered my voice. "I was so big I broke my mother's pelvis."

"Say what?" Deborah stared at me. "I never heard of such a thing."

"It's not common, but it can happen. That's what my parents said."

"Hmm. My twins were big too. Sam Junior was seven pounds, nine ounces. I had to have an emergency C-section." Deborah patted her stomach. "But it was all worth it once I saw those beautiful babies."

"I understand that's how mothers normally respond. But not mine." I shrugged and said lightly, "I was too much for her, and she couldn't handle it, so she just left."

"Who told you that?"

"My father. And my stepmother, the Botox queen." Candy was also the one who'd let slip—after too much eggnog one Christmas—that my "free-spirited hippie mother" had wanted to name me Angelica.

"When did your mama leave?"

"The week after I was born."

Deborah's eyes brimmed. "And she never contacted you afterward?"

"Not once."

"She must have had a powerful reason for leaving. It's not an easy thing for a mother to leave her child."

I snorted. "That's a crock. Not everyone has that famous warm and fuzzy maternal instinct. Even your own mother."

My hand flew to my mouth. "I'm sorry."

"Guess it's not just me who suffers from foot-in-mouth disease." Deborah gave me a crooked smile. "For the first nine years of my life, my mama took real good care of me and my brothers and sisters. But the babies kept on coming and the money didn't. My daddy got sick and lost his job, and we didn't have no insurance. When he died, there was nothin'. Mama worked as a waitress, but there still wasn't enough money."

She got a faraway look in her eyes. "But Mama was real pretty, and the men started coming 'round. There was one who even took us out for ice cream in his big, shiny car. Mama thought if she could find another good man to marry, he could take care of us." Deborah sighed. "But what man's going to take on seven children that aren't his?"

Her fingers tightened on the purple fabric. "Mama found a man, all right, but he wasn't a good one. She started staying out all hours, and I'd be left home alone with the rest of the kids. He's the one who got her hooked on heroin."

Deborah stared off into the distance again. "That last time Mama came home and asked Granny for money, I could see in her eyes that she loved us, but she was ashamed. That's the last look I ever saw in my mama's eyes . . ."

"Are you ladies all right?" The shoe clerk cleared his throat. "Did you want to try on any more shoes?"

Deborah swiped at her eyes and stood up. "I think we've bought enough today. Besides"—she winked at him—"you don't want us to be cryin' on no leather. That salt water would shrivel those designer shoes right up."

· · · ·

"Mama, are you playing fairy godmother?"

"You see any wings on this body?" Deborah looked up from her easy chair in front of the ottoman where she was applying coral polish to my toes.

"I tried to just say no, but she wouldn't listen." I shot Lydia a helpless look.

"Best not even try. When Mama gets an idea in her head, there's no stopping her."

"Is that so, Miss Lydia?" Deborah fixed her daughter with a piercing gaze. "I had the idea for you to come back to Decatur, but that didn't work."

"That's because I put my foot down. You'll have to do that too, Freddie."

"I would, but I don't want to get polish all over your beautiful furniture."

"If you don't stop moving, *I'm* going to get polish on it."
Deborah stuck the applicator back in the tube for a fresh brush full.

"That's a pretty color." Lydia spied the shopping bags next to
the end table. "Ooh, what'd you get?"

"What *didn't* we get is more the question." I began ticking
items off on my fingers. "Clothes, shoes, makeup . . ."

"Can I see?"

"Help yourself."

Lydia riffled through the bags, pulling out items and holding
them up. "This is some good mascara. Halle Berry wears it. It will
really bring out your eyes, Freddie."

"That's what I told her." Deborah gave her daughter a pleased
smile.

"How much did your mother pay you to say that?"

"Nothing. You really have some pretty green eyes. You need
to show them off more." Lydia pulled out the new mascara wand
and approached. "Now look up."

"I know how to put on makeup."

Deborah snorted. "Then how come you're not wearing any?"

"What's the point?"

"Quit talking if you don't want me to poke you in the eye,"
Lydia said. "There, now. That's better." She fished a small mirror
out of her purse and held it up. "See?"

· · · ·

The Oprah audience burst into thunderous applause as the new
and improved me strode confidently across the stage to greet the
queen of all TV. My shiny, highlighted reddish-brown hair in its
new flattering cut gleamed under the lights; my porcelain skin
took on an ethereal, Nicole Kidman glow; and my gorgeous green
eyes between lush lashes practically melted the camera lens.

Oprah did the split-screen before-and-after shot, and even I was amazed at the transformation from frumpy creature with mousy brown hair and unremarkable features to amazing sex goddess.

The few scattered men in the estrogen-heavy audience clapped and whistled, and I noticed women in the front row wiping away empowering tears. Afterward, when I left the building, I was mobbed with backstage Johnnies wanting my autograph or a date.

"Ooh." Lydia breathed in sharply, bringing me back to the present. She put her hand on her stomach.

"What is it? You okay?" I asked.

"I'm fine." She expelled a long breath, patting her stomach as she did. "Just Braxton Hicks."

"Oh, is that what you've decided to name the baby?"

Deborah guffawed, and Lydia giggled.

"What?"

Lydia giggled some more. "Braxton Hicks is the name for a preterm contraction. False labor."

"And I would know that how?" I mimicked one of my favorite *Gone with the Wind* scenes. "I don't know nothin' 'bout birthin' no babies." Then felt my cheeks flame in embarrassment. Wasn't that one of the scenes that African-Americans found so insulting?

But Deborah just snorted. "Ain't that the truth!"

I gave her a mock withering look and pointedly turned back to Lydia. "So what *do* you plan to name the baby? Have you picked out a name yet?"

She shot a defiant glance at her mother. "Well, Mama likes Rachel or Rebecca . . ."

Deborah nodded. "Good biblical names, both of them."

Lydia continued. "But I'm leaning toward Kenya or Keshia if

it's a girl and maybe Malcolm or Jamal if it's a boy." She gave me a secret smirk. "Although I'm also thinking of Little Bow-Wow."

Deborah glowered. "No grandchild of mine is going to be given a name that sounds like it belongs to a dog. Or even a rapper."

"Relax, Mama. I was just teasing you. Can't you take a joke?" Lydia lifted her chin. "Although . . . since *I'm* this child's mama, choosing his or her name is my responsibility and my prerogative."

Deborah opened her mouth and then quickly closed it again.

"If I ever have a daughter," I jumped in, "I want to name her Kate. I've always loved that name. So strong and classic. Unlike Freddie." I grimaced. "I hate my name. Always have. Especially when my Dad insists on calling me Fredericka, which is even worse."

"So why don't you change it?" Lydia asked.

"You can't do that."

"Sure you can. It's your name—you can do whatever you want." Lydia shot Deborah a conspiratorial grin. "Hey Mama, remember my friend Puké?"

Deborah shook her head. "What kind of parents would name their baby girl that, especially with Green as a last name? I don't blame her for changing it to Renee the minute she turned eighteen."

Hmmm . . . now, there's an idea . . . I leaned back in my chair, thinking about my Oprah debut and total transformation. And murmured, "A Kate could handle anything."

· · · ·

"Now, tomorrow, you remember to do your eyes like Lydia showed you," Deborah instructed as I said good night.

"Yes ma'am. Anything else?"

"Mmm-hmm. When I see you at that open house, you better be wearing your new skirt and not one of those old black ones."

I saluted. "Ma'am, yes ma'am."

When I got home, I curled up in the tub with the first volume of the romance series Millie had given me. Reading about the plain-Jane governess who was transformed into a beautiful swan and whom the lord of the manor fell in love with, I sighed and peered over my paperback, admiring my coral toes over the bubbles.

I'm really not that big on clothes or makeup, but I do love a good pedicure!

:: *chapter eight* ::

N ice cat." Shane peered over my shoulder at the rendering of
the orange cat I'd just drawn in icing atop the carrot half-
sheet cake for Hal Baxter's open house.

"You think so?" I bit my lip and surveyed the drawing. "It's
not too Garfield looking?"

"Not at all. This cat looks real. You going to do a dog too?"

I exchanged pastry bags and metal tips and began outlining
the shape of a yellow Lab. "Yep. And probably a bird too. I don't
want to discriminate. I think Dr. Hal's an equal-opportunity
vet." I held back my shudder so I wouldn't smear the frosting.
"Although I draw the line—or in this case, not—at hamsters or
anything in the rodent family."

"Aww. But hamsters are so cute." Nicole wiped the cookie
crumbs from the display-case tray she'd just brought back from
the front. "Don't you think so, Shane?"

"Yep. We always had hamsters growing up."

"Me too! What about you, Millie? Did your kids have
hamsters?"

"Nope. I'm with Freddie on this one." She shuddered.
"Hamsters are too much like mice. Todd really wanted one when

he was little, but I got him a puppy instead. I'll take chewed shoes any day over chewed toes."

Shane laughed. "Hamsters don't chew toes. Neither do mice."

"Tell that to Ben," Millie said.

"Ben?"

"You know. The movie."

"What movie?" Shane, movie geek of the universe, scrunched his eyes in confusion.

"*Ben.*"

"Ben who?"

"*Ben*, the movie. About the rat? Came out in the early '70s. Michael Jackson did the theme song." Millie sang a snatch of it in a silly mock falsetto.

Nicole and Shane gave her a blank look.

She sighed. "Never mind. You're too young." Millie turned to me. "You remember it, don't you?"

I shook my head. "I wasn't born till the late '70s. But can we stop talking about rats and mice, please? They creep me out."

Anya poked her head through the door. "Nicole? Where are those cookies?"

"Coming right up." She lifted the tray of sugar cookies and followed Anya to the front, stopping to whisper in my ear as she walked by. "Great job on the cake, Freddie. Dr. Hal's going to *love* it."

. . . .

I wasn't about to wear my new clothes or even my new makeup to work because I knew Anya would make some smart crack or give me one of those withering, pitying glances. So I waited until everyone had left before retrieving my hanging outfit from the car. As I did, I glanced at my watch. I'd really have to rush to get there and have the cakes set up in advance of the six o'clock open house.

In the restroom, I peeled off my work clothes, splashed some water on my face, ran a baby wipe beneath my arms, and dabbed on some Secret. Then I pulled on the coral skirt and black T-shirt and unzipped the little pink polka-dotted bag Deborah had insisted I needed for all my new makeup.

No time to do the whole rigmarole she and Lydia had taken me through last night—concealer, foundation, powder, blush, shadow, mascara, eyeliner, lipstick. I just slapped on a little mascara and coral lipstick and hit the ground running.

Good thing I'd kept my work clogs on till I got in the car.

Shane had already removed the cakes from the walk-in and loaded them into my car for me, so I was good to go. Ten minutes later, I pulled up in front of Happy Paws. I kicked off my clogs and pulled on the new sandals from the bag in the back seat. Then I picked up the chocolate-fudge cake in its pink box, took a deep breath, and picked my way carefully to the entrance on the uneven flagstone walk.

"Freddie!" Hal stood in the doorway beaming and looking almost spiffy in a white cotton open-necked tunic over khaki shorts. His eyes flickered to my cheeks, and he started to say something but checked himself.

"You look great." He nodded to the box in my hands. "Can I help you with that?"

"Actually, the other cake's still in the car. Could you bring that in?"

"Of course. Can't wait to see it." He winked. "And eat it."

"Thanks." I entered a large waiting room filled with multi-colored balloons and streamers.

"There you are!" Deborah, who was a fuchsia-clad marvel from the top of her head to the tips of the toes peeking out through her sandals, looked up from a platter of cold cuts she was unwrapping. "I was startin' to worry." She glanced at my feet with satisfaction as I made my way to the buffet table. "I knew that polish would be perfect with those shoes."

"Freddie, you certainly look nice," Samuel said. "That skirt's a beautiful color."

"Didn't I tell you?" Deborah grinned, but her grin quickly faded to a frown. "Where's your belt?"

"Oops." I looked down at my undefined waist. "I must have left it in the bag in the car. I'll go get it."

"Not so fast." Her eyes zeroed in on my cheeks. "What'd you do to your face?"

"My face?"

"You got black dots all under your eyes."

My hands flew to my cheeks. No wonder Hal had looked at me strangely—the same Hal who was fast approaching the entrance, cake in hand.

"Quick, go in the restroom and clean up your face," Deborah said. "I'll go get your belt."

"But I need to get the cakes set up."

"You can do that when you come back. Now, go!" She gave me a little push.

. . . .

"What a cute cake." A Britney Spears blonde in white shorts and a red baby tee with a diamond (or more likely rhinestone) belly-button stud stopped in front of the cake table where Hal was chatting with a few middle-aged men. "That picture looks just like my sweet little kitty."

The trio of graying baby boomers sucked in their guts. "My cat looks just like that too," the short one with the bad comb-over said. "I call him O.C. for orange cat. What's your cat's name?"

"Princess Aurora," she purred, her eyes locked on Hal.

"From Sleeping Beauty?"

"Exactly." She slipped an arm through his. "How refreshing to meet a guy who knows his fairy tales. I can't wait for you to meet my sweet princess. She'll just love you."

I picked up a fruit skewer and nibbled on the pineapple at the end, doing my leaning thing again and all the while yearning to take my skewer and pop that rhinestone out of the Britney wannabe's taut, tanned tummy.

"Popper?" Deborah thrust a hors d'oeuvres tray beneath my nose. "Jalapeño popper?" She leaned over and whispered, "Careful you don't drip pineapple juice on your new shirt. What you doing in the corner, anyway? How can anyone see you there?" She gave me a little push. "Go mingle."

Fortunately, Brooke and Jon chose that moment to arrive. Brooke's eyebrows arched in surprise at the sight of me. "Wow. Can this be my roommate? You look great! You should wear color more often. Don't you think so, Jon?"

"Mmm." But he was focused on the lavish buffet spread.

Brooke eyed the meatballs and deli meats askance. "Anything for the noncarnivores?"

"Try these cheese-stuffed mushrooms," I urged. "The jalapeño poppers are really good too."

Jon popped a mushroom into his mouth and moaned. And Brooke followed suit.

"Aren't those great?" Hal asked, having extricated himself from the Britney wannabe. "I told Deborah I had some veggie-saurus friends."

"Veggiesaurus?" I frowned.

"Yeah, you know," Jon said. "From *Jurassic Park*?"

"Never saw it."

"What?" Both men looked at me as if I were from another planet.

"It's one of the coolest movies ever," Jon said.

"Especially in surround sound." Hal's eyes gleamed. "That roar of the T-Rex is amazing."

"Oh yeah." Jon high-fived Hal.

"Men and noise." Brooke rolled her eyes. "That and a car chase is all they need in a movie. Oh, and explosions. They need explosions."

"Don't forget the beautiful babes," Jon teased. "That scientist chick was pretty hot."

"Smart and feisty, I'll grant you, but a little too skinny for my taste." Hal gave me a slow smile that made me blush as I realized, *He's flirting with me. He's actually flirting.*

Deborah, who was passing by with another tray of hors d'oeuvres, stopped and patted Hal on the back. "Now, there's a man who knows what's what." She extended the tray to him with an inviting grin. "Cheese puff?"

"Thanks." He wolfed one down and grabbed another. "Mmm. These melt in the mouth. Delicious." Hal turned to me. "And thank *you*, Freddie, for recommending A Taste of Honey. A taste of heaven is more like it."

Deborah beamed. "We'll have to add that to our advertising."

"Speaking of taste"—Hal glanced at his watch—"when do you think would be a good time to serve the cake?"

"Ooh, honey, you're gonna love Freddie's cake," Deborah said. "That girl can bake."

I felt the heat higher on my face. "Now would probably be good." I turned to make my way to the cake table when a familiar voice behind me caught my attention.

"I just got a dog, so here I am," Jared was saying. "Besides, there's free food. What's not to like?"

I whirled around in time to see the lissome brunette by his side giggle and give him a playful punch. My sudden movement caught Jared's eye, and he looked my way. Praying my blush wasn't too noticeable, I gave him a shy smile.

Which he never even saw, since he looked right past me.

"Freddie? Something wrong?" Hal asked. "I thought we were going to cut the cake."

"Of course." I followed him to the table, with Brooke and Jon close on our heels.

"First, I want to get a picture of your masterpiece for posterity." Hal turned to my roommate. "Brooke, you brought your camera, right?"

I stepped off to one side, but Hal steered me back behind the cake, his arm around my shoulders. "No, no. I want you in the shot. The artist with her creation."

If I could have sucked in my upper arms the way I sucked in my stomach, I would have. I wasn't prepared for male contact. But Deborah was lovin' it. Out of the corner of my eye, I noticed her giving me a big thumbs-up.

Hal released me to give a little welcome speech, and Deborah hurried over to help by slicing the chocolate cake while I cut through the kitty on the carrot cake. "Can I have a corner piece, please?" Hal asked with a boyish grin after finishing his speech. "Cream cheese frosting is my favorite. And would you think I was a total pig if I asked for a small piece of chocolate too?"

Jon and Brooke made snorting sounds.

"Not a total pig—maybe just a half." I blushed. Boy, I was really on tonight.

Brooke opted for a piece of chocolate, and Jon chose carrot cake.

As the veggie twosome drifted away, taking bites off each other's plates, Jared approached with the flavor of the week on his arm. He shot Deborah a megawatt smile, deepening his killer dimples. "Hey there. Good to see you again." Then he glanced at the cake knife in my hand and at last connected the dots. "Hiya, Frankie. How's it goin'? Good to see a Jorgensen's cake here. Can't wait to wrap my mouth around a piece again."

"Freddie, this is delicious. You're a marvel." Hal kissed me on the cheek—and I nearly dropped the cake knife on my bare toes. He stuck out his hand to Jared. "Hi, there. Hal Baxter. Welcome to Happy Paws."

"Jared Brown." Jared shook Hal's hand, then turned to the woman beside him. "And this is Tiffani."

"With an *i*," she added, fluttering her incredibly long lashes at Hal while Jared continued the introductions.

"Tiffani, this is Deborah and Fra—Freddie from my church."

"Carrot or chocolate?" I extended a piece in each hand.

"Oh no. None for me." Tiffani shrank back, flicking a quick glance at my hips. "Do you know how many calories are in just one slice?"

"Ten thousand?" Deborah asked innocently as Jared relieved me of the carrot-cake slice.

"Not in a Jorgensen's cake."

My heart sank. What was Anya doing here?

"At our family bakery we use only the finest ingredients—no cheap, fattening shortening, like most places." Anya's eyes flicked to Deborah, dismissing her in a glance. "Don't worry," she assured Tiffani. "A small piece wouldn't be more than a couple hundred calories."

Jared's date checked out Anya in her tight jeans, low-cut lacy camisole, artfully tousled hair, and four-inch heels. "Okay, I'll take a teensy sliver of chocolate, please."

I set down the larger piece in my hand and cut a new slice while Anya schmoozed Tiffani and Jared. I had to hand it to her. She really had it down to an art form. Tiffani never even realized my boss was homing in on her date. And even though Anya probably had a good ten years on Jared, she wouldn't let that stop her. Unless you looked really closely, she hid her age well. Amazing what expensive makeup, the latest fashions, and a wee touch of cosmetic surgery will do.

Samuel approached his wife. "Excuse me for interrupting, sug', but could I get you to help me with something at the buffet table?"

Deborah excused herself, as did Hal moments later when a client approached with a question about his sick gerbil, leaving me alone with Anya, Tiffani, and Jared's dimples.

Tiffani's cell blared out "Someday My Prince Will Come." She flipped it open. "Hi, this is Tiffani with an *i*," she said in an ultra-perky voice. Her eyes grew huge. "Shut up! Really? When? Omigosh. I'm *so* there!" She snapped her phone shut. "Sorry, sweetie, but I have to run. Prada and Jimmy Choo are having a special 70-percent-off sale for only the next hour. Gotta go." She blew him a kiss and raced off.

"Seventy percent off? Wait for me!" Anya sped after her.

And now Jared and I were all alone with his dimples.

He stuck out his delicious lower lip in a pout. "Don't you want to go too?"

"Nah. I'm not exactly the fashionista type. What you see is what you get."

Jared looked closely at me, as if seeing me for the very first time. "Well, I certainly do like what I see. Give me a woman who's not blown about by the fickle winds of fashion any day. A real woman. Classic. That's you, Freddie." He leaned in close . . .

"Freddie?" Anya's amused voice popped my fantasy bubble. "You with us, Freddie?"

I flushed. "Sorry. I was daydreaming."

Anya giggled and shot Jared a coy glance. "I'll bet I can guess about what."

My fingers itched for a banana cream pie.

• • • •

When I got home, I shucked off my new outfit and changed into some comfort clothes. Tigger was dirty, so I settled for Eeyore instead.

I powered up my laptop and read my blogger bio again to make sure I hadn't revealed too much. I wasn't comfortable telling the whole world my name, what kind of work I did, or even the city I lived in. The last thing I needed was some weird stalker with a penchant for big women and cream puffs to show up on my doorstep someday.

Name: Betty Bigg
Gender: Female
Location: Northern California

About Me: I'm a single, thirtyish, big woman, working and living in a midsized city in northern California, who feels like the invisible woman because of my size. Can you relate? This blog is my safe place to rant. If you're a big woman--or man--who feels like the world doesn't notice you, I hope you'll chime in. One request: no diet talk allowed.

Satisfied with my bio, I started right in on that day's blog entry:

Friday

So, speaking of men and being invisible, this guy I know and kind of like (okay, I admit it, I sort of have a little crush) never can remember my name. I was at this party tonight and started to hyperventilate when I spotted him coming my way. I sucked in my stomach and smiled at him as he approached.

But he walked right by. Never even noticed me, even though everyone else said I was looking good.

Later, I was in a group with someone else he knew, and he finally said hello. But he got my name wrong. Again.

It didn't help that my skinny boss from the Netherworld showed up and embarrassed me.

A lot of skinny women do that to big women in general. It's like we're an affront to their thin perfection or something. We're their worst nightmare. They probably look at us and think they're only a few Twinkies and a couple of cartons of Ben & Jerry's away from, horrors!, looking like us.

What I don't get is what's the big attraction to skinny women anyway? Okay, forget I asked that.

I have this new friend: a funny, zaftig, gorgeous woman totally comfortable in her own skin. And she has a sweet, wonderful man who adores her just as she is. All of her. Every inch.

Why can't more men be like him?

I reviewed my post to make sure there were no typos or spelling errors, and that's when I noticed I had two comments on my first post. Nervously, I read the first one.

Dear Betty,

You rock! I, too, am a "big woman," and this kind of stuff happens to me all the time. The guy in the bookstore ignoring you due to your size--try restaurants, stores, trains, planes, and automobiles. I'm twenty-one and in college in Massachusetts. The guys on campus walk past me all the time without even seeing me. It's like I'm a ghost or something. I notice them checking out the size 4 hotties, but they never give this size 14 girl a second glance. (Okay, I lied. I'm mostly a 14 in skirts, but in jeans, it's just not happening. There I'm a solid 16.)

Hey, I have a great idea! We should start some kind of big-woman commune or fat-girl farm. There's strength in numbers. If we band together, they can't ignore us. Right? I'm thinkin' maybe somewhere in the middle of our two coasts? Ohio, perhaps? Or Kansas?

What do you think?

Mad in Massachusetts

I stared at the screen. *I don't think so.*

The summer I was thirteen, my parents sent me to a fat farm where I ate rabbit food, ran around a track, and worked out with weights every other day. By the end of nine weeks, I'd only sweated off twenty-seven pounds, which wasn't nearly enough to satisfy my father.

I buried my head in Zsa Zsa's fur, then responded.

Hi, Mad in Massachusetts,

Not Kansas. I'm all out of ruby slippers, although I do have a small dog. I'm thinking one of those four-letter Midwest states with an *I*--Ohio or Iowa. Except . . . don't they have a lot of humidity in the summers? I don't do humidity.

Somewhere more temperate perhaps. Not tropical, though.

Bathing suits are not my friends.

Betty B.

I read the next comment and promptly deleted it. Eew! Big women were definitely *not* invisible to this guy.

Hi, everyone!

Me, again. Thanks to those of you who are reading my blog (all two of you ☺). And please accept my apologies for the X-rated nature of one of the comments that came in, which I just deleted. This is a G-rated site with perhaps an occasional foray into PG. For this reason, even though I prefer to remain anonymous, I can no longer allow anonymous responses. Thanks for understanding.

I appreciate the gentleman's (and I use that word loosely) sentiment about admiring big, beautiful women, but that's not exactly the kind of attention I had in mind.

:: *chapter nine* ::

How'd the open house go? Tell me everything." Millie, who was filling in this Saturday for Shane, pushed a cup of tea my way. She looked at me closer. "Hey, are you wearing makeup?"

"A little."

"It looks good. What brought about this change?"

"Deborah thinks I need to stand out more and not just blend into the background."

"Good for her! I've been telling you that for years, but you wouldn't listen. I think I need to meet this Deborah." The corners of Millie's mouth curved upward. "So, did the vet like your gorgeous cake?"

I sipped my tea and nodded. "So did everyone else." I thought of the tiny blonde with the tight tummy and princess cat.

"And did you have a good time?"

Walking to the double doors, I peered through the window to make sure the coast was clear. "Yeah. Until Anya showed up."

"*Anya* went to that open house?"

"Uh-huh."

"Since when does Anya deign to go to those kinds of things?"

"Since she decided a vet, although admittedly not a real *doctor*, is at least in the same ballpark as one."

"Poor Anya," observed Millie. "She loves money, but she can't ever decide if she wants to make it or marry it."

"Yeah," I murmured. "Poor Anya."

. * . *

My diamond toe ring flashed in the sun as I strode purposefully to the podium in my stop-sign red sandals. The shoes and my curve-hugging red silk dress set off my gleaming chestnut locks, specially arranged for this trip to the podium to accept the award for Woman Entrepreneur of the Year.

The applause thundered in my ears as I gazed over the diverse crowd of top movers and shakers—mostly women, but a few men, including a beaming Jared and Hal—noshing on Deborah's famous appetizers.

"Thank you. Thank you." I waved at them to sit down. "Please. Continue to enjoy your wonderful food from A Taste of Honey. Isn't it delicious?"

More thunderous applause.

"My friend, Deborah, is an amazing cook."

Further applause.

"And an even more amazing friend." I shot her a dazzling smile. "If it weren't for Deborah, I wouldn't even be here today accepting this amazing award. Deborah's the one who believed in me and pushed me to start my own company, Reeka's Specialty Cakes." (No way was I calling it Freddie's.) I motioned for her to come join me.

"Girl, the first time I saw one of your beautiful cakes, I had a feeling you were destined for great things." Deborah's booming voice needed no microphone as she wound her magenta-clad self

through the crowd. "Then I tasted one. Mmm-hmm. And I knew."
She reached me and enveloped me in a happy hug.

"Thank you, Deborah. For believing in me and pushing me
to leave the nest and try going on my own."

The clapping resumed.

I held up my hand. "I would be remiss if I didn't thank
another woman too. An equally talented, smart, and amazing
woman who gave me my start in the bakery business and showed
me the ropes."

Anya, in a beige suit that didn't go well with her complexion,
started to stand.

"Millie Ames, would you please come up here?" I asked.

Millie, looking elegant in a navy dress with white piping,
touched my arm in acknowledgment as she joined me on the
podium.

I basked in the triumphant moment, nodding and smiling at
the cheering crowd. Three strong women standing together,
exulting in our accomplishments.

The only thing missing was Oprah.

• ∘ • ∘

Millie touched my arm again and cleared her throat. "Freddie?"

I blinked.

"Did you hear what I said, Freddie?" Anya, wearing not beige
but a pale salmon that matched her painted-on peaches-and-
cream complexion, gave me a pointed look. "Or were you daydreaming again? I don't know how you ever get any work done."
She descended into whine mode. "You have no idea the responsibility involved with owning your own business and how hard it is
when people don't pull together . . . I can't afford to pay you for
overtime when you're wasting time with your head in the clouds."

Anya set an address down on the counter. "I need you to deliver the Yancey/Clark wedding cake because I have a meeting with a potential new client." She fluffed her hair. "I figured going to that goofy open house last night was a smart business move. And who knows? Maybe a personal one too." She gave me a knowing smile. "That Jared Brown is pretty hot."

I held back my grimace by sheer force of will. "You mean Jared's your new client? That's who you're meeting with?"

"Absolutely. Over lunch." She grinned. "Did you get a look at his dimples? Mmm. He goes to your church, right? Maybe I'll have to give this church thing a try after all." Anya smoothed down her short skirt and said over her shoulder on her way out to the front. "Oh, and you can take the rest of the day off today after you deliver the cake."

The door swung shut behind her.

"Well, wasn't that big of Lady Bountiful—letting you have the afternoon off when you only work half a day on Saturdays already?" Millie shook her head. "Unbelievable." She sent me a tentative look. "I'm sorry."

"For what?"

"For not standing up for you and for letting Anya talk to you that way. If I weren't a year away from retirement, I'd really give her a piece of my mind." Millie lifted her shoulders in a helpless shrug. "But I really need that retirement. And besides, who else is going to hire an arthritic sixty-four-year-old?"

"It's not your fault, Millie. And it's not your place. Don't worry about it." I gave her a slight smile. "One of these days, maybe I'll grow a backbone." Adjusting the pastry bag in my hand, I carefully piped icing onto the sides of the white, raspberry-filled cake, writing out *James and Kayla Forever* on alternate layers.

The back door opened, and Shane breezed in.

"I thought you had the day off," Millie said.

"I did. My family was going to Marine World for my nephew's birthday, but he got sick, so they had to cancel the party." Shane grabbed an oatmeal cookie from the cooling rack. "Figured I'd see if you guys needed any help."

He ambled over to where I was working. "Cool!" he exclaimed, leaning closer. "Where'd you get the idea to put words on the cake?"

"The bride saw a picture in one of those celebrity wedding magazines." I stood back and surveyed my handiwork. "The difference is, in that photo, it was just the word *Love* repeated around each layer. More words are a little trickier."

Millie grunted. "At least she changed her mind from what she originally wanted."

"What was that?" Shane wolfed down his cookie.

"'A cord of three strands is not quickly broken'—plus the scripture reference from Ecclesiastes."

"Just how big did she think the cake was?"

"Exactly." I changed the tip on my pastry bag. "I love that scripture, but to make it fit even on the widest bottom layer, I'd really have to scrunch the writing." I began adding Swiss dots to the nonwriting layers. "And even then, people wouldn't be able to see the words at the back."

"Was she bummed?" Shane grabbed another cookie.

"At first. And so was her mother. But then she decided she'd have the verse imprinted on the wedding napkins and programs instead."

"Programs?" He stared at me. "For a wedding?"

"Sure. When's the last wedding you went to?" I smoothed over a dot that looked more square than round and piped on a new one. "Everybody has programs now listing the names of all the attendants, the order of service, the songs that will be sung—"

Millie grunted. "Sounds more like a Broadway production than a wedding. When I got married, we didn't have all that stuff." The corners of her mouth quirked into an ironic smile. "Maybe that's why my marriage failed. If I'd had all those bells and whistles, surely we'd still be together."

"I think I'll just elope when I get married," Shane said. "Who needs all that stuff anyway?"

"Um, that would be the bride," answered Nicole, who'd pushed through the swinging doors in time to hear Shane's comments. "Most girls dream of their wedding day for years and have it all planned. Right, Freddie?"

"I guess." I thought back to my wedding that never happened. The wedding I'd dreamed about for years, then planned so carefully. I'd had the church, the dress, the music, the food, the flowers—everything all arranged, and it had all gone up in smoke. Thankfully, I was able to get my money back for the dress. (Since we'd decided against having the wedding in California, my father had refused to pitch in a penny.) As for the rest . . . I let cheater Greg deal with the fallout. Especially since the wedding—or nonwedding, as it turned out, was in his hometown.

But that was all ancient history. I shook my head to clear it.

Nicole looked at me. "Your eyes look really pretty today, Freddie," she said shyly. "That mascara really shows them off."

Yeah. It's just too bad it can't help the rest of my body. Right?

"Thanks." I piped my last dot with a flourish. "There." I stepped back and surveyed my handiwork. "What do you think?"

Nicole sucked in her breath. "It's beautiful. I love it! You have to do my cake when I get married."

"Deal." I stole a look at Shane, who was doing all he could to hide his rapt adoration from Nicole.

But she was lost in dreamy wedding land and never noticed.

"Remember that pretty cake in that old movie, *Father of the Bride?*"

"Ooh, I saw that on video with my sister," Nicole added. "They had that beautiful reception at her parents' house."

Millie sighed. "I love Spencer Tracy."

We gave her confused looks. "I just remember Steve Martin and that goofy wedding planner guy who talked funny," I said. "And those swans in the bathtub."

"Swans? In the tub?" Millie's eyes widened. "What are you talking about?"

Movie geek Shane came to our rescue. "It's two different movies—the 1950s original and a 1991 remake. The 1950s one had Spencer Tracy and Elizabeth Taylor. The remake was Steve Martin and had a wedding planner . . . and the swans."

"But why would they be in the bathtub?" Now Millie looked confused.

"To keep them warm," Nicole explained. "The day of the wedding, there was an unexpected snowstorm in Southern California, so they had to keep the swans in warm water and defrost the tulips with hair dryers. It was pretty funny, but it all worked out in the end, and the wedding was perfect."

"We've had our share of mishaps too," Millie said. "I remember, years ago, it was a hot August day, and I was delivering a cake—in a van without air conditioning, no less. I went around the corner too fast, and the whole thing tipped and fell." She shuddered. "The icing had started to melt, so it was this big gooey mess—kind of looked like Neapolitan ice cream all mixed together. I was an absolute wreck and didn't know what to do—the cake was totally unsalvageable. But the bride and groom were this wild and crazy couple in their late thirties, and they decided to just eat the cake out of the back of the van."

"You're kidding!" Nicole's big eyes grew even bigger.

"Nope. The top layer was still pretty good—it hadn't smashed together like the rest of it—and they just took great big handfuls of the cake and fed it to each other. The photographer took pictures of them sitting in the back of the van, eating the cake. And the guests got a real kick out of it."

"Cool," Shane said.

Millie nodded. "Now, that's a good way to start a marriage—being fun and flexible." She grimaced. "Unlike others I can think of. Freddie, remember that time when we decorated the cake with those gorgeous cascading red roses down the front, and when we got there, the red totally clashed with everything?"

"Uh-huh. It wasn't pretty."

"How come?" Nicole asked.

"The groom's mother had changed the bride's color scheme without telling us," I explained. "She was pretty much paying for most of the wedding because the bride didn't have any family or money. So she decided she got to choose the colors, and *she* liked lavender and purple. But she forgot to notify us."

"Whoa." Shane shook his head. "Wonder if they're still married."

"How awful." Nicole's eyes flashed. "I'd have killed the mother and my fiancé too, if he didn't stand up to his mom."

"Definitely not a good way to start a marriage," Millie said. "That's why when my son got married, I just bit my tongue and went along with everything, even though his bride's tastes were totally different from mine. It is the bride's day, after all."

"Which is why we want to make the cake as perfect as possible for her." I slid the finished James-and-Kayla cake into the freezer and pulled out the Yancey cake with the tilted-hearts motif I'd gently pressed into the sides with an aluminum cookie cutter.

"What about the groom?" Shane protested. "Doesn't he get any say at all?"

"Not much." Nicole smirked. "It's all about the bride. You just have to show up."

"But that's not fair."

"You've got a lot to learn about weddings, my boy," Millie said. "But you'll catch on fast around here."

"Traditionally, the groom and his family are in charge of the rehearsal dinner," I explained as I boxed up the Yancey layers.

"And the honeymoon." Millie gave Shane a sly glance. "And by the way, if I were you, I wouldn't recommend camping— unless you marry one of those rugged outdoor types. Most girls—if you take 'em to a nice hotel or bed-and-breakfast, they'll be much more inclined to feel romantic."

"I hear that." Nicole munched on a cookie.

Shane blushed. "Back to the wedding . . . are you telling me the guy has no say about all the food and stuff?"

I tilted my head at him. "Don't they teach you this stuff at cooking school?"

"Not so far," he said. "And I just think it's kind of weird that the groom is totally out of it like that."

"Well, you can have a groom's cake." I scrunched my face at Millie. "Remember that ugly armadillo one with the gray frosting in *Steel Magnolias*?"

"How could I forget?" She shuddered. "With the red velvet cake inside that looked like blood when Shirley MacLaine cut into it."

"Eew." Nicole grimaced. "Not at *my* wedding."

Shane rested his chin in his hand, deep in thought. "I think I'll have a hamster cake," he said. "I know I could do one—if I could find the right pans."

. . . .

When I arrived at the church parking lot half an hour later, I was delighted to see Deborah's cheery catering van by the back door, standing open. I pulled in next to her and carefully retrieved the first of two sets of layers for the four-tiered cake from my car.

Two years ago, when I first started working at the bakery, I'd tried to carry the full cake all together, but the top layers were too heavy for the spindly plastic pillars holding them up. To my horror, those two layers tipped and fell. I knew the story of Millie's wedding cake disaster, but somehow I didn't see the couple at this upscale wedding eating their cake out of the back of a van.

Terrified that Anya would fire me, but even more afraid I might ruin the bride's big day, I called Millie, sobbing.

"Come on back and we'll fix it," she said. "Don't worry. I have a couple of layers in the walk-in for a birthday cake I haven't decorated yet. It'll be fine."

Thankfully, the birthday cake was the same flavor as the wedding cake. By the time I returned, Millie had nearly finished icing the top two layers. All I had to do was repair one small section at the bottom by scraping off some dented roses and piping on new ones. When I transported the cake that time around, I separated it into two levels and waited to assemble it until I got to the reception site.

The bride never knew her cake had been destroyed and rebuilt. In fact, this same bride sent a gushing letter to Anya after her honeymoon, saying how much everyone loved the cake and how they thought it was one of the most beautiful wedding cakes they'd ever seen.

Millie and I saw no reason to clue Anya in to the near disaster. But I always transported multitiered cakes in separate sections after that.

Today I slowly navigated my way through the open door of the multipurpose room next to the sanctuary with the top two cake layers. I sucked in my breath. "Oh my." The standard bland box of a room had been transformed into a beautiful rose garden, with varying shades of pink, red, and yellow cabbage roses everywhere.

Short crystal bowls of roses dotted the blush-colored, linen-clad tables, white tin cones of cascading pink roses hung from mock Grecian columns dotted around the room, and two latticed garden arches flanked the head table, festooned with climbing roses. Beneath one arch, a swan fountain atop a skirted table dispensed fizzy pink punch into a punchbowl pond. The other arch, with its empty skirted table in the center, beckoned me.

The only thing missing in that splendid room was the caterer.

"Hey, Deborah," I called out. "It's Freddie. Where are you?"

Silence.

"Samuel?"

Nothing.

They had to be here. Their van was outside, and I saw containers of food stacked on the table near the kitchen.

I shrugged and set the bottom tiers of the chocolate cake in the middle of the cake table under the white latticed canopy. Then I returned to my car and retrieved the top two layers, which I set off to one side. I sprinkled some shredded coconut atop the icing of the larger bottom layers to prevent the new layers from sliding. Then I carefully lifted the top layers by their slightly larger cardboard base and positioned them atop the bed of coconut—always a tricky maneuver. You have to center the layers just right so they'll line up.

Whew. Got it. And now, for the final touch.

I removed the half-full pastry bag from its Tupperware home in my purse and piped out a beaded border of icing around the edge where the two sets of layers joined, to hide the cardboard. Bag in hand, I slowly circled the entire table, making sure there were no missed spots or smudged areas. Thumbs and fingers had a way of slipping and messing up the cake during positioning.

Sure enough, there was a slight dent at the bottom from my right thumb. I quickly filled it in. Then I stepped back and surveyed the final result. Perfect—although the tablecloth had gotten slightly crooked from my cake ministrations. I tugged it into place and looked around.

Still no sign of Deborah or Samuel. Now I was beginning to worry. Where were they?

Just as I whipped out my cell to call Lydia, Deborah appeared wearing a yellow pantsuit that perfectly matched the yellow cabbage roses in the decorations. Did the woman dress to match the décor at all her gigs? "There you are. I was getting worried. I thought you'd been abducted by aliens or something."

"Might as well have been," she said in a glum tone that was uncharacteristic for her.

"Why? What's wrong?"

"Our help didn't show."

"Oh no."

"Uh-huh. And this isn't the first time either." She scowled beneath her yellow turban. "That's what comes from hiring a ditzy teenager whose mind's too full of boys and shopping to focus on work."

"So what are you going to do?"

She lifted a tray of containers full of food and carried it to the kitchen, with me following. "We couldn't get a signal in here, so

Samuel's outside around the corner, calling the temp agency." She sighed. "He probably won't get through. They're not usually open on Saturdays."

"What about Lydia? Doesn't she help you out on weekends sometimes?"

"She's at home resting. She had a hard week at work, and I didn't want her overdoing it." Deborah removed the tubs of cold salad from the tray and set them on the counter. "I told her to stay home today and just chill out. I figured we'd be fine 'cause Heather was working, but then Heather flaked out on us. Again."

"For the third time," Samuel said, rejoining us.

"For the last time." Deborah banged a pan on the counter. "Three strikes with me, and you're out." She sent a beseeching look to Samuel. "Any luck, baby?"

"Sorry, sug'. Just got the answering machine. I pressed the number for emergencies, but all I got was voice mail."

Deborah continued to work as she fretted. "Well, we don't have time to waste. Good thing it's a small wedding, or we'd really be up a creek without a paddle." She sighed. "But we're still really going to have to hustle."

"I could help if you like." I offered.

"*Could* you?" Her face lit up. "Would you?" Her eyes flicked to the cake table. "But don't you need to get back to work?"

"I'm done for the day. This delivery was the last thing on my schedule." I held out my hands, palms up. "Just tell me what to do."

Deborah set down the platter of food in her hands and enveloped me in a crushing bear hug. "Thank you, Jesus!"

"Yes, Father, amen!" Samuel said.

Deborah released me and turned to her husband. "Give this girl an apron, babe." She winked. "We want to make sure we protect her nice black outfit."

:: *chapter ten* ::

Deborah nodded to the kitchen as I tied the Taste of Honey apron behind my back. "If you'll start dishing up the cold items and set them at this end of the table, Samuel and I will take care of the hot food. You do know how to display food, don't you?" She gave herself a little shake. "What am I saying? Of course you do. You're an artist. Since they'll be serving themselves from both sides of the table, the main thing is to make sure you duplicate each item on both sides. Two Caesar salads, two potato salads, two vegetable trays—you see?"

"No problem."

I headed to the kitchen and began removing items from the fridge.

"And there's lots of fresh parsley to use as garnish," Deborah hollered after me.

"Got it." I filled the two hollowed-out watermelon baskets with fresh fruit from the large plastic container and removed the plastic wrap from two of the cheese trays, adding parsley at strategic places around the edge to offset all the orange and yellow slices.

But it still wasn't quite right. I rooted through Deborah's supplies until I found what I was looking for. I added a large cluster of red grapes to the center of each cheese tray and then rewrapped them in plastic, which I'd remove at the last minute.

Deborah had already chopped all the vegetables for the fresh-veggie platters, so all I had to do was transfer them from their plastic containers to each platter. I fanned celery sticks, baby carrots, cauliflower, green onions, mushrooms, and broccoli on each cut-glass plate, then cut the tops off two bell peppers, scooped out the seeds, and set the whole peppers in the center of each platter for the fresh bleu cheese-and-walnut dip.

Deborah hummed gospel songs as she worked, and when she wasn't humming, she kept up a steady stream of chatter.

"This bride was smart," she said. "She told me she knew everyone would be hungry waiting for them while they had their wedding pictures taken, so she wanted us to serve some hors d'oeuvres to take the edge off till they could get here and have their buffet lunch with the guests." She grunted. "I've been at too many weddings where everyone stood around starving while the photographer took his time." Deborah looked at her watch. "We've got about fifteen minutes before folks start arriving. Once the hors d'oeuvres are done, how 'bout if you and Samuel serve them, and I'll replenish the salads and cold trays as needed?"

"Serve?" I shot her a horrified look. "As in offering platters of food to groups of strangers?"

"That's normally how it's done."

"But I'm not good in front of people. I'm more a behind-the-scenes kind of girl."

"Well, it's time we changed that." She slid a tray of stuffed mushrooms into the oven. "What are you afraid of anyway? They're just people. They're not going to bite you."

"You sure about that?"

"I promise. And if any of them do, you just bite right back."

She removed the plastic wrap from a tray of crab puffs and slid them onto the rack beneath the mushrooms. "Serving comes with the territory. We're all servants when you get right down to it. That's what the Lord calls us to do—serve one another."

Leave it to her to put a biblical spin on it so I couldn't worm out of it.

Fifteen minutes later, Samuel was working one side of the room while I took the other. "Crab puff?" I extended scripture-imprinted cocktail napkins to an older couple and, using the silver tongs Deborah had given me, placed a puff on each napkin.

"Can I have two, please?" the silver-haired man asked. "I'm hungry."

"No problem."

I made my way through clusters of people dispensing crab puffs until I noticed my supply was getting low. On the way back to the kitchen, I spotted two heavyset women doing the big-girl leaning thing over in a corner. Sending them a warm smile of recognition, I approached. "Would you like an hors d'oeuvre?"

"No thanks. I'll just wait for the buffet," the brunette in a purple silk pantsuit said.

"Me too," echoed her auburn-haired friend in a black Payne Tryon dress I'd recently thought of ordering from their catalog. "I don't want to spoil my appetite."

I did a quick look around and saw that everyone was engaged in conversation and not paying the least bit of attention to either them or me. "Oh, go ahead," I whispered. "No one's looking. And even if they are, I'm blocking their view. It's still going to be another half hour or so before the buffet opens, and these crab puffs are really delicious."

They giggled in big-girl solidarity and scarfed down the remaining four puffs. "Thanks."

"No problem. I got your back."

An hour later, Deborah's gorgeous buffet had been picked clean. All that remained were a couple of olives and a few grapes.

I carried the remaining serving dishes to the kitchen, where Deborah was humming a hymn as she washed platters. After setting down the dirty dishes, I picked up one of the platters to dry. "I've been wondering . . . what made you choose Daystar Fellowship?"

"You mean instead of one of the black churches in town?"

I flushed. "I guess."

"Well, we tried a couple of all-black churches when we first got here and felt at home right away. It was real nice and comfortable—a lot like home. But sometimes we're not supposed to feel comfortable. You know what I'm sayin'?" Deborah handed me a platter and fixed me with a penetrating stare. "We didn't feel the Lord was calling us to any of those churches.

"God called us to Daystar—we're not sure for how long, but at least for now. They need a little bit of seasoning and color, and we're here to provide that. Besides"—she flashed me a broad smile—"if we hadn't come here, you and I would never have met."

I couldn't help smiling back at her.

The strains of "Butterfly Kisses" wafted to the kitchen, signifying the father-daughter dance.

Deborah fluttered her hand over her heart. "Oh, I'm glad my baby's not here today. This is the song she danced to with her daddy at her wedding."

"Has she heard anything from her husband? Donnie, was it?"

"Not a word." Deborah sighed. "That boy sure fooled all of us. I wish he'd shown his true colors before they got married—then my baby wouldn't be goin' through so much heartache now."

"Not necessarily." I wiped hard at the plate in my hand.

"What was his name?" Deborah asked gently.

"Who?"

"The man that done you wrong."

My eyes slid to hers, expecting to see pity, but all I saw was love and compassion. "Is it that obvious?"

"Not to everyone, but I'm well-acquainted with heartache."

"Greg." I sat down on a kitchen chair. "His name was Greg. I caught him in bed with the best man's sister the week before our wedding."

"Oh honey, I'm so sorry."

"Me too." I gave a short laugh. "Although I don't know why I was so surprised." I looked down at my tree-trunk legs. "She was thin and beautiful."

Deborah splashed a handful of water at me. "You stop that right now! He didn't leave you 'cause of your size. He left 'cause he's a jerk." Her ample bosom heaved with indignation. "And even though I never met him, I think you're well rid of him." Her voice softened. "Honey girl, God has something better planned for you. I just know it."

"Well, I wish he'd hurry up and reveal the plan to me. I'm not getting any younger, you know."

The kitchen door swung open, and I jumped up as a well-dressed forty-something woman in a pale pink suit and matching sandals strode in. "Deborah? Everything was wonderful. You and your crew did a fabulous job. Thank you so much. Everybody's raving about the food—especially those delicious crab puffs." She cut her a sly glance. "I don't suppose you'd give out the recipe, would you?"

"Can't, Mrs. Clark. Old family secret." Deborah smiled to soften her refusal. "But I'd be happy to make them again for you or your friends for a dinner party, corporate event, whatever— just say the word."

"I certainly will. Do you have some extra business cards I can pass out?"

Deborah pulled a fistful out of her apron pocket. "This enough?"

"Plenty. I'll trade you." Mrs. Clark handed three crisp, green hundred-dollar bills to Deborah in exchange. "For you and your helpers." She shook her hand. "Thank you again. And now I need to go see the bride and groom off." She smiled and tripped away in her pink sandals.

Deborah passed me one of the bills, then plopped down on a chair. "Whew! What a day. You really saved our butts, Freddie."

"You sure did." Samuel, who had joined us, squeezed my shoulder. "Thank you." He flipped open his cell phone. "I'm going to call Lydia now and check on her." He frowned as he held his phone up, trying to get a signal. "Guess I'll have to go outside again."

I put my feet up and nibbled on the lone remaining crab puff. "Mmm. So, is this the same kind of food you served back home?"

"Pretty much," Deborah said. "Unless it was a real down-home soul-food wedding. Then it would be barbecue or fried chicken and catfish, cornbread, and plenty of greens."

"Greens? You mean salad?"

She snorted. "*Greens*. Turnip greens with pot liquor."

My eyes widened. "Is that moonshine?"

Deborah guffawed. Then she snorted. Her whole body started shaking, and her eyes began to water. I got her a glass of water, but she shook her head, unable to speak.

"Lydia says she's—" Samuel, who'd just returned to the kitchen, stared at his wife. "You okay, sug'?"

She wiped at her streaming eyes. "Freddie . . . asked . . . if . . ." She held up her hand and gasped out, ". . . pot liquor was *moon-*

shine." She clutched at her stomach, going off in another gale of laughter.

"Moonshine?" Samuel's dignified eyebrows arched into his salt-and-pepper hair. Then he slapped his knee and joined in his wife's raucous laughter.

"What is so funny?" I put my hands on my hips.

"You can sure tell you've never been to the South. Honey, pot liquor is juice from the turnip greens, seasoned with ham hocks or salt pork, sometimes hot sauce. Best stuff there is." She expelled a gust of air and fanned herself. "I might have to go home and change my clothes. I like to have wet myself."

She turned to Samuel. "How's our baby?"

"Hungry. She asked can we bring her something home?"

"Let me guess. She wants onion rings and more tapioca." Deborah shook her head. "I bought that girl a whole case of tapioca pudding two weeks ago. She's having some powerful cravings."

"She comes by it naturally," Samuel said. "I seem to remember having to keep a certain someone well stocked with jars of marshmallow cream and beef jerky."

"Beef jerky?" My eyes slid from Samuel to Deborah.

"I had a strong craving for salt."

"Ah. So you didn't actually dip it in the marshmallow cream then?"

"Says who?" She sent me an innocent look. "You have to mix the two flavors and textures together to satisfy the craving."

I shuddered. "Remind me never to get pregnant."

. . . .

At home, I took a long, hot bubble bath, grateful that Brooke wasn't home and I had the house to myself. After all that mingling and serving today, I'd used up most of my social skills. Plus

I was tired, and my feet were killing me. But it was a happy kind of tired.

I sank lower into the soothing bubbles and bath salts, putting my ears under water to be lulled by the roar of the ocean. When I resurfaced, I heard a familiar scratching noise. Zsa Zsa pushed open the door I'd left slightly ajar and padded over to the tub.

"Hi, baby. Were you lonely?"

She stood on her hind legs and extended her front paws in a vain effort to reach the edge of the tub.

This dog had a strange affinity for bubbles and bath salts—as I'd discovered quite by accident the first week Brooke brought her home. I'd been soaking in the tub, my left arm trailing over the side, when suddenly something licked my fingers.

I screamed and shot out of the water like a cannonball.

Zsa Zsa huddled in a corner of the bathroom, trembling and whimpering pitifully.

"Freddie, you all right?" Brooke hollered from outside my closed bedroom door.

"Yeah, now that I know there's not a rat in the house."

"Huh?"

"Tell you later." I shouted.

Shivering, I sank back into the warm water, casting a baleful look at the white bundle of fluff. "Little dog, you almost gave me a heart attack."

Zsa Zsa laid her ears back and gave me a one-eyed mournful look that cut straight to my heart.

"I'm sorry. I didn't mean to scare you." I patted the outer side of the tub. "Come here, girl," I soothed. "It's okay. It's all right."

She bounded over and began licking the tile floor.

"*Now* what are you doing?" I peered over the edge of the tub and noticed a slight puddle where some of the bathwater had sloshed over the side. Zsa Zsa was eagerly lapping it up.

"Poor thing. Are you thirsty?" I pulled the plug to let out the bathwater and grabbed my towel from the rack, wrapping it around me as I stepped out of the tub. Rinsing out the bowl that had earlier held my sugar-free chocolate pudding, I filled it with water and set it next to the tub. "There you go. Some nice, fresh water."

Zsa Zsa sniffed at the bowl and turned up her nose. Then she began licking my dripping legs in earnest.

Light at last beginning to glimmer, I tried a little experiment. I sat down on the edge of the tub and swirled my hand in the fast-draining bathwater. Then I extended my wet hand to Zsa Zsa, who licked it greedily.

"Gee, I guess Calgon really takes you away, doesn't it?"

The funny thing is, Zsa Zsa loved bathwater, but not swimming pools. When Brooke first brought her home, she bought one of those little plastic kids' swimming pools and tried to coax Zsa Zsa into it, but the puppy would have none of it.

Brooke finally scooped her up and actually set her in the water, but Zsa Zsa jumped right out.

"That's really strange," Brooke said. "Most dogs love to swim— that's where the term *dog paddle* came from. But Zsa Zsa's acting more like a cat."

"Or a princess. A princess who eats paperbacks."

Princess was right. Zsa Zsa loved to be groomed and pampered.

Anytime she heard me blow-drying my hair, no matter where she was in the house, she'd come scampering down the hall into my room and whine at the bathroom door till I let her in. She'd sit there expectantly on the bathroom rug, staring hopefully at me with her one eye and wagging her tail to beat the band.

"What? What do you want?" I pretended not to know. "Do

you want this?" I'd show her the blow dryer, and her tail would take on a propeller life of its own. I kept waiting for liftoff.

Zsa Zsa would lower her head while I fluffed the fur on her back on low speed so that the heat wouldn't be so intense for her little body. Then she'd lie down on the rug and roll over, turning her stomach my way for a little tummy action. I'd direct the heat up and down the length of her body, and she'd throw her head back in Stevie Wonder ecstasy.

Tonight, she followed my motions hopefully with her one eye as I stepped from the tub and toweled off. I pulled on my blue fleece robe dotted with white clouds, twirled a Q-tip in my ear to sop up the excess water, and removed my blow dryer from the cabinet.

Zsa Zsa did her happy dance.

Once we were both blown-dry to perfection, I picked up my Bible from the nightstand, intending to continue with my nightly reading of Psalms. I liked to try and read one or two before I went to sleep. But tonight, for some reason, I couldn't focus. I kept reading the same two verses in Psalm 37 over and over: "Refrain from anger and turn from wrath; do not fret—it leads only to evil. For evil men will be cut off, but those who hope in the Lord will inherit the land."

Antsy, I got up and decided to surf the Net. I read the headlines of the day and got depressed, so decided to blog instead.

Saturday
Today I was at a wedding, and my heart ached for two attractive, albeit "big" girls who were on the sidelines, looking on while the men flocked to all the smaller women.
Story of my life.
As I passed a table of slim, well-dressed couples, I overheard an older woman saying to her husband about

one of the girls, "It's such a shame she's so big . . . she really has such a pretty face."

Change the broken record already. I've heard that all my life. And I'm not alone. *American Idol* judge Paula Abdul even said it on national TV to the amazing, albeit big, Mandisa.

I'm only guessing here since I don't know her and have never met her, but I'll bet with Mandisa's wonderful presence, faith, and vitality, she has guy friends. You could tell the male contestants liked her and appreciated her talent. But . . . would they ever date her?

I've had guy friends too, especially in college. I was a nice person, a great listener, and a safe place to go to get that female perspective when they had girlfriend problems. And their girlfriends didn't get jealous either. Why would they? What man in his right mind would ever leave one of them for a fat girl?

Even if she does have "such a pretty face."

The two big girls at the wedding today also skipped the wedding cake. And I know why.

Taking a random, totally unscientific poll here now . . . Are you a dessert-in-public or a dessert-in-private person?

I'm the latter. I learned long ago that I had to be. And I'm guessing that if you're a big woman like me or the two girls at the wedding, you're also a dessert-in-private person.

It's a total self-defense maneuver--because you know that if you dare to take even a bite of dessert in public, the rest of the world will swoop down on you like vultures and tear you to bits.

"Well, no wonder she's fat! Look at her eating that cream puff."

"Is she really going to eat that chocolate eclair?"

"There are starving people in China . . . who does she think she is, eating that tiramisu?"

"There ought to be a law."

Or even, kindly but condescendingly, "It's just so sad . . ."

With this sort of pressure, there's no way you can enjoy that yummy piece of cheesecake or Mississippi mud pie . . . so instead you go inhale a whole pint of Ben & Jerry's chocolate-chip cookie dough in the safety and privacy of your own home.

I don't know about you, but I'm a little tired of that.

So all you dessert-in-private or closet dessert eaters (and I'm talking to myself here too), it's time to come out of the closet and eat your dessert in public!

. . . .

I signed off and burrowed beneath the covers. But when I reached up to shut off my bedside lamp, I noticed the light on my answering machine blinking. It had gotten shoved to the far back corner of my nightstand again, thanks to Henry and Eliza, who were always chasing each other around the house and jumping on furniture and moving things or knocking things over.

Whenever I see my answering machine flashing, I have this little game I play with myself. I imagine the most amazing, life-changing phone call—like from Publisher's Clearing House or Oprah or my long-lost mother or something equally fantastical—saying:

"Congratulations! You've won a million dollars in our sweep-stakes!"

Or, "Freddie Heinz, come on down! You've won an all-expense-paid trip to Europe, *after* we give you a complete makeover on our show."

Or . . . "Freddie, I'm so sorry I ever left you. It was the biggest mistake of my life. I promise never to leave you again . . ."

Tonight I thought up a new possibility: "Congratulations! This is Ikea calling to inform you that you were recently the one-hundred-thousandth visitor to our store, so you've won one hundred thousand dollars! Please hurry down and claim your prize without delay."

Whoa. If I had a hundred thousand dollars to burn, I could quit my job and not have to put up with Anya's shabby treatment any longer. And I could take a trip to Italy or Greece, where the men like women with a little more meat on their bones. I'd meet some dashing Greek god who'd sweep me off my feet, and we'd eat moussaka and baklava in the Plaka in Athens and break plates and yell *Opa!*

That would work.

Or . . . maybe the message was from Jared. Maybe after spending time with Anya today, he'd seen through her brittle mask and all that makeup to who she really was deep down, and he'd decided he'd much rather be with a real woman who was kind and warm and loving. My lips curved in a smile as I imagined his message.

"Freddie? Hi, it's Jared. I've been wanting to call you for a while. It seems like fate that we keep running into each other. I know you've seen me with a lot of skinny bimbos, but they were just placeholders while I got up the nerve to call you. You're the woman I want. The woman I want to take home to Mom and Dad. Please call me."

I held off pushing the button a millisecond longer just to enjoy the fantasy. Once I pushed it, I'd have to deal with reality.

I sighed and hit play.

"Freddie?" My stepmother's squeaky voice got even squeakier when she was excited. "I couldn't wait to call and tell you! Today I was talking to one of my girlfriends, and she told me that her daughter had that gastric bypass surgery and has already lost *a hundred and thirty pounds* in just six months! Isn't that amazing? She showed me before-and-after pictures, and Nadine is just a shadow of her former self!"

Candy paused, and I could hear her taking a sip of something—probably one of the berry wine coolers she chugged like Kool-Aid. I always wondered if she knew how many carbs those things had. "Anyway, she said her health insurance covered it, so I was thinking . . . maybe that's something you might want to consider? And here's the best news of all." She paused for dramatic effect. "I discussed it with your father, and he said that if your insurance doesn't cover it, he'd be willing to pay for the whole cost. Your father is such a generous man. Why he's always—"

I slapped the erase button, shaking.

Gastric bypass surgery? Isn't that surgery for people who need to lose at least a hundred pounds? Or even two or three hundred?

Yes, I know I'm a big girl, but I don't have an extra hundred pounds to get rid of. I looked in the mirror, turned sideways, and sucked in my stomach. Sure, I could stand to lose thirty, maybe even forty or fifty pounds, but that's still nowhere near a hundred.

I sucked in my cheekbones. Of course, if I wanted to go the anorexic model route, I'd lose eighty. But would my life really be better? If I lost a ton of weight, would I then get the happily-ever-after I yearned for? The husband? The baby (minus the weird food cravings)? The perfect job? Would I then be confident, witty, someone who was always at ease . . . ?

Or would I still be just plain old me? Thinner. But no better.

:: *chapter eleven* ::

That's it! You've got it!"

Shane sent me a triumphant smile as he held up his wooden skewer with its pink icing rose.

"Now just lift it off and transfer it to the top of the cake, like so." I demonstrated with my own skewered rose, and Shane followed suit, lifting his rose off the tip of his thin wooden canvas and placing it next to mine on the sample cake.

"Perfect!" I said. "Another week or so, and you'll be ready to do a wedding cake all on your own. You're a natural."

Shane flushed with pride.

It was Sunday afternoon, and Brooke and Jon were on a day-long bike ride, so I'd seized the empty-kitchen opportunity to give Shane some extra cake-decorating lessons. There was never time at work, and he was eager to ratchet up his on-the-job education.

"In fact," I said, "why don't you finish the cake while I get us some lunch?"

"Serious?"

I rummaged through my shelf containers, pulling out some Italian sausage I'd hidden from Brooke's veggie eyes in my orange Tupperware, along with a couple of sun-dried tomato tortillas, an onion, and some red and green bell peppers. "Sure. You can do it. I have confidence in you. And besides, if you mess up, we'll just eat the evidence, and no one will be the wiser."

While Shane practiced his flower-making skills, I browned the sausage in a large skillet and sliced the onion and peppers. I added the vegetables to the skillet, and while they cooked with the meat for a few minutes, I quartered a cantaloupe and filled two of the cantaloupe gondolas with red seedless grapes and kiwi slices.

Then I drained the finished sausage mixture, sprinkled in a few drops of bottled Italian dressing, tossed in a little shredded Mozzarella, and filled each tortilla with the mixture, rolling it up and then slicing each Italian burrito in half to make what I called my bada-bing wrap. "Okay, lunch is ready."

"Freddie, I think you're in the wrong business," Shane said a few minutes later, his mouth full of peppers.

I brushed a tortilla crumb from the side of my mouth and pouted. "Okay, intern, I know you want to take over my cake-decorating place, but don't kick me out of my day job just yet."

"No . . ." He swallowed and took a drink of milk, then gestured to his sandwich. "I mean you're a really good cook."

"Hello. That's just a sandwich, cake boy. Anyone can make a sandwich."

"Not necessarily." He shuddered. "My mom made the worst sandwiches ever—fried Spam, tons of Miracle Whip, and those shiny, overprocessed, fake cheese slices. Ugh." He took another bite. "And you're forgetting that dinner you made at Millie's last movie night." He licked his lips. "Those pork chops were great."

"And easy." I lifted my shoulders. "All I did was dredge them in crushed pecans."

"All I did was dredge them in crushed pecans," he mimicked.

"And those pecan-crusted chops were way better—and healthier—than the Shake'n Bake we had growing up."

"I never even tried Shake'n Bake," I said wistfully, thinking of all the dry, tasteless baked chicken breasts I had consumed as a child.

"Didn't miss anything," he told me fervently. "Why do you think I'm in cooking school anyway?"

"To meet girls?" I asked innocently.

He snorted. "Heck no. With my mom's cooking, it's a matter of survival!"

. . . .

"Hey, Deborah, want to go with me to that new weight-loss class they announced in the bulletin today?" I was giving her a ride home from church a few weeks later since Samuel and Lydia had to go out-of-town car shopping for Lydia.

"No thanks. Not for me."

"But it's biblically based."

"Well, I would hope so, since it's offered at church." She cut me an impish grin.

"Why don't you want to go?" I'd been sure she'd jump at the chance, and it would be some fun girl-bonding time.

"Honey, I've shelled out money to every weight-loss program out there: Jenny Craig, NutriSystem, Atkins, Dr. Phil—you name it, I've done it. They're just not for me." Deborah shifted in the passenger seat. "It would be one thing if I had this delicate bone structure and weighed as much as I do 'cause I keep stuffing myself with sweets and junk food all the time." She held up a warning hand. "And yes, I know I like my cake, but I don't eat it every day—just now and then as a treat. Plus, I don't have diabetes, my blood pressure's good, and I'm healthy as a horse. I'm just a big woman."

She thrust her arms out in front of her. "You see these wrists? These aren't the wrists of some tiny, delicate woman." She stuck her sandal-shod foot on the dashboard and pulled up her pants leg. "Ankles, either. I'm a big-boned woman, and I come from a long line of beautiful big-boned women. My mama was five foot nine, and my Granny Marsh was bigger than that—a giant. It's in my genes."

"Would those be stretch jeans?" I slid her an innocent look.

"Is there any other kind?" She punched my leg. "Listen to you, girl, being all sarcastic and bold."

"What can I say? You're rubbing off on me."

"Good. Then I hope this will rub off on you too." She patted my arm. "Honey, you're not a tiny woman either. You never will be," she added gently. "And that's okay. Face it—you're just not built that way."

I looked down ruefully. "I'm pretty sure God didn't do all this."

She snorted. "So you could stand to take off twenty or thirty pounds. Who couldn't? But God definitely made you big—made us both that way. And we're both of us fearfully and wonderfully made. We should celebrate that, not be ashamed of it."

"Easy for you to say. You're married to a great guy who loves you just the way you are."

"That's the only kind to marry. It's the kind of man I'm praying for you to meet."

My turn to snort. "You better pray hard."

"Honey, if the Lord can send me a man who appreciates me in all my beautiful black bigness, he can certainly do the same for you."

I gave her a doubtful look, and she placed her hands squarely on her hips. "You think all men are looking for those matchstick women in Hollywood? It just ain't true, I promise you. And the ones that throw up all the time? That's nasty—no man wants that. Besides, all this weight obsession is setting an awful example for young girls." Deborah huffed. "Girls are dieting at nine and ten now. That's just not right."

"But what about childhood obesity? They say it's an epidemic."

"I know, but that's 'cause them kids are eating so much junk food and sitting in front of the TV or their computers all the time instead of going outside and playing and getting exercise. And 'cause their mamas are too busy to cook dinner, so they bring in more junk food." She wagged her finger. "Better watch out. You got me on my soapbox now. We're way too obsessed with looks and weight in this country—especially here in California. We spend so much time and energy focusing on the outside, our insides are all rotten."

She sighed. "Maybe if we spent more time taking care of the poor rather than buying expensive diet foods and obsessing about our own bodies, we'd all be better off." She shook her head. "When we were in Africa, we didn't have time to worry about our weight. We were too busy feeding hungry children and seeing that they got an education . . ."

I pulled up in front of her house and cut the engine. "So, I guess that's a definite no to the weight-loss class then?"

"Ya got that right." She chuckled. "Sorry about the lecture, though. Why don't you come on in and have some lunch?"

"After all that, now you want to eat?"

"Uh-huh. It's lunchtime, and I'm hungry. But don't worry." She clambered out of the van. "I've got some leftover turkey from last night, and I'll just cut it up and add it to a green salad. And for dessert . . . no cake, I promise." Deborah smiled at me as she unlocked the front door. "Just a fresh fruit salad. Samuel went to the farmer's market yesterday and got me a flat of strawberries and some blackberries and melon."

I followed her into the kitchen, where she punched the blinking answering machine and began removing stuff from the fridge.

"Hi, Mama. Hi, Daddy. How y'all doin'?" A mellifluous male voice filled the kitchen air. "I thought you'd be home from church by now. Sure am missin' y'all. And your cookin', Mama—'specially your red beans and rice and your pecan pie." He groaned. "No one else makes it as good as you. Lydia, you better be takin' good care of yourself and that nephew of mine. And don't be giving me any of that "might be a girl" stuff—I'm ready to teach that boy to pitch." His voice grew animated. "Hey, Daddy, Coach says he's putting me on third base. We got a big game comin' up Tuesday. Wish y'all could be here to cheer me on. But that's okay," he teased. "There's a certain young lady in the stands who'll be rooting for me. You'd like her, Mama. She goes to chu—"

The answering machine cut off.

Deborah picked up the phone and punched in numbers. "Freddie, the turkey's in the fridge. Can you start chopping it for me while I call my boy back? I need to find out about this girl." She harrumphed. "At least this one sounds like she goes to church."

"So Isaiah's a bit of a ladies' man?"

"Of a sort. But mostly it's girls throwin' themselves at him all the time. He's a good-looking boy." She made a face. "Voice mail." Deborah left a message for Isaiah to call her back and then turned to me. "I think later this afternoon I'll make that boy a pecan pie so I can send it out to him tomorrow."

"Aw, aren't you the sweet mom?" I foraged in the fridge for greens and tossed the salad.

"Well, I don't know about that." She grabbed a box of whole-grain Wheat Thins and handed me two iced teas. "Let's eat. I'm hungry."

"Do you have any Splenda?"

"Can't live without it. And here's the fruit salad." She handed me a bowl of jewel-toned slices. "See, I eat healthy too." She studied me.

"What? Do I have something in my teeth?"

"No . . . I was just thinking. Although I won't go with you to a diet group, I'd like you to join me instead."

"Where?" I shot her a wary look.

"To my water aerobics class."

"Your what?"

"Water aerobics. You know, exercise in the water?"

"Uh, wouldn't that involve a bathing suit?"

"Usually. Unless you want to wear one of those rubber wet-suit things."

"Eew. Even worse." I shook my head. "I haven't worn a bathing suit since I was ten, and I don't intend to start wearing one now. I'm not about to inflict that on the people of America."

"Shoot. You think you're the only big woman out there? Look at me."

"You're married."

"So?"

"So you're off the market. No way I'm going to let any man see me in a bathing suit."

"It's a women's class," Deborah said patiently. "There's no men there. And besides, you know that dieting's not the only way to lose weight. You gotta get a little exercise." She gave me an innocent look. "And wouldn't you rather exercise with a bunch of women like me than in a gym with men?"

. . . .

I sneaked a peek in the locker room mirror.

Just as I thought. A beached whale. One of those black-and-white killer whales. I could definitely kill someone with this body.

Deborah had finally convinced me to check out the water aerobics class at her gym. So here I was, Tuesday after work, hiding in the locker room. Stuck like that kid in *A Christmas Story* who got his tongue stuck to the telephone pole.

Only it was my bottom that was stuck to the locker-room bench.

I just knew that the second I walked outside that room in my bathing suit, California would have one of its infamous earthquakes. The concrete would crack, women and children would run screaming for cover, and grown men would quake in abject terror.

Sunday afternoon after lunch, Deborah and I had gone on another shopping trip so I could buy a suit. She kept pulling out bright reds, oranges, pinks, and florals, but this time I'd held firm. For me it was basic black or nothing.

When she picked me up after work, she peered closely at my white tunic and black palazzo pants. "You got your bathing suit on under those clothes?"

"Of course."

"You do know they have locker rooms at the gym."

"Yes. But I'm not changing in front of other people."

"It's not people. It's ordinary women like you and me."

"That's fine. I'll go to the locker room to remove my pants and shirt, but I'm not going to strip down to the altogether."

"Okay, Miss Shy and Demure." Deborah chuckled. "Guess it's nice to see modesty hasn't gone completely out of style."

Only it had—in that locker room, at least. I hadn't seen this many naked women since high-school gym class. At least I wasn't the only one with hail damage on my thighs. Even the skinny girls had cellulite. I stared down at my flip-flops, pretending an absorbed interest in my coral polish, which was just beginning to chip.

"Ready, Freddie?" Deborah twirled in front of me in her neon-pink bathing suit and a cute bathing cap dotted with rubber daisies. My eyes zeroed in on the rubber cap. "Uh, should I be wearing one of those?"

"Nah. We don't go underwater. I just don't like to make other folks uncomfortable with my alopecia." She winked. "Let's go, girl!"

I pried my recalcitrant thighs from the bench, wrapped my beach towel around my waist, and cautiously followed her out.

My plan was to drop the towel at the last possible second at the edge of the pool before I entered the water. That way my massive white flesh would only be seen by the rest of the world for a split-second before being immersed. However, there were signs everywhere that said, "Please place belongings on tables or chairs so others won't trip on them." So, being a good little sign follower (and not wanting to get arrested by the pool police, especially in a bathing suit), I dropped my towel on a chaise lounge that was probably a good six yards from the pool.

As I traversed those interminable six yards, I knew how the convicted felon in *Dead Man Walking* felt.

But the earth didn't move and the ground didn't shake.

And something even more amazing: not one person in or around the pool was paying the least bit of attention to me. No one recoiled in horror, whispered behind their hands, or scooped up their children and ran from the premises.

Tentatively, I stuck one toe in the water. Then another. The water felt good. I couldn't remember the last time I'd been in a pool.

Definitely not in high school. Rather than expose my big self to bathing-suit ridicule, I'd chosen volleyball as my P.E. elective so I could wear knee-length shorts and an oversized T-shirt instead.

Was my last pool experience as a child? Vague memories of a blue plastic wading pool with colorful fish on the sides surfaced.

I could see my seven-year-old self in a pink Sleeping Beauty bathing suit, laughing and splashing happily in the water while my stepmother sunbathed nearby in a white bikini.

All at once a shadow fell on me, blocking the sun. "You idiot, what were you thinking?" my father thundered. "Get her out of that water. She looks like a pink elephant. Do you want all the neighbors to see?"

That had been the end of my water-baby days.

Until today, of course.

As I hesitantly looked around the outdoor pool, I was delighted to see women of all shapes and sizes in the class. Several were even bigger than me. In fact, I suddenly realized that, with one exception, I was the smallest one in the group.

That was a first. Maybe this wouldn't be so bad after all.

"Hi, Deborah. How's it goin'?" asked a sixtyish woman in a leopard-print one-piece with a chest bigger than Pamela Anderson's buoys.

"Any better and I'd have to be twins, Roxanne." Deborah turned to me. "This here's my friend Freddie. It's her first time."

"Hiya, Freddie. Welcome." She nodded her not-found-in-nature-red head. "You're in good hands. Deborah knows all the moves."

"Thanks," I said. "Good to know."

The warm water was welcoming and made me feel almost weightless. *So this must be what it's like to be thin.* I took a couple of buoyant steps and felt like an astronaut bouncing around on the moon's surface.

"Hey, Roxy, you going out dancing afterwards?" asked a dark-haired woman in a lime-green bathing suit, who sported a fairy tattoo on her fortyish shoulder.

"Sure am. Line dancing every Tuesday night. You want to—"

"Okay, ladies, let's all move to the center of the pool and get ready to start." A stocky brunette in a white tank top and bicycle shorts that hugged her healthy, well-muscled frame turned on a portable CD player and strode to the side of the pool as sounds of Motown filled the air.

"Welcome to Aqua Sports. I'm Judie, and today all of our exercises will have a sports-related theme." She demonstrated on the concrete. "We're going to start with some warmups. Let's just do some gentle marching in place. That's it. Bring your knees up. Get those arms pumping."

I pumped the best I could, feeling the resistance of water.

"Okay, now we're going to kick it up a notch and start jogging." She pointed to the shallow end. "Let's all jog down that direction."

We did it en masse, looking like a school of tropical fish in all our bright colors.

All except me in my Orca suit. I was tempted to run and scream "Free Willy!"

Judie hollered. "Okay, now we're going to go cross-country skiing." She stretched out her arms in front of her, one after the other, as if she were digging ski poles in the snow. "And be sure you're moving your opposite leg from your arm."

Was she kidding?

For a woman with no rhythm, that was definitely a challenge. Plus, Judie was facing us, so we were supposed to do the opposite of her movements. Confused, I decided to follow Deborah instead.

After several more sports-related exercises, Judie segued into the "sport" of percussion—apparently consistency of theme wasn't her strong suit. "Let's go ahead and play the bongos," she said, slapping rapidly at an imaginary drum set in front of her.

We followed suit, patting our hands hard and fast on our

pretend drums, pushing the water down on each side of our body and then in front.

"Come on, ladies. Work it, work it!"

We worked it. So much that afterward, when we climbed out of the pool and made for the Jacuzzi, my arms and legs felt like rubber.

"I feel like a real California girl in a hot tub and everything now." Deborah patted her bathing cap. "The only thing missing is my long blonde hair."

"Just get you a wig, girl," leopard-print Roxy said.

"And George Clooney," her friend in lime green added slyly.

"George Clooney nothin'." Deborah shook her head from side to side. "Denzel's my man. Uh-huh."

"I hear that," a mahogany-skinned woman in a tomato-red suit said. "That is one fine-lookin' brothah."

"You can say that again." Roxy smacked her lips.

Deborah giggled. "But as fine as Denzel is, and as much as I enjoy lookin' up at him on the silver screen, I'm plenty happy with the man I got at home. My Samuel is my Denzel."

"Go ahead, rub it in." Lime Suit sighed. "At this point, I'll take George or Denzel or Samuel . . . or even a Herbert."

"Did you say pervert?" Roxy waggled her painted-on eyebrows.

Lime Suit giggled and splashed water at her. "You're bad."

I shifted. The hot churning water felt great, but after a few minutes the jets itched. I caught Deborah's eye. "I think I'm starting to get a little pruney."

She stood up in all her majestic hot-pinkness. "Well, y'all, we got to get goin' now. See you Thursday. All right now?"

"'Bye, Deborah. 'Bye, Deborah's friend."

"Freddie," Roxy reminded them.

"'Bye, Freddie."

Back in the locker room, I changed inside one of the stalls—grateful I'd remembered to throw some underwear into my purse.

Deborah's giggle floated over the metal door. "Girl, you're so funny."

As I was blow-drying my thick, mousy-brown hair in front of the mirror, she gave me a wistful look. "You got yourself a nice head of hair there. Although . . ." she cocked her head, "you should think about jazzing it up some.

You ever thought about dying it red?"

· · · ·

"My turn, now, to pick the place," I said as we drove away from the gym. "Have you been to Bramwell's?"

"What's Bramwell's?"

"My favorite bookstore. *And* they have the best hot chocolate anywhere. Good coffee too, apparently, but I'm not a coffee drinker, so can't vouch for it personally."

"I wonder if Lydia knows about it." Deborah fanned herself. "It's a little warm for hot chocolate. Maybe I'll get an iced coffee."

Fifteen minutes later, we were in the café, placing our order at the counter. (I didn't want to risk my usual invisibility treatment or have Deborah make a scene with the clueless clerk.) She ordered a piece of cheesecake with her iced coffee while I had my usual.

Deborah noticed someone at a nearby table reading *Beloved*. She grimaced. "I tried to read that 'cause my girl Oprah loves it so much, but I just didn't get it. Made me feel stupid."

"You too? I like books that make me think, but not ones that give me a headache."

"I feel that." She picked up her fork, then laid it down again. "In my book club back in Decatur, we read this one thick old novel that had won a mess of awards, but none of us could make sense of it. It was boring. Nothing ever happened." She sipped her iced coffee. "I like a little more action in my fiction."

"Me too. So what were some of the other books your group read?"

"Let me think." She closed her eyes and recited. "*Uncle Tom's Cabin, Rebecca,* and *Christy.*"

"Oh, I love *Christy!* Fabulous book. And *Rebecca.*"

Deborah nodded. "I tried to read some more Daphne Du Maurier, but just couldn't get into *Jamaica Inn.*"

"Me either. Too dated. I like more contemporary mysteries."

"Yeah, like the alphabet lady or that one caterer who's married to the cop."

"Exactly." I sent her a teasing smile. "So, Ms. Caterer, have you solved any mysteries on the side?"

Deborah stood. "The only mystery I want to solve is trying to find the bathroom before my bladder bursts."

I pointed to the far end of the café, and she hurried off.

Flipping the pages of the in-store book review I snagged from another table while I waited for Deborah to return, I took a sip of water and another bite of my dessert.

"Hey, have you read that Betty Biggs blog?" a woman's voice beside me asked.

I choked on my lemon bar.

:: *chapter twelve* ::

I coughed and washed down the crust lodged in my throat with another swig of water, in the process stealing a furtive glance at the table next to me.

Two middle-aged plus-sized women in stretch jeans and T-shirts—one blue, one red—carried on an animated conversation over their mochas.

"I love that blog. My daughter turned me on to it." Red T-shirt answered her friend. "Betty tells it like it is."

"She sure does. Do you know I've had that same thing happen to me? In this very bookstore, in fact."

"No. Really? You mean"—and here Red Shirt lowered her voice so I had to strain to hear without being obvious—"not getting good service because of your size?"

"Good service. Hah! How about *any* service?" Blue Shirt sent a frown to the lanky kid behind the counter, who was too busy playing with his cell phone to notice. "Although I must admit it's improved a little lately."

"Maybe he read Betty's blog too." Red Shirt giggled.

"Let's hope. It should be required reading for every skinny server in America."

I tried not to preen.

Blue Shirt continued. "I also agree with what Betty said about men giving big women dirty looks when they see them eating dessert." She sipped her mocha. "Women do it too. I think they're worse than men. But why shouldn't we eat what we want in public? We're not harming anyone. Not like smokers."

"You're right." Red Shirt giggled. "So . . . want to split a piece of cheesecake or maybe one of those yummy-looking brownies?"

"Try the cheesecake," said Deborah, who'd just returned and heard the last part of their conversation. "It's delicious, especially with that raspberry sauce they drizzle over the top." She sat down and proceeded to polish hers off, but not before offering me a bite.

"No thanks." I drank my water slowly so I wouldn't have to engage in conversation that might drown out the T-shirt ladies.

"So where do you suppose Betty lives?" Red Shirt asked after taking a bite of cheesecake and giving Deborah a thumbs-up. "She said northern California."

"Probably San Francisco or somewhere in the Bay Area."

"You think?"

"Sure. She's probably some high-powered lawyer or corporate type," Blue Shirt said. "Has to be, with that kind of chutzpah."

"Well *I* think she's a famous author."

I cupped my hand over my mouth to hide my pleased smile.

"What's wrong, Freddie?" Deborah asked. "You about to sneeze?"

I nodded and squinted my eyes in a fake sneeze pose. I shook my head. "I hate it when that happens! Don't you? When you have to sneeze and can't?"

"Uh-huh." Deborah stood and stretched. "You ready to go? *Cops and Lawyers* starts in fifteen minutes, and that's my favorite."

. . . .

I went home and struck a series of different poses in front of the mirror.

First, I was a high-powered lawyer. Grabbing my new polka-dotted makeup bag, I pretended it was a briefcase.

Then, a famous author. I plucked my reading glasses off my nightstand and tried to look all scholarly.

A stand-up comedian? I tried to do a Robin Williams shtick, but no one can do Robin but Robin.

Lying down on my futon, I looked up at the nondescript beige ceiling. I wasn't any of those things. I was just a big, fat invisible baker living in a rented room and working for a woman who treats me like dirt.

But I wasn't going to let her push me around anymore.

I punched my pillow.

I am woman. I'm a big woman. Hear me roar!

. . . .

It was Wednesday night at the meat market. Also known as the singles group at church.

I don't know why I even bothered going. Most of the people there, male and female, were just trolling for dates—some more effectively than others. But I hadn't been in a while, and I knew I needed to meet other singles. Deborah was becoming a good friend, but she was happily married with a devoted husband and kids.

And sometimes, to be honest, that was hard to be around.

Picking a piece of Zsa Zsa's white hair off my new olive skirt, I noticed from my leaning vantage point at the back of the room that Jared had zeroed in on a Malibu Barbie type with bleached hair and matching teeth and a skimpy T-shirt stretched over her considerable assets.

"You might want to cover your eyes," a husky male voice with a slight trace of a to-die-for English accent said behind me.

"Excuse me?" I turned around hoping for Colin Firth and got a cross between Colin Farrell and Ewan McGregor.

Not a bad combo at all. In fact, really, really good. Kind of stocky, but taller than me, with thick reddish-brown hair that flopped down over his Ben Franklin specs.

He gestured with his plate toward Malibu Barbie. "She could take you out with that laser-beam smile."

"I thought men loved women with perfect teeth and perfect hair." *And perfect boobs.*

"Hey, not all men. Perfection is highly overrated." He stuck out his hand and grinned, revealing a slight gap between his front teeth and gorgeous hazel eyes behind his glasses. "Hello. I'm Simon."

"Freddie." I shook his hand, then cast about for something witty to say to keep the conversation going. "Pizza or egg rolls?"

"Pardon?"

Yeah, that was real witty, all right.

Tonight was international potluck night. Everyone was supposed to bring a dish from another country, so most of the guys had brought pizza or Chinese take-out, although one enterprising type had pushed the envelope and brought microwave mini tacos.

I flushed and jerked my head at the table. "The male offerings for the night are mainly Italian or Chinese. Unless you count the cold McDonald's French fries."

"Now, that's just wrong," he said in that fabulous accent.

What is it about English accents—even just the slightest hint of one—that made me and every other red-blooded American girl go all weak in the knees? I locked my knees in self-defense.

"The only way to eat fries," he continued, "*especially* from McDonald's, are fresh and hot from the drive-through window."

"Exactly." Emboldened by a man who had publicly confessed his love of fattening fast food—and in church, no less—I ventured another question. "So, what *did* you bring?"

"Shepherd's pie. I wanted Britain to be properly represented."

"Ah, I *thought* you were English."

Duh. Could you be any more lame? I braced myself for his sarcastic reply as visions of the acerbic-tongued judge Simon Cowell from *American Idol* danced in my head.

But this Simon was all graciousness. "Actually, me mum's English, but my dad was a Yank, so I'm only half." He smiled again, revealing that adorable David Letterman gap before he laid his accent on a little thicker. "And what about you, then?"

"Mostly German and Polish, but with a little Scandinavian and Dutch thrown in."

"That explains the porcelain complexion." He gave me a lazy George Clooney smile that made my face flame. "But I meant, what did you bring? I'm guessing you came straight from work . . ." His eyes flicked to the table. "Sushi or Stouffer's?"

"German potato salad."

"From the deli?"

I shook my head. "Homemade."

"Really?" His eyes lit up. "With bacon?"

"Of course."

"Let's go." He grabbed my hand, a determined look in his eye.

"Where to?"

"The buffet table, before everyone eats up all your potato salad."

"I think we'll be safe. I don't think hot potato salad is a big California crowd pleaser."

But my new acquaintance was on a mission. Dragging me in his wake, he bulldozed past clusters of loud singles, male and female, giving none a second glance—although plenty of the women gave him one. "Where is it?"

I pointed to a spot between the lasagna and the fried rice. "But it's probably cold by now." He dropped my hand to start filling his plate.

"That's okay. I can nuke it." His eyes honed in on the pass-through window. "That's a kitchen over there. Right?"

"Uh-huh." I followed him into it.

"So, how long have you been going to this church?" Simon asked as he opened the microwave door. Even in here, he had to raise his voice to be heard over the meat-market din.

"About a year or so."

He stuck his potato salad in the microwave, covered it with a paper towel, and punched in forty-five seconds. "And how do you like this singles group?"

"It's okay."

"Just okay?"

"It's fine. For a singles group. They're not really my thing."

"What *is* your thing?"

The microwave dinged, and I was saved from answering as he removed his plate, took a bite, and closed his eyes as he chewed, not saying a word.

"Do you like it?" I bit my lip.

"I don't like it." His eyes flew open. "I *love* it. I want the recipe."

"What? Are you a chef or something?" I teased.

"As a matter of fact, I am. I even own my own restaurant."

"You're kidding."

He shook his head as he continued to eat.

"So, how long have *you* been going to this group?"

"This week is my first time." He wiped his mouth on his napkin. "I actually belong to an Episcopal church downtown, but they don't offer much in the way of singles, so I thought I'd scope out this potluck tonight."

"And what's the verdict?"

He gave me another lazy grin that did strange things to my stomach. "So far, so good." He glanced over at my plate of carrots and celery. "Is that all you're eating?"

I nodded.

He groaned. "Not you too."

"Not me too, what?"

"Watching what you eat. Every woman I know is on a diet. Why are women so obsessed with diets?"

"Why are men so obsessed with thin women?"

"I think I said this earlier . . . not all men. Personally, I prefer a nice healthy woman with some curves and substance."

I rolled my eyes. "Yeah, right. You mean like Jennifer Lopez, right?"

"No, I mean like Queen Latifah. Or that actress that used to be on *The Practice*."

Yeah. That's what Greg said before he slept with his best man's skinny sister. "Then you're in the minority."

"Guess so. Always have been. When I was a kid, I was more interested in helping my mom make dinner than playing football." He pushed his glasses up. "I cooked my first family dinner when I was six—grilled peanut-butter-and-banana sandwiches with Kraft macaroni and cheese on the side." He shrugged. "What can I say? I've always kind of been the odd man out. But that's okay. I'm secure in my masculinity. It's just the rest of the world that's not."

"Maybe if you spit and scratched, you could join the good ol' boys club."

"Nah. I think my hog's all I need for entry."

"Your hog?"

"My Harley." He puffed out his chest.

"Of course. That explains the black leather jacket in June. Doesn't it get hot, though?"

"A little. But I'm a big safety-first guy, so I don't mind a little heat. And speaking of heat—I slaved for hours over a hot stove making that shepherd's pie. Won't you at least try some?"

"Well, when you put it that way . . ." I let him lead me back to the buffet table, ignoring the gaggle of young, hard-bodied girls with exposed midriffs and taut tummies trying to catch his eye.

Although I admit, I did suck in my stomach.

Simon scooped a large helping of his shepherd's pie onto my plate and looked at me expectantly.

"Don't I need to nuke it?"

"Nope." He pointed to the table. "Sternos."

"Oh, I didn't even see that there. My friend Deborah—she's a caterer—uses those too."

I took a bite. "Mmm. Who knew hamburger could taste so good?"

"That's ground sirloin, I'll have you know. Only the best. No fatty chuck."

"It's delicious. And how handy to have the meat and mashed potatoes all in one dish."

"Vegetables too. Can't forget to mind your peas and carrots." He smiled.

"That's like minding your p's and q's, right?"

"Ah, you watch BBC TV, don't you?"

"Love it. Especially the Inspector Lynley mysteries and *Monarch of the Glen*."

He swallowed his last bite of potato salad. "So what do I need to do to get the recipe?"

"You mean in addition to walking on hot coals barefoot?"

He nodded.

"And bringing home the bacon?" I grinned. "Actually, I had to cook the bacon for my potato salad in the middle of the night last night."

"Why?"

"My roommate's a vegetarian. Can't stand the smell of meat."

"Good thing you didn't go for steak and kidney pie then."

"Kidney? Eew. Even this carnivore wouldn't touch that with a ten-foot pole." I shuddered. "I'm no vegetarian, but you'll never catch me eating kidney. Or heart. Or tongue. Now, liver, on the other hand . . . that's a different story."

"Liver and onions?" He began to pant. "With bacon or without?"

I hesitated, reluctant to admit it. Then decided to go for broke. "With. The only way to go."

"I couldn't agree more. What about pâté? Chicken, duck, or vegetarian?"

"Actually, I've never had any."

"You're kidding. *Never?*"

"Nope. What can I say? I don't get out much."

"Sorry." He laughed. "Was I sounding pretentious?"

"Only a little. If you'd started talking about caviar and the lovely bouquet of your favorite red wine, I'd have had to call in the snob police."

He backed up in mock horror. "Anything but that. Actually, I like pretty basic foods overall, but I confess to a weakness for pâté. You should stop by my restaurant and try some. On the house."

"What's the name of your restaurant?"

"Friar Tuck's."

"After the drunken priest in *Robin Hood*?"

"He wasn't really a drunk," Simon protested. "I think of him more as the epicurean of the Merry Men—one of the first foodies, if you will."

"I thought that honor went to Nero."

"Nah. He was more into music."

We laughed together. I hadn't had this much fun talking to a guy in ages. Usually I felt all awkward and tongue-tied. But talking to Simon was, I don't know . . . comfortable. Easy.

Shauna, the marathon runner, sidled over, a tiny pink sweatsuit subbing for her usual tight bicycle shorts. "Hi, Frankie . . . who's your friend?"

"Uh—"

"Actually, *Freddie* and I were just going outside to get a little air," Simon said politely. "Will you excuse us, please?" He led me away.

At the door, he turned to me. "You don't mind if we get away from everyone for a few minutes, do you?"

I hesitated.

He grinned and held up his hands, palms out. "I promise I'm not a stalker, and I'll maintain a respectable distance."

"Well . . ."

"Hold on a minute." He tapped the shoulder of a nearby woman I didn't know, who was chatting to a girlfriend. "Excuse me."

She turned and gave us a quizzical glance.

He extended his hand to her. "Hi. I'm Simon. What's your name?"

"Lynn." She shook his hand.

"Lynn, I'm wondering if you'd mind doing me a favor?" He turned on his boyish charm and laid his accent on thick.

"Depends . . ." She shot me an uncertain look.

I lifted my shoulders in a "you got me" expression.

He nodded in my direction. "This is Freddie, and we've just met. I've invited her to go outside so we can hear each other without having to shout. But since she doesn't really know me, she's a little cautious—understandably so." He winked. "For all she knows, I could be an ax murderer or Jack the Ripper or an Amway salesman or something."

Lynn and her friend giggled. I did the trademark eye-rolling thing.

"Would you mind keeping an eye on us through that door right there, and if you see me getting a little too close for comfort or doing something inappropriate—like, say, whipping out an ax from my back pocket and brandishing it at her—could you just give a shout and maybe bring a couple of big, beefy guys out to save Freddie? I'd really appreciate it."

She giggled again.

Simon nodded to a bench just visible through the open door. "We won't go any farther than that, so if all of a sudden you can't see us, call the cavalry. Okay?"

"Sure." She giggled yet again and gave me a look that asked, How'd you ever hook up with this cute, funny guy? If you don't want him, I'll take him.

"Well that's a novel approach," I said. "Do you use that often?"

He motioned me out the door. "Nope. First time."

Who was he kidding? But I decided to play along. "Oh, I get it. You've got my defenses all lowered now, but it's just a warmup for the next time, when you really will pull out your portable ax."

"You got me." He ushered me over to the bench and wiggled his fingers in a wave to Lynn watching from inside.

Grateful to see the bench was concrete rather than one of those flimsy wooden-slatted ones, I sat down, carefully adjusting my new olive skirt so it wouldn't bunch around my thighs.

Simon sat down next to me, but not so close that he invaded my space. Clearly, this guy had read *Boundaries*.

"So," he said, "whaddya say we get the résumés out of the way?"

chapter thirteen

Résumés?"

"You know; the basics." Simon ticked them off on his fingers. "Name, age, occupation, marital status, favorite color, food, dysfunctional family members . . ."

He pointed to himself and began to recite: "Simon Wesley Shattuck. Thirty-one. Chef and restaurant owner. Never been married—although I was briefly engaged until she dumped me for a podiatrist."

My left eyebrow did its quirking thing.

"She had corns and plantar fasciitis," he explained. "This way she'd have free treatment for life."

"Ah."

"I also had my heart broken in the seventh grade when Kari McConnell dumped me for Brock the basketball star." He took off his glasses and wiped them with his shirt. "What kind of name is Brock anyway? Sounds like something from a Western romance novel. But never mind." He put his glasses back on. "Favorite color is blue. Favorite food . . . ?" He frowned. "That's a little harder. Let's see . . . fresh cracked crab. Fish and chips. A great filet, medium-rare. Authentic German potato salad . . ." He sent me a crooked smile.

"No Italian?"

"Oh, of course! Good fresh pasta, osso bucco, risotto . . . I make an amazing mushroom risotto." He puffed out his chest. "Also a great lasagna, if I do say so myself."

I stiffened. Greg had made—and later, effectively demonstrated—that same claim. Time to change the channel from the Food Network. "And dysfunctional family members?"

"Well, other than Uncle Lou, who liked to drink a little too much wassail at Christmas, I'm afraid I come from a fairly functional family." He sent me an apologetic grin. "My folks were crazy about each other. They met when he was stationed in England, got married, and promptly had three kids—bing, bada, bing. I'm the youngest and the only boy. One sister's married and living in Fresno, and the other's here in town, as is my mum." A shadow crossed his face. "Unfortunately, Dad died when I was eleven."

"I'm sorry. Are you close to your mother and sisters?"

"Yeah. They're great. A little overprotective now and then"—he made a face—"but that's only because they love me."

Must be nice.

"What about what you *don't* like?" I asked. "You can't get a true picture of someone unless you know what they hate as well."

"That's easy," he said. "Jerry Springer, rap music, and Siamese cats." He lifted his shoulders. "What can I say? I was scarred for life as a little boy by those two evil cats in *Lady and the Tramp*."

How cute is that? A man who admits his fears—goofy as they may be.

"I forgot one more," he said. "I confess to not being a big fan of reality TV shows. Except *American Idol*, which is more of a talent competition."

"Exactly! Who was your favorite last year? And don't be mean like the judge who shares your name."

"Mandisa. What a powerhouse!"

I nodded agreement.

"Okay, your turn."

"Huh?"

"Your résumé."

"Mine's not as interesting as yours." I grimaced and took a deep breath. "Fredericka Brunhilde Heinz."

"Ouch. So where're the long yellow braids and winged helmet?"

"I left them at home. Besides, I prefer Puccini to Wagner. And speaking of music, I like just about everything. Except yodeling and hip-hop."

"Yeah, I'm not too big on hip-hop yodeling either."

I shook my head in regret. "We're probably missing out on the next hot trend—gangsta lederhosen."

"Have you been peeking in my closet, Miss Rabbit Trail?"

"Okay, okay. Point taken." I continued with my résumé. "Almost thirty. Never married, although I was engaged once too, but it didn't work out." I frowned. "Not sure what my favorite color is. Guess I never really thought about it before." I thought of how Deborah was always trying to get me to add some color to my wardrobe. "Green, maybe?"

"Favorite movie?" I ducked my head and scrunched my eyes shut. "*Dirty Dancing.* I watched it over and over again as a kid. My stepmom loved it."

"Nobody puts Baby in a corner," he quoted.

"At least not when Patrick Swayze's around." I grinned. "I love *Chocolat* too." I turned my hands palms up. "What can I say? I work in a bakery."

"Really? I *knew* we were kindred spirits." His hazel eyes gleamed behind his glasses. "Where do you work?"

"Jorgensen's." I lowered my voice just in case Anya had spies in the singles group. "I'm the resident cake lady."

"No way! I love their cakes—especially the Danish layer. Mmm. So *you're* responsible for that decadent concoction."

"Oh no!" That's all I needed—Anya thinking I was trying to steal her family's thunder. "The recipe's been in the Jorgensen family for generations. I think old Mr. Jorgensen's mother brought it over from the old country. I just follow the directions," I said. Then, in the interest of full disclosure: "Mostly."

"So do you like to cook too?" Simon asked, standing to stretch. "Besides baking cakes, I mean?"

I stood up too so I wouldn't have to crane to look at him, although I wasn't sure exactly what to do with my hands. Too bad this skirt didn't have pockets. "To be honest, I don't cook that often." *These days, anyway. No one to cook for.* "Sacrilege to a chef, I know."

He lifted his shoulders in a resigned shrug. "Most people don't anymore. Cooking at home's becoming a lost art. But I guess that's good for us restaurant types."

"So what kind of restaurant do you have?" I decided relaxed at my side would be the best bet.

"English."

"Really? I've heard English food is pretty bland and boring." Did those words really just come out of my mouth? Way to knock a guy's profession and his country. Well, his mother's country, at least. I clutched at my skirt where a pocket should have been. "Not that I would know," I added hastily.

"Was your shepherd's pie bland?"

"No."

"Well then." He sighed. "England used to have a reputation for bad food, but not anymore. Now a lot of restaurants and pubs are becoming more continental in flavor."

"Have you traveled a lot in Europe? How old were you when you lived there?"

"I was born in England and spent the first seven years of my life there. Then my dad got transferred to Germany for three years—"

"Ah, so that's where you developed a taste for German potato salad."

"Actually I never had this kind of potato salad in Germany. Oh, but the schnitzel and sauerbraten, the spaetzle and strudel . . ."

"All *s* foods," I observed.

"Oh, they use other letters too: beer and bratwurst and *Brötchen*. And *Pommes Frites mit Mayonnaise*—although that term's mostly French, I think"

"Pommes Frites?"

"French fries."

"With *mayonnaise*?" I shuddered.

"Hey, don't knock it till you've tried it. But it has to be real mayonnaise, not Miracle Whip." It was his turn to shudder. "You ever been to Europe?"

"No, but I'm dying to go someday. The farthest I've been is Chicago."

"Ah, the windy city. Great town." In a clear, light baritone he sang a snatch of the song Sinatra made famous.

"What next? You cook, you sing, you ride a Harley. Is there no end to your talents?"

He grabbed my hand and twirled me to him in a jitterbug move. "That's why the ladies call me a Renaissance man."

I stepped on his foot. "And that's why I'm not a Renaissance woman." My cheeks burned. "Sorry. I have absolutely no rhythm."

"Maybe you just haven't had the right partner." He gave me another slow smile.

Does this guy know the effect he has on women?

He released my hand.

Of course he does.

"And your dysfunctional family members?" he asked, breaking the mood.

"Trust me. You don't even want to go there." I shivered. "It's getting kind of cool. Maybe we'd better go back in."

Was it my imagination or did I see a flicker of disappointment in his eyes?

"Yeah, it's getting a little late."

My imagination. He followed me through the door.

"I see he brought you back safe and sound," Lynn, our guardian, said with a smile. "No axes."

"Nope," I told her. "But thanks for keeping an eye out. I appreciate it."

"Thanks, Lynn." Simon winked at her. "If you ever need guard duty references, let me know."

We returned to the buffet table to claim our food. "I see the vultures have been busy while we were gone," Simon said, picking up his empty casserole dish.

"Even my potato salad." As I leaned over to lift the dish, I overheard Jared's Malibu Barbie talking to a girlfriend.

"Oh yeah," she said. "When I want to feel good about myself, I go to Gap. I mean, those mirrors? Every single one makes me look like a newborn *babe*. Absolutely hot. Thighs just the right size."

I stole a glance at her thighs in their tight jeans. And shook my head.

"Then I go to Sears." She shook her head, eyes wide and woeful. "One look in their mirrors, and I want to kill myself."

Simon caught my eye and rolled his. "Freddie, you ready to

go?" He walked me out to my car. "It was great talking to you tonight. I hope to see you again soon . . ."

He seemed to hesitate. Was he going to do it? Was he going to ask me out? What would I say? I tried not to look too nervous.

He pushed his glasses up on his nose. "You'll come to my restaurant won't you? Don't forget. Friar Tuck's."

Disappointment and relief washed over me. I hid them both with a blithe, "Right. The epicurean, not the drunk."

He gave me a jaunty smile. "That's right. And if you come, I'll introduce you to the joys of pâté."

Well, that's kind of asking me out. Wonder if Deborah would like to go out to dinner soon.

.   .   .   .

At home I jumped on my blog even before I put on my jammies:

Wednesday

Mirror, mirror, on the wall,

Who's got the skinniest thighs of all?

Why are we so fixated by what we see in the mirror?

Take tonight. I was at this party where I overheard this slip of a girl talking about mirrors. She couldn't have been more than a size 4, tops, and she was complaining about how fat she looked in a dressing-room mirror.

If that woman thinks she looks fat, what hope is there for the rest of us?

Most women I know are always complaining about how they need to lose weight--even the size 2s. I could never let those women know my size. Sure, they can look at me and probably guess, but they don't actually know.

Unless, of course, they work in women's clothing at some department store.

Remember gorgeous Kate Winslet in *Titanic*? When that blockbuster movie first came out, all the entertainment TV shows and magazines went on and on about how big and "voluptuous" she was--and she was only a size 8!

What is it with Hollywood? Could we have a reality check, please?

I was thrilled a few years ago when a new sitcom featured a larger-than-average single young woman on the boob tube. Since TV adds ten pounds, she was probably only a size 10, maybe a 12 at the most. And she was absolutely adorable, with long, gorgeous red hair, beautiful eyes, a fabulous smile, and a cherub face. A year or so later, when I picked up a celebrity magazine, I was dismayed to see that this same curvaceous woman had lost fifty pounds. To celebrate her new size 6 figure, she'd also had her fabulous hair cut and dyed blonde--making her indistinguishable from the bevy of Hollywood blonde clones.

The same thing happened with a redheaded teen actress whose freckles and curves were a welcome respite from the shallow sea of blonde anorexia. But once she got a couple of hit movies under her curvy belt and turned eighteen, she, too, fell prey to the Hollywood clone machine. She dropped twenty pounds, dyed her hair blonde, and completely lost her unique appeal.

I don't need to worry about that happening to me if I ever head to Tinseltown. I don't care if blondes have more fun or not, it's just not me. Besides, I'd have to lose way more than twenty pounds to fit in. (Good luck with that!)

The thing is, maybe we shouldn't spend so much time looking in mirrors. Sure, it's good to make sure you don't have spinach in your teeth or mascara smudges under your eyes. But maybe we should spend a little more time looking at what's going on inside of us. Is the person we see in the mirror the same person the God of the universe sees?

:: *chapter fourteen* ::

Freddie, hurry up with that birthday cake!" Anya snapped, startling me. "The customer will be here any minute, and I don't want to keep her waiting."

I scraped the now-smeared *Happy* script off the top of the cake and began again. "I'm almost finished." As Anya clattered back to her front counter domain in her three-inch stilettos, I added under my breath. "I only got the order three hours ago."

Most bakeries in town asked for a forty-eight-hour notice on a cake, but Anya liked to live on the edge—and make more money—so she advertised our "last-minute" cakes (with a minimum turnaround time of three hours) and charged accordingly. Problem was, she wasn't the one living on the edge—we were.

"Why doesn't she just rename the bakery McCake's while she's at it?" Millie glanced at the still-swinging door. "I think someone got up on the wrong side of the bed this morning."

"No, I think it's more that the latest guy she met isn't interested," Shane offered. "Nicole told me Anya's been calling and texting him all over the place, but he's not returning her calls."

Ah. That explained it. I'd wondered last night when I saw

Jared with his Malibu Barbie. I boxed up the birthday cake with a lighter heart.

Securing the plastic lid on the plastic bucket of buttercream, I slid the airtight container onto the rack beneath my work station to join the other plastic buckets of frosting. I mean icing. I called it frosting when I first started work at Jorgensen's, but Millie quickly corrected me. "Frosting is what housewives use," she said. "We're professional bakers." She giggled. "Old Mr. Jorgensen told me that when I first started, so I'm just carrying on the tradition." (I saw no point in telling her that the bakers in the big Chicago bakery where I apprenticed didn't seem to care what they called it.)

Another thing Millie taught me when I first started working at the bakery that really surprised me was that the icing—except for the cream cheese stuff—didn't need to be refrigerated. In fact, it was better if it wasn't, much easier to spread. As long as we kept the buttercream (made with top-grade shortening, not butter) in an airtight container at room temperature—not close to the oven or any heat—it was fine. We turned around so many cakes on a constant basis that it didn't have a chance to go bad.

Shane carried the completed birthday cake out front, and I removed the next pink order form from the walk-in door—a half-sheet chocolate baby cake for a luncheon shower tomorrow. That coupled with the wedding cake for Saturday afternoon and the Danish layer cake for the silver wedding anniversary Saturday night would keep me busy for a while.

The phone rang, but I knew better than to pick it up. Anya liked to be the voice as well as the face of Jorgensen's. Everyone had strict orders not to answer the phone when she was working—unless it went to a third ring, because that meant she was busy with a customer.

I continued to mix the eggs into the chocolate batter, the steady whir of the mixer lulling me into a daydream as I replayed last night's fun conversation with Simon the chef. Then Shane's voice intruded: "Freddie, phone call."

"For me?" My head snapped up.

"Uh-huh. And Anya's not happy." He made a face as he recited: "You know the policy of no personal calls at work unless it's an emergency."

"Thanks. I'll get rid of whoever it is really quick." I wiped my hands on my apron and picked up the extension. "This is Freddie. How can I help you?"

"That's a good question, young lady." My father's cold voice froze the line. "You can start by not being rude to my wife."

"Excuse me?"

"Candy said she called you nearly a week ago, and you haven't returned her call," he continued in a clipped tone. "Your mother and I made what I think was a very generous offer—for a very expensive surgical procedure, I might add. The least you could do is give us the courtesy of responding."

I clenched the phone. "Look, this isn't a good time."

"Well, you'd better make the time, young lady." As my father continued to harangue me, I heard another sound on the line— soft breathing. I wasn't sure if it was Candy or Anya listening in. With my luck, probably both.

"I'm sorry," I said in the most professional tone I could muster, "but I'm afraid I have to get back to work now. I'll talk to you later."

And I hung up, shaking.

Millie gave me a concerned look. "You okay?"

"I'm fine." I lifted my shoulders in what I hoped came across as a casual shrug and rolled my eyes. "Parents."

"I hear ya." Shane did his own eye-roll thing.

I turned back to the finished cake batter, steadied my shaking hands, and began pouring the wet chocolate mixture into the first pan.

The phone shrilled again and I jumped, slopping batter onto the floor.

Nicole stuck her head through the door, a worried frown puckering her forehead. "Uh, Freddie, it's for you again."

Carefully, I set the large mixing bowl down. Carefully, I stepped over the chocolate puddle on the floor at my feet. A little less carefully, I snatched up the phone and hissed through clenched teeth. "I said this isn't a good time."

"Freddie?" Deborah's distinctive Southern voice was like honey on a wound. "What's up?"

Was it her breathing I heard, or someone else's?

"I'm sorry, Deborah, but I really can't talk right now. Can I call you later?"

"Sure, honey. Whenever you're free. Y'all take care now, ya hear? And girl?"

"Yes?" I tried not to sound impatient, wanting to get off the line before Anya had a cow.

"I'll be praying for you. Sounds like you need it."

"Thanks. I appreciate it." I clicked off. As I turned to return to my work station, the double doors flew open.

"Two personal calls?" Anya slammed through the door, her stilettos slapping angrily against the tile. "What have I told you about personal calls at work?" Her chest heaved beneath her white silk camisole, drawing my eyes to large splotches of red and white above the lace bodice.

"I'm sorry," I said in an even tone as I began to walk back to the counter. "I didn't ask either of them to call, and if you'll notice, both conversations were very brief. I told them I'd need to call them back later."

"You need to do better than that." Anya followed behind me, spitting her words out in staccato machine-gun bursts. "You need to tell your family and *friends*"—she sneered at the last word—"that you're not allowed personal calls at work. At all."

I whirled around. "Were you listening in on my pho— Watch out!"

Too late I saw the spilled batter and Anya's delicate sandals fast approaching. My warning wasn't fast enough. Her strappy Jimmy Choos connected with the gooey mess, and her bronzed tanning-bed legs shot out from under her.

Horrified, I watched the whole thing as if in slow motion— her flirty yellow skirt flying up umbrellalike to reveal way more of my boss than I ever wanted to see. (I've never understood the whole thong appeal. Maybe it was because I didn't have the body to wear one, but it just looked really uncomfortable to me. In grade school we called those wedgies.)

Anya's skirt fluttered down again as she fell and landed smack on her bottom in the middle of the chocolate puddle. Shane, who had rushed to grab her during her freeze-frame free fall, slipped too. He landed on top of her in an undignified tangle of arms and legs.

Beside me, Millie sucked in her breath.

"Oh my gosh. Are you okay, Anya?" I asked.

"No, I am not okay," she screeched. "I'm covered in chocolate, my favorite shoes are ruined, and my air supply is being cut off." She pushed at Shane's chest. "Would you get off me, you big idiot?"

Shane scrambled to get up but kept slipping in the sticky goop like Lucille Ball in a vat of grapes.

Millie made a strangled gurgling noise beside me, and I could tell she was trying not to laugh. I also knew that if I met her eyes, I'd be done for.

Trying to keep a straight face, I planted my feet clear of the spattered batter and tried to help Shane to his feet. He continued to slip and slide, laughing so hard he couldn't get up.

Forcing my lips into a straight line so no snorts or laughs could escape, I then extended a hand to Anya, but she slapped it away. "Now you try to help? This is all your fault."

She placed her chocolate-smeared palms on the floor on either side of her narrow hips and tried to push herself up, but couldn't get any traction and slipped again. She let fly a string of expletives. "On top of everything else, now I broke a nail."

A dripping Shane tried to be Mister Gallant and help her up, but she snarled, "I can do it myself, clumsy boy. Just throw me a towel."

He found her a dishcloth next to the sink. She wiped her chocolatey hands, then gripped the pine leg of the sturdy wooden island with her left hand and the lower metal shelf beneath the counter with her right and pulled herself up, slipping and almost falling again in the process.

Quickly I turned my head away, afraid my face would betray me, but I couldn't hide my shaking shoulders. Millie's and Shane's shook too, but they weren't in Anya's direct line of vision.

"You think this is funny?" she spat out. "I'll show you funny. You're fired, Freddie. I've had it with you."

"But it was an accident," Millie said.

Anya glared at her. "You want to be next?" She scooped a clump of batter off her skirt and flung it in the sink. Then she yanked off her stilettos and squished her way to the back door. "Make sure you don't let the door slam your big butt on the way out." She stormed out. Moments later we heard her BMW spin gravel as she roared out of the parking lot.

Nicole cautiously pushed open the double doors. "Is it safe to come in? I saw Anya's car leave." She looked at a chocolate-smeared Shane, her eyes widening. "What the heck happened back here?"

Shane, still a little bit in shock over what had just happened, looked at me. Millie looked at Shane. Both of them looked at me, and we all burst out laughing.

"Aw c'mon guys, that's not fair," Nicole said. "Share with the rest of the class."

But we were all too far gone to speak. The three of us were on the laughing jag to end all laughing jags, complete with streaming eyes and sore stomachs. Any minute now I expected us to float upward on a cloud of laughter like the guy in *Mary Poppins.*

Millie tried to pull herself together. "Well, you see," she gasped out, "Freddie spilled some batter, and when Anya came back to give her what for about the personal phone calls, she"— Millie clutched her side and doubled over in another gale of laughter.

"She was really giving it to Freddie," Shane continued, "and you know how Anya is when she gets mad. So she clicks after Freddie in those silly shoes she's always wearing, and then she slips in the batter—"

"And then Shane tries to help," I picked up the story, "but he slips too and lands on top of Anya, and now she's really losing it. It looked like something from *Skating with Celebrities*—without the ice." I pointed at Shane's chocolate-blotched clothes and started giggling anew.

"All that was missing from the whole scene was a cream pie in the face," Millie snorted.

"Well . . . we've still got a banana cream out front," Nicole said with a wicked glance at Shane. "If you like, I can bring it back here and finish the job."

"Hey!" he protested, then grinned at her. "Think I'll stick with chocolate."

"Of course, I'm now unemployed thanks to my slip-up." I giggled at my pun. "Or Anya's slip-up."

But Shane had turned sober. "That's right," he said. "I can't believe she fired you! What are you going to do now?"

"Anya fired you?" Nicole's hand flew to her mouth. "Oh Freddie, I'm so sorry."

"Don't be." I shrugged out of my white coat. "This makes the third time . . ." I stopped to confirm with Millie. "Third time this year, right?"

She scrunched up her eyes in thought, then nodded. "Yep, today marks number three."

"Really?" Nicole's baby blues grew even wider.

"Oh yeah. Anya explodes now and then into a screaming fit, and it's best to just get out of the way when that happens," Millie said with a wry smile. "Unfortunately, Freddie's the one who always seems to get hit by the flying shrapnel."

"And speaking of flying shrapnel"—I grabbed my purse from under the counter—"sorry to leave the mess for you guys to clean up, but it won't be long before Anya gets back, and it won't be pretty if I'm still here. You think this is bad, you ain't seen nothin' yet. Millie, can you and Shane bake the shower and anniversary cakes for me, please? Anya should cool off in time for me to decorate them."

"Sure." Millie shooed me out the door. "Now, scoot. And don't forget dinner's at six. And it's your turn to bring the salad."

· · · ·

As I drove home, I punched in Deborah's number on my cell. "Hey there. I can talk now."

"You okay?" Her concern resonated in my ear.

"I am now."

"So what was happening when I called earlier? You didn't sound too good."

I blew air out through my teeth. "I forgot to tell you we're not allowed personal calls at work, and yours was my second of the day—right on the heels of the other one."

"I'm sorry. Hope I didn't get you in trouble."

Before I could tell her everything that happened, Deborah rattled on. "So, who was the first call from? That nice vet, Hal? I think he really likes you."

"And I think you're crazy. But no, it wasn't Hal," I retorted. "It was my father. But I don't even want to go there."

"No problem. So where are you calling from now? Are you outside taking a break?"

"Nope. I got fired."

"Say what?" Deborah's shock boomed in my ear. "Because I called?" Her righteous indignation flared up. "I'll go over there right now and clear that up with your boss."

"No. No." I hastened to reassure her. "It's not your fault. Don't worry. It's not the first time she's fired me, and it won't be the last."

"What?"

"It's just this power game Anya likes to play from time to time." I filled Deborah in on all that had happened and finished with a sigh. "It won't stick."

"Why you let her play you that way?"

"That's just how Anya is." I shrugged my shoulders even though she couldn't see them. "Not a lot I can do about it."

"Oh yes, there is," Deborah said with a snort. "You can stand up for yourself. Or if you want, this big black woman will come stand up with you."

"No, no, that's okay. I'll handle it. But thanks." I sought to distract her. "So why did you call earlier, anyway?"

"To see if you were coming to water aerobics with me again tonight. I thought you could come for dinner first, if you like. Samuel's grilling some steaks, and we're having baked potatoes and a mess of grilled vegetables too."

"Sounds delicious. But I'm going over to my friend Millie's from work. I'll catch you next time, okay?"

"I'll hold you to it, girl."

:: *chapter fifteen* ::

Honey, I'm home," I sang out to Zsa Zsa. Usually at the first sound of my key in the lock, she would come hurtling down the hall to greet me, and by the time I opened the door she'd be quivering with excitement and jumping up and down saying, "Hold me, hold me. You've come home at last. You didn't abandon me after all."

This happened whether I was gone one hour or one week. That's the wonderful thing about dogs. I love coming home each day to that wagging tail and those sloppy kisses.

I know. Sappy. So sue me.

But today, there was no little white fur ball to welcome me.

"Zsa Zsa?" I looked in the living room, where a snoozing Eliza curled up at the end of the couch. She lazily opened one eye at the sound of my voice, then shut it again. Henry ambled by on his way to the kitchen, leaned over to give my legs a friendly rub, then strolled on past. I heard him lapping water. But still no sight or sound of Zsa Zsa.

I checked the kitchen. Empty save for Henry.

The dining room? Still nada.

I hurried to my room.

The first thing I saw was the paperback of *Moby Dick* I'd recently brought home from Bramwell's—shredded on the floor. I followed the paper trail around to the other side of the bed, where at last I found my furry little bundle of energy lying listless on a pair of my flannel pants.

She didn't even lift her head at my approach.

My heart caught in my throat. Had I killed my dog with a classic?

Hurrying over to Zsa Zsa, I scooped her up in my arms. She whimpered and gave me a pathetic look out of her lone eye. And when I touched her nose, it was hot and dry. I called Hal Baxter's office, and he told me to bring her over.

. . . .

I handed him the remains of the shredded paperback. "I think she ate *Moby Dick*."

"Wonder if it tasted like chicken. Or in this case, tuna." He grinned.

I didn't smile.

"Sorry. Bad joke." He examined Zsa Zsa and took her temperature. "Dogs don't normally eat paper."

"This is no normal dog."

"With a name like Zsa Zsa, I kind of figured that." He stroked her fur. "Yes, you're a pretty girl, aren't you? In the future, however, you might want to skip the classics. If I were you, I'd try a little Louis L'Amour." He palpated her abdomen, did a few more checks, then handed her back to me. "Just a little indigestion. She'll be fine in a little while."

"Isn't there any medication I can give her to help?"

"Afraid not. She's just suffering the consequences of her dietary indiscretion. But chances are, this, too, shall pass, and once it does, she should be back to her normal frisky self." He gave me a reassuring smile.

"That's good to know. Thanks. I appreciate your fitting us in on such short notice." I turned to go.

"Uh, speaking of short notice . . . are you the spontaneous type?"

"Not usually."

"You should try it sometime. Like tonight for instance. How'd you like to go out to dinner with me? And not KFC."

Whoa. Was he asking me out on a date?

Last night, Simon. Well, sorta kinda. And tonight, Hal. What's going on? I must be giving off some mysterious kind of man-attracting scent (pheromones?) or something. Wish I'd known how to do that before.

Truth was, I hadn't had a date in ages. Not since the disastrous blind one Millie set me up on with her dentist nephew from Modesto. I'll never forget the look on his face when he first saw me— ouch. And can you say "bored out of my molars"? I'd sworn off blind dates after that. And I was pretty wary of the whole dating scene.

I looked at Hal. Ah, I get it. He's trying to make amends for his insensitive crack about Zsa Zsa. Good thing I've got a legitimate excuse.

"Sorry," I said. "I've already got plans for tonight. In fact, I was going to ask you if you think it's okay for me to go out tonight and leave Zsa Zsa. Should I be keeping watch on her or something?"

"It should be fine. Although it could be a little messy. You might want to keep her in the garage while you're gone."

In the garage? Princesses don't stay in the garage. I called Brooke at work.

"Sure," she said, "I'll be happy to keep an eye on Zsa Zsa tonight."

"How about another night?" Hal asked when I flipped my phone shut. "I have a meeting Friday, but what about Saturday?"

I searched his scruffy face looking for traces of ulterior motive and saw nothing but friendly interest. Plus a few small crumbs from lunch snared in the beard.

This was too weird. Maybe my instincts were playing tricks on me.

Or maybe it really is a date.

. . . .

"Well, Miss Nibs really got hers today." Millie pulled her chicken, rice, and Campbell's cream–of–mushroom soup bake out of the oven in her compact blue-and-white galley kitchen. Since she and I took turns cooking, the culinary offerings varied widely. I loved to try out more ambitious menus, while Millie's cooking was purely down-home. But the food was always good, and the company was better. I liked it so much, I was still a little nervous about having Nicole join us Saturday for our "special" movie night.

"That had to be one of the funniest things I ever saw," Millie went on. "I just wish I'd had a camera. If we had a digital one and knew how to download it right, we could post pictures on one of those Internet dating sites she belongs to."

"Now, that wouldn't be nice." My good Christian girl kicked in. *Funny, but not nice.*

"And since when has Anya ever been nice to you? Or to me, for that matter." Millie transferred the contents of the pan to our waiting plates. "If her parents could see how she treats her employees, they'd be rolling in their graves," she added with an edge to her voice. "And if her grandpa were still here, he'd turn her over his knee and give her what for."

"But none of them are here, so Anya pretty much has carte

blanche." I tossed the spring mix salad with frise, blue cheese, and pecans that was my contribution to dinner. "So what happened after I left? Did you and Shane get the cakes finished?"

"All set and just waiting for your decorating prowess, my dear." She looked at her watch. "Speaking of Shane, wonder where that boy is? If he doesn't get here pretty soon, dinner's going to be cold." She furrowed her eyebrows. "Now, what was I going to tell you? Something about cakes . . ." Millie snapped her fingers. "I know! We got another Danish layer order in after you went home—a special birthday one for Sunday that Anya okayed and said she'd deliver, so I just doubled the recipe. It's cooling in the walk-in, just waiting to be put together and iced tomorrow."

"Thanks." I plucked a pecan from the salad and nibbled on it. "Wonder how long it will take for Anya to call me in the morning?"

"You mean the queen of denial?" Millie snorted. "I'd say the soonest would be nine thirty or ten."

"You want Ranch or my homemade raspberry vinaigrette?"

"Do you even need to ask?"

"Ranch, it is." I poured the Hidden Valley over her salad. "I just thought maybe you might get adventurous and try something different for a change."

"Why should I?" Millie said. "I know what I like and don't see any reason to change it. And that goes for movies too."

"So what are we watching tonight?" I followed her into the living room and helped her set up three wooden TV tables in front of the couch and her recliner.

"*Some Like It Hot*, with Jack Lemmon and Tony Curtis. You're going to love it—one of the funniest movies ever made. I watch it at least twice a year." She headed back to the kitchen for drinks. "You want milk or water?"

"If it's one-percent, I'll take milk."

The doorbell rang. "About time." She opened the door to an out-of-breath Shane. Millie put her hands on her hips. "And where have you been, young man?"

"Sorry. I had a clothing emergency. I spilled Starbucks all over my jeans and had to go back home to change."

"And you couldn't call?"

"Hey, come on, guys," I said. "Food's getting cold."

Millie settled into her recliner and started the movie as we all chowed down.

"This is a *comedy*?" I asked a few minutes later as we watched a bunch of men get machine-gunned in a garage in what Shane explained was the St. Valentine's Day Massacre.

"Oh yeah," he said. "Just wait."

I didn't have to wait long. Seeing Jack Lemmon and Tony Curtis trying to walk in girdles and heels was hilarious. The actors played two down-on-their-luck musicians who witnessed the massacre and needed to hide away from the Mob, so they dressed in drag and joined a girl band.

"That Tony Curtis made a pretty good-looking woman."

"Tony Curtis made a good-looking man," Millie said with a sigh. "Quite the heartthrob in his day."

"Are you wishing you were Janet Leigh?" Shane asked her with a smirk.

"The *Psycho* lady who made me afraid to get in the shower?" I shivered at the frightening teenage memory. "What'd she have to do with Tony Curtis?"

"They were married—"

"Shh," Millie said. "You're going to miss Marilyn's entrance and Jack Lemmon's great line."

A larger-than-life black-and-white Marilyn Monroe sashayed onto Millie's big-screen TV in all her oozing voluptuousness and

vulnerability. Quite the combination—and one that got the attention of every male in sight. Including Shane.

"Look how she moves," Jack Lemmon's thunderstruck character said to Tony as she passed by them. "It's like Jell-O on springs."

Definitely a lot of jiggling and wiggling. I don't know any
women who walk like that these days. I checked the DVD to see
what year the movie was made: 1959.

Like the rest of the world, I'd seen Marilyn's too-familiar like-
ness plastered on everything from posters to purses, but I'd never
quite understood the appeal. I thought other old actresses from
the time were much more beautiful—like Grace Kelly or Audrey
Hepburn or especially Ingrid Bergman.

But watching Marilyn now, I finally understood. She was a
unique mixture of curvy femininity and wide-eyed, girlish vulnerability—all wrapped up in one breathless, undulating package. No wonder men were obsessed with her.

I was sashaying down the train platform in my own red stilettos and a swirly white halter dress, my matching little white dog
tucked adorably in my red handbag, when the phone rang.

Millie hit pause, and while she talked to her out-of-state
daughter and Shane browsed through Millie's DVD collection, I
decided to call Brooke and check in. "How's my little Zsa Zsa?"

"Much better now that she's shed herself of that whale,"
Brooke said. "She's almost her old self now."

"Can you put her up to the phone, please? I don't want her
to think I deserted her."

"Sure thing, Fred. Hang on."

I waited a few seconds for Brooke to pick the puppy up. Then
I crooned, "Hi, baby. Mommy's glad you're all better now. I'll see
you soon."

I flipped my phone shut and looked up to find Millie shaking her head at me. "What?"

"Don't you think it's a little ridiculous to talk to an animal on the phone?"

"Zsa Zsa's not an animal. She's family." Although before falling in love with her, I'd probably have thought the same thing—not that I'd admit it to Millie.

"Whatever you say, mush girl." Millie reached into the microwave for the popcorn I'd brought—light butter—and handed me my diet root beer.

"So, Shane . . . are you ever going to get the nerve up to ask Nicole out?" I teased.

He blushed. "Oh, I don't think she'd ever go out with me. She could have her pick of any guy."

"But you're a great catch," Millie said. She winked at me. "And that's why we're having our Saturday-night gig—to give you a little help."

"Oh no, leave me out of it." I held up my hands. "I'm not good at this matchmaking stuff. If I was, I'd have found a match for myself long ago."

"But how could you meet anyone from the back room of the bakery, or hiding yourself behind a book?" Millie asked. "I'm really glad you met this Deborah. She's helped you come out of your shell and blossom."

"I think you're mixing your metaphors there."

"You know what I mean."

"Yeah, Deborah's great. I really like her. She has a really nice family too. Her husband worships the ground she walks on."

"Must be nice."

"I hear ya. I didn't know men like that even existed anymore."

"Hey!" Shane protested. "Am I invisible or something?"

"No. Just too young," Millie said, giving him a sweet smile. "At least too young for me or Freddie—which is too bad since you're a good guy and we both picked a couple of bad ones our first time around." She picked up the remote. "But good riddance to bad rubbish is all I can say. There's always going to be bad apples, but that doesn't mean they all have worms." She snaked a glance my way. "I believe God has just the right man out there for you. Maybe a certain vet?"

Or maybe a certain chef?

. . . .

This time when I got home and opened the door, Zsa Zsa bounded up to me, wagging her tail. "That's the baby I like to see." I scooped her up and carried her into my room, snuggling my nose in her fur.

Fur that was the same color as Marilyn's hair.

Thinking about the tragic movie star, I Googled her. And was surprised at what I found.

Thursday

I've decided I was born in the wrong century.

I just watched a Marilyn Monroe movie from the 1950s, and can I just say that woman had some serious curves! Can you say voluptuous with a capital V? Every man within a hundred-yard radius was drooling over her. Yet by today's Hollywood standards, she'd be considered fat.

Sure, I've seen pictures of Marilyn over the years. Who hasn't? They're everywhere. Coffee mugs, T-shirts, mouse pads . . . talk about overkill. But this was the first Marilyn Monroe movie I ever saw (*Some Like It Hot*). And you know what? She was funny and sweet and vulnerable. All those things together in one curvaceous package. No wonder men tripped over themselves for her. So I Googled her to learn a little more, and guess what I found out? She often wore a size 14 or 16!

Whoa! Not too much smaller than what I usually wear, so I'm in good company.

Okay, so she was two dress sizes smaller than me. Just don't start telling me that a 14 back then was the same as today's 10 or 12. Let me enjoy this moment in the big-girl sun.

And don't worry, I'm not going to dye my hair blonde and sing "Happy Birthday, Mr. President" in a breathless voice anytime soon. But I think that maybe, just maybe, I'll walk a little taller now. And a little prouder. And maybe even act a little more sexy. 'Cause if there are only a couple of dress sizes between me and Marilyn, then I'm so *not* a fat girl. I'm just a big girl with curves. And you know what?

Real women have curves.

Remember those recent Dove beauty ads where they had women of all shapes and sizes in their underwear? And not any of that Victoria's Secret stuff either—tiny wisps of nylon and lace—but basic white cotton for basic women. Real women. Big women. Wasn't that the coolest thing?

Gotta run. I need to add that movie *Real Women Have Curves* to my NetFlix queue.

:: *chapter sixteen* ::

The phone rang at nine forty the next morning when I was giving Zsa Zsa a bath. Not wanting to stop in the midst of rinsing off her doggie shampoo, I let the machine answer it.

"Freddie?" Anya's fingers-on-chalkboard voice punctured the air. "Where *are* you? You're late. Mrs. Anderson is going to be here in an hour to pick up the cake for the bridal shower luncheon. Hello? If you're there, pick up."

Zsa Zsa let out a little whimper.

"It's okay, baby," I soothed. "Don't worry. She's not here. She can't hurt you."

Zsa Zsa did her doggy thing and shook her wet fur, spraying me in the process as Anya continued to talk into the machine. "You still have to finish up the wedding cake for tonight too. Since you're not answering, I'll just assume you're on your way."

Her voice clicked off.

I toweled off Zsa Zsa, then sent her into blow-dry heaven, brushing and fluffing her fur. "There you go. Aren't you a pretty girl? So soft."

I washed my hands, combed my hair, and applied a little of my new makeup. When I went to get dressed I noticed my answering machine had two messages. The first one was the one I'd heard while bathing Zsa Zsa. I skipped over the rest of it and hit play again.

"Freddie?" Anya's voice was a little more frantic now. "It's ten to ten. Where are you?"

She must have called again while I was blow-drying Zsa Zsa.

I looked at my watch: two minutes to ten. Plenty of time to get to work, finish up the cake, and not ruin the bridal shower surprise. I slipped on my rubber-soled work shoes and ducked out the back door before Zsa Zsa could see me leave.

. . . .

"Morning, everyone."

Shane and Millie heaved a collective sigh of relief. "I'm so glad you're here. Anya's been going cr—"

The double doors from the front flew open. "Has anyone heard from Fr—Oh, Freddie, you're here. Good. Mrs. Anderson will be here in less than half an hour to pick up her cake." She nodded to the iced but undecorated sheet cake on the island in front of Shane and started to say something else, but instead turned and returned to her public domain.

Even Anya knew better than to push it after yesterday.

Shane handed over the pastry bag filled with pink icing. "I told her I'd decorate the cake if you didn't show, but she doesn't trust me with the fancy stuff yet."

I outlined a tilted pink umbrella in the upper right hand corner. "Anya has a problem with trust." I nodded to Millie. "Remember when I first started—how long it took her to let me solo without your help?"

Millie nodded. "Three months. And this was *after* you had apprenticed with that big bakery in Chicago."

I wrote "Welcome, Little One" on the left-hand side and changed tips to draw the shower of pink booties cascading from beneath the umbrella. "Don't worry, Shane. Your day will come." I stole a glance at the double doors and handed him the bag of yellow icing. "In fact, why don't you do the yellow booties for me?"

"For real?"

"Sure. If Millie doesn't mind keeping an eye out for Anya."

Millie scooted to the doors and assumed sentry duty. "No problem."

I gave Shane space to work. "Good job. Like I told you, you're a natural." I exchanged my pink bag of icing for his yellow one. "Now, why don't you just finish up the border and we'll be all set."

He piped a border of pink flowers around the base, ending with a flourish.

"Oh that is so cute!"

Shane and I both jumped as Nicole came up behind us.

"How adorable," she cooed. "Don't you just love baby stuff?"

"Ix-nay on the Shane-ay," Millie warned, scooting quickly away from the doors.

Shane thrust the pastry bag at me and busied himself with the pink cake box as Anya strode back in. "Mrs. Henderson is here a little early." Her eyes flicked with relief to the finished cake, and she uttered a grudging "Nice job" to me. "Shane, box it up and bring it out."

"Whew, that was close," he said, pretending to wipe sweat off his brow when he rejoined us. He looked at Nicole. "I thought you were off today."

"I am. I just came to pick up my check and to confirm our plans for tomorrow night."

"Our plans?"

"Yeah. Remember?" Her gaze swept the room uncertainly. "We're all going over to Millie's to watch that old movie."

"*The Best Years of Our Lives,*" Millie prompted. "Unfortunately, *someone* here has a date and can't make it."

Nicole looked at Shane. "You have a date?"

Was that a trace of jealousy I detected?

"Not Shane." Millie flicked her eyes at me and began to sing. "If I could talk to the animals . . ."

A radiant (and was it also a little relieved?) smile lit up Nicole's beautiful face. "Ooh, are you going out with that vet, Freddie? I could tell he had a thing for you. What are you doing? Where are you going?"

"I'm not sure." I blushed. "Just to dinner somewhere. It's no big deal. I don't think it means anything; he probably just wants to thank me for my help at the open house."

Millie and Nicole exchanged a knowing glance. "Right."

I pulled one of the two Danish layer cakes out of the walk-in and started to decorate it. The second one I'd finish in the morning since we didn't need it till Sunday.

"Millie, what would you like me to bring for tomorrow night?" Nicole asked.

"Just your sweet self. I've got dessert already taken care of, and Shane's making us dinner."

"You are?" Nicole gave Shane a teasing look. "What's for dinner?"

"You'll see." A small smile tugged at his lips.

"Aw, come on. Give us a hint," Nicole said.

"Nope. You'll just have to wait and see." He sent her an anxious look. "You don't have any food allergies or anything, do you?"

"Just to Brussels sprouts." Nicole shuddered. "And it's not really an allergy. I just hate them. They're all round and slimy, and they stink. Ick."

"That's how I feel about snails." Millie wagged a finger at Shane. "So don't be feeding us any of that *escargot* stuff."

"Not to worry."

"Well, I'm off." Nicole gave a little wave. "See you all in the morning."

Anya stuck her head through the double doors. "Shane, I need you to come replenish the oatmeal-raisin."

"Oh, Anya, don't forget," I said, "I have to leave at three thirty today for my doctor's appointment."

"Just make sure the cakes are ready to go for tonight and tomorrow before you leave."

"Doctor's appointment?" Millie asked as Anya's head disappeared.

"Just my annual physical. No big deal."

Except I knew they'd inflict the Chinese water torture thingy on me. Or, to be a little more precise, the scale torture. (I measure them about the same—in units of pain.)

This time, though, there's a silver lining. At least this torture would give me new material for my blog.

· · · ·

Friday

There's nothing worse than getting weighed at the doctor's office. My weight is never the same as my scale at home. Maybe that's because I don't have a digital scale, but one of those ancient ones that came over on the Mayflower. It has one of those dial gizmos at the top, which I set to five pounds less than zero to allow for that whole variation in floors thing.

Hey, it works for me--until I have to go to the doctor's office and get weighed on their perfectly calibrated scales. (Or so they say!)

That's what happened to me today. I had my annual physical. Which meant I also had to face the dreaded annual weigh-in.

One of the problems is they don't subtract for clothes. Everyone knows you're supposed to allow at least seven pounds for fabric weight. My bra alone weighs probably a good two pounds. Not to mention my control-top underwear. And, of course, my shoes. I personally think they should even take off for heavy makeup. But they don't. What you see on that sliding bar is what goes on the chart for posterity. So that's one gripe I have about weigh-ins at the doctor.

My other is the fact that they always announce the weight in a loud voice so that everyone can hear. You think they'd know better. The two things women have lied about since time immemorial are their weight and their age.

I have no problem with my nearly-thirty age--well, most of the time, except when yet another tiny twenty-year-old gets engaged. And I know that more and more women are revealing their weight these days, once they've lost seventeen pounds on their favorite diet or on reality TV shows. But my weight is a private and confidential matter. Just between me and my doctor.

And his staff, the visiting pharmaceutical reps, and the entire waiting room.

I vote that we rise up and ban scales from all doctors' offices. In fact, let's just ban all scales everywhere--except at meat-packing plants. Are you with me?

When I finished my daily blog entry, I scrolled back up to my last post to see if there were any comments. Whoa. Several. Someone was getting popular.

Betty Bigg, we'd like to honor you with this award for Blog of the Year. Your public service blog was selected over hundreds of thousands around the country for the help it has provided to women everywhere. Thank you for shining a light in the darkness and for being a beacon to all big women who feel invisible and overlooked by society.

Most of the comments were short and sweet. A lot of "right on," "I hear ya," and "You go, girl! You rock!"

This last one had a familiar ring:

Hey Betty,

My friend Lynette and I love your blog, and we're wondering if you can settle a bet. She thinks you're a lawyer or some big corporate muckety-muck, but I think you're an author. Which one of us is right? There's a piece of chocolate cake riding on your answer.

Curious in California

Had to be one of the T-shirt ladies I overheard at Bramwell's. But which one? Blue Shirt or Red Shirt? I couldn't remember, but I supposed it really didn't matter. I smiled and continued typing.

Dear Curious in California,

Sorry. You're both wrong, so I guess I get the cake. ☺ I'm not a lawyer or author, but I can tell you that I do help make people's happily-ever-after dreams come true.

Betty

. . . .

The phone rang while I was logging off my computer.

"Freddie? Can you hear me?" Deborah's voice sounded strange. All tense and out of breath.

"Deborah, what's wrong?" I heard strange sounds in the background—thumps, rustles, indistinguishable words, and other noises I couldn't place. "What's going on?"

"Lydia's gone into labor. We're taking her to the hospital right now."

"Oh my gosh." In the background I could hear Lydia groaning and Samuel's soothing voice. "Which hospital?" I kicked off my slippers and searched frantically for my shoes. "I'll be right there."

"No, no. That's okay. Actually. I'm calling to ask a huge favor." Her voice grew fainter. "There, there. It's okay, baby girl. Don't worry. Mama's right here with you. We'll be there soon." Now it grew more urgent. "Samuel, can't you go a little faster?"

She returned to me. "Sorry. You still there?"

"I'm here. Just tell me what you need. Anything."

Her words tumbled over each other quickly. "I have a booking tonight I'm hoping you can cover for me. The backup caterer I had in place for this very reason chose this weekend to go to Disneyland on the spur of the moment, leaving me high and dry. If it were any other client, I'd consider canceling. But this dinner has the potential to bring us a lot more business—some corporate accounts we've been want—"

Deborah's voice turned soothing, and I could tell she was talking to Lydia again. "That's fine, baby, you're doin' good. Breathe now, slow . . . slow it down . . . like they taught you at Lamaze. There you go."

Her normal voice returned, with a twinge of panic. "Any way you can help me out?"

I hesitated. But only for a second. "Of course," I said. "Just tell me what to do."

"Thank you! Consider yourself being hugged right now." She

grew businesslike. "It's a small dinner party on the east side of town, and everything you need is all packed in the van, ready to go. My recipe binder's on the passenger seat, and the menu is clipped to the front, along with the address . . . Okay, baby, that's good . . . big cleansing breath now. That's right . . . breathe that pain out. It's okay, baby girl. It's okay," she soothed. "We're almost there—Freddie, where was I . . . ?"

"The van's all packed with everything I need."

"Almost everything." She sighed. "I'd just stuck the short-cake in the oven when Lydia started having contractions, and in all the excitement I forgot about it, so it burned, and now there's no dessert. I was planning to serve strawberry shortcake. Mrs. Harris specified something with either strawberries or raspberries." She sighed again. "Apparently one of her guests requested it."

"Don't worry, I'll handle it." I could hear Lydia groaning in the background. "I got your back."

"Thanks! Let's see now . . . you'll find the van keys in the flowerpot by the front door and . . . oh, I just know I'm forgetting something, but I can't think!"

"Don't worry. Everything will be fine. If there's anything I know, it's how to follow a recipe. No problem."

I could hear sirens in the background. "Gotta go," she said. "We're pulling into Emergency now. If you need me, just call me on my cell." She paused, and I could hear her saying, "What?" to someone.

"Sorry, Freddie, I forgot. We can't use cells in the hospital. Uh—"

"Never mind. I'll be fine." I said it as much for myself as for her. "Stop worrying. I'll handle it. You just take care of Lydia and give her my love. I'll come by the hospital afterward."

"Thanks. You're a lifesaver." Deborah's words rushed out. "I'll be praying for you."

"I'll be praying for *you*—and for Lydia and the baby. Now, go! Bye." I flipped my phone shut.

Then I started to hyperventilate.

Help, Lord!

:: *chapter seventeen* ::

I looked at my watch—five twenty-five. Deborah hadn't said how long the food would take to cook—or even, for that matter, what the menu was. I hoped it wasn't anything too complicated. I wasn't a professional like her. I drummed my fingers on the desk, thinking. If the van was already loaded, that sounded like she was planning to head out soon.

I looked down at my nightshirt.

What should I wear? Deborah always sported a variety of colorful outfits at her catering events, but I'd only seen her working weddings and, of course, Dr. Hal's open house. For an upscale dinner party in someone's house, perhaps we needed something a little less obtrusive? I closed my eyes and thought back to the catered events my parents had held over the years. No vivid colors like Deborah usually wore popped out at me. Instead, a series of nondescript black pants and white shirts hove into view.

Grabbing one of my many pairs of serviceable black pants from a hanger—glad now that I hadn't chucked all of my wardrobe staples at Deborah's urging—I searched through my closet for the lone white Oxford shirt I knew I had in there somewhere. At last I found it wedged in between my winter wool blazers. I pulled it out and examined it with a critical eye—a little wrinkled, but it would have to do. No time to press it. I figured the Taste of Honey apron would hide a multitude of evils, including—I hoped—my thunder thighs.

Yanking my new catering uniform on, I scraped my hair back into a ponytail, grabbed my purse, and flew out the door. And the first red light I came to, I tilted down the rearview mirror and swiped on some foundation and lipstick.

First stop was the bakery. I unlocked the back door, punched off the alarm, and made a beeline for the walk-in. There I grabbed the already-decorated Danish layer cake, sitting ready for tomorrow's anniversary celebration, and the plastic tub of whipped topping—*not* Cool Whip. Setting the cake on the counter, I took a cake knife and gently lifted off the "Happy 50th Anniversary" lettering, which I flicked into the trash. I pulled my favorite icing spreader from the knife rack, scooped up a big hunk of whipped cream, and spread it over the top to cover the indentations from the writing.

Then I returned to the walk-in and grabbed a basket of fresh raspberries, which I rinsed and patted dry and rimmed along the top edge of the cake. Beautiful!

Quickly I boxed up the cake, reset the alarm, locked the door, and sped toward Deborah's, knowing I'd have to return after the dinner party to finish up the other Danish layer cake before morning. At least I wouldn't have to start from scratch and bake one. In the walk-in, I'd spotted the iced layers Millie had prepared for Sunday's order. All I'd need to do was decorate them with "Happy Anniversary" and some flowers and flourishes, then replace that second cake on Saturday.

It should all work fine as long as Anya didn't find out.

And provided I didn't get stopped for speeding.

At Deborah's I found the keys, unlocked the van, and set the cake in the backseat, making sure to wedge it firmly next to the box of packed food so it wouldn't slide. Then I hopped into the driver's seat and reached over to pick up Deborah's yellow recipe binder with the bumblebee buzzing across the top.

As my eyes flicked down the menu, I realized I was going to need reinforcements to pull this off. I punched in a number on my cell. "Shane, I need your help. How'd you like to earn fifty bucks?"

. . . .

Twelve minutes later, I pulled up in front of an elegant Tudor-style home on the chichi side of town. Following Deborah's instructions, I pulled the van around to the back, shooting up a prayer as I slid open the side doors to start unloading.

Please, God, don't let me mess this up for Deborah. And please let everything go well with Lydia's delivery.

Shane's Geo Metro with its one burned-out headlight pulled in behind me. He hopped out, a mirror image of me in black pants and white shirt.

"Boy, am I ever glad to see you." I tossed him an apron.

"No worries. I'm always happy to earn a little extra cash."

I lifted out the cake, and Shane followed me with the box of provisions. The back door swung open at my knock to reveal a plump middle-aged woman in a Hawaiian muumuu and flip-flops. "Mrs. Harris?"

She grunted. "Not likely. I'm the housekeeper. You'd better come on in and get cracking. Her ladyship expected you ten minutes ago and is starting to freak out."

She ushered us into an ultramodern state-of-the-art kitchen with slate floors, pale maple cabinets, stainless-steel countertops and appliances, and a huge pristine island in the center beneath a gleaming pot rack of La Creuset cookware that looked as if they'd never been used.

"I'll let her know you're here." The housekeeper disappeared through an arched doorway.

Shane and I began unloading the food. He held up the shrimp packed in ice. "So what's the menu?"

"Shrimp cocktail, spinach salad, shrimp scampi on a bed of rice pi—"

"There you are at last." A slim, tanned woman with a honey-blonde bob stepped through the archway. "I was beginning to wo—" She looked around. "Where's Deborah?"

I pushed down the butterflies playing hockey in my stomach and smiled. "Deborah had a family emergency, so I'm standing in for her." I wiped my hand on my apron and extended it. "Hi, I'm Freddie."

She frowned and shook it briefly, then tugged at the pearls nestled in the bodice of her beige silk blouse. "The caterer I normally use is on vacation, and this is a very important dinner for my colleagues on the charity board. Deborah came highly recommended, and I don't appreciate some helper taking charge in her place." She glanced at the jeweled Rolex on her arm. "But my guests will be arriving soon, so I guess you'll have to do."

"Mrs. Harris?" Shane sent her a deferential smile. "Hi. I'm Shane, and I'll be helping Freddie with your dinner tonight. She's Deborah's partner, and you couldn't be in better hands. Freddie's an absolutely *amazing* cook. Now, if you'd like to show me the dining room, I can get things set up in there." He steered her out and winked over his shoulder at me.

I shook my head and continued unpacking the box of food, frowning as I looked again over Deborah's menu for the evening.

Shrimp cocktail seemed a trifle pedestrian for the chichi Mrs. Harris. We needed something with a little more *wow* factor.

My eyes lasered around the kitchen, zeroing in on the crystal martini glasses on the glass shelves at one end of the room.

That's it! I'll make seafood martinis instead. I remembered a cooking show on the Food Network where the chef whipped up a batch of seafood martinis—although I think he used lobster rather than shrimp. And maybe mangos and red peppers?

I'd just have to improvise.

My eyes lit on a couple of avocadoes and tomatoes ripening on the window ledge. When Shane returned, I was dicing the tomatoes.

"Partner?" I raised my eyebrows.

"Well, you are partnering with Deborah to help her out tonight, right? I didn't lie"—he grinned—"just put a spin on the situation to make her comfortable so you and I could work undisturbed. Now, tell me what you want me to do, boss lady."

I nodded to the avocadoes. "If you could peel and dice these and mix them in with the tomatoes, that'd be great. Thanks." I pulled down a couple of saucepans and looked at my watch. "When did Mrs. Harris say her guests will start arriving?"

"About fifteen minutes."

I poured chicken broth into one saucepan to boil and some butter and olive oil in another. "So . . . are you excited about tomorrow night?"

"Huh?"

"Your date with Nicole."

"It's so not a date—we're just going over to Millie's to watch a movie," Shane said. "You're the one with the date."

"Hang on a sec." I held up my hand and cocked my head to one side, hearing the sound of muted laughter. "Sounds like her guests got here a little early. We'd better get a move on."

"Want me to get started on the salad?" Shane asked.

"Perfect. And while you do that, I'll finish up the appetizers." I spooned the tomatoes-and-avocado mixture into the bottom of each martini glass and mounded the shrimp on top.

"This is really a cool kitchen, huh?" Shane tossed the slivered almonds, raisins, crumbled bleu cheese, and mandarin oranges with the spinach leaves. "I always wondered how the other half lived."

"Me too. Love all the space." I thought of the cramped galley kitchen in Brooke's small house as I taste-tested my makeshift seafood martini with Deborah's homemade cocktail sauce. "Mmm, good, but it's missing something." I zinged up the sauce with a little lemon juice and finished off my creation by zesting a few lemon curls atop each glass. "There."

"Now, let's see. What next?"

My eyes lit on the pink bakery box I'd placed on the counter just inside the back door when we first arrived. "Oh my gosh. I forgot to put the cake in the fridge." I scuttled over and grabbed it, then began looking around the hi-tech kitchen for a refrigerator. I opened cabinet after cabinet and several drawers until at last I found a refrigerated drawer—nearly empty. I eased the cake in next to a block of cheddar, a wedge of parmesan, and some bottled water. When I closed the drawer and looked up, Shane was disappearing through the archway into the dining room with the martini appetizers on a silver tray.

I added long-grain rice to the butter and oil in the saucepan, sprinkled in a little salt and pepper, then added butter, lemon juice, and parsley to some sautéed garlic in a frying pan. Then I poured the boiled chicken broth over the rice, covered it, and turned down the heat to simmer. Placing the shrimp in a shallow baking dish, I poured the butter mixture over the shrimp and stuck the baking dish in the oven. Then I checked my watch.

Amazingly, everything was on schedule. I'd just slide the garlic bread in during the final ten minutes, and we'd be good to go.

Shane returned a few minutes later with the empty hors d'oeuvres tray. "Those seafood martinis rocked. They scarfed 'em down." He frowned. "All except one guy who couldn't have any 'cause he's allergic to seafood."

"What?" My heart plummeted. "But seafood's the main course."

Mrs. Harris rushed in. "I see you've just heard about my guest's allergy. I'm so sorry. It was news to me too." She sent me a stricken look. "Is there anything else you can serve him?"

"Well . . . we have a wonderful spinach salad and some rice pilaf . . ."

"But what about the main course? Can't you substitute something else for the shrimp?" A worried frown puckered her brow. "He's the new chairman of our charity and one of the biggest contributors. I don't want him to go hungry. There's got to be something in the fridge or freezer you can use." She began yanking open drawers in a frenzy.

"Aha!" She held up the block of cheddar with a triumphant smile. "I've got some marvelous imported English cheddar. Couldn't you do something with that?"

You mean besides hit myself in the head *with it?* "We'll take care of it. Don't worry." I pasted on a bright, confident smile.

"No problem." Shane relieved her of the cheese. "We're like the Boy Scouts—always prepared." He gave her a little salute.

"Well, I'll leave you to it then," she said nervously. "I'd better get back to my guests."

"Always prepared?" I snorted once she was gone. "I'm so not prepared. And the rest of this dinner will be ready in"—I checked my watch—"just under ten minutes now. What in the world can I come up with in ten minutes?"

Shane began cutting thick slices of cheddar. "You'll think of something. Anya makes you jump through hoops all the time, and you always sail through. This will be a piece of cake." He grimaced. "Sorry." Then he rooted around in the cupboards until he found a box of gourmet water crackers, which he fanned with the cheese onto a small plate. "Meanwhile, I'll give Mister Allergic something to snack on. That guy looked seriously hungry." He waved and did his Terminator impression. "Ah'll be baaahck."

I took a deep breath. Okay, steady. You can do this. Don't freak out. There's gotta be something in this culinary museum that's edible. Just think. If you were some kind of meat, where would you be hiding? Slowly I pulled open the drawer next to the refrigerated one where I'd stored the cake. A rush of frosty cold air hit me in the face.

Ah, the Holy Grail. Thank you, God.

Inside the freezer I found a frozen bunch of black bananas, a couple of Wolfgang Puck frozen dinners, and a large salmon that looked like someone's fishing-trip trophy.

Really batting a thousand now. But wait, what's that?

I dug down deep and struck the mother lode—a package of frozen chicken breasts. "Eureka!"

"What'd you find?" Shane set the empty cheese plate on the counter.

"Only our salvation." I held up the chicken.

"Sweet." He looked at the clock above the stove. "You want me to put in the garlic bread now?"

I nodded as I pried loose two of the thinner chicken breasts. Sticking them in the microwave to thaw, I rooted through the cupboards until I found some Italian-flavored breadcrumbs. These I sprinkled into a shallow bowl with some freshly shaved parmesan and some cracked ground pepper.

Shane tossed the spinach salad with a raspberry vinaigrette and carefully arranged the portions on salad plates. Then, at a nod from me, he transported the tray of plates into the dining room.

I cracked the lone egg I discovered in the back of the fridge drawer into another shallow bowl and whisked it together with a little olive oil. Then I added olive oil to another large frying pan, dredged the chicken breasts through the egg mixture and the bread crumbs, and transferred them to the sizzling olive oil.

While the chicken was cooking, I melted a little butter in the smaller frying pan and added some fresh parsley to it that I'd snipped from Deborah's food box.

Shane returned from the dining room and checked my progress. "See? What'd I tell you? Piece of cake."

"No, that comes later." I grunted. "More like a piece of I'm flying by the seat of my pants here."

"You're doing great," he soothed. "Don't sweat it."

The timer dinged, and Shane removed the shrimp scampi and garlic bread from the oven while I fluffed the rice pilaf with a fork to see if it was done. Not quite. Maybe another two minutes.

I turned the chicken and covered the pan with a lid to make it cook faster.

Shane lined a porcelain basket with an oversized cloth napkin and filled it with the garlic bread, sealing in the warmth with the folded-over ends of the napkin. Then he removed a large Wedgwood platter from the built-in china cabinet at the end of the kitchen and set it on the counter for me.

"What else you need, boss lady?"

"Can you grate some more fresh parmesan please?"

"No problem."

I fluffed the rice again. Finished—and just in time, too. I spooned it onto the serving platter, making sure to leave enough in the pan for our chicken man. Then I topped the rice with the shrimp scampi and some bits of parsley.

Shane's stomach growled as he reached for the platter. "Oh is that for me? You shouldn't have."

"Hands off, helper boy. I'll treat you to a Big Mac when we blow this popsicle stand."

"I can hardly wait."

"Why don't you take in the garlic bread now, and when you come back, I'll have chicken man's plate ready to go."

"Whatever you say." He picked up the bread basket. "You know, you're really good at this, Freddie. A natural. If only Anya could see you now."

I shuddered. "If she saw both of us now, she'd fire our butts."

"Ain't that the truth." He winked and disappeared through the archway.

I tested the chicken, relieved to find it done, and removed it to a smaller platter along with the rest of the rice. I drizzled the cooked parsley and butter over the top of the chicken and finished off the plate with a liberal sprinkling of fresh parmesan.

"All set?" Shane rejoined me.

"Let's do this."

He carried in the shrimp-and-rice platter while I followed behind with the chicken. Too late, I realized I'd forgotten to ask Shane which guest was the allergic one. But Mrs. Harris noticed my hesitation and flicked her eyes discreetly to a balding man at the end of the table.

"Here you go, sir." I smiled and set the plate down in front of him. "I hope you'll enjoy your Tuscan chicken."

* * * *

When we returned to the kitchen, Shane and I both collapsed on barstools at the island.

"If I were a drinking woman, I'd say give me a dry martini right about now." I affected a British accent. "Shaken, not stirred."

Shane rubbed his eyes. "I'd rather have a Corona."

I reached down into the refrigerator drawer and grabbed a couple of bottled waters. "Here's the next best thing."

Shane tapped his water bottle against mine. "Here's to you, Queen of the Caterers. Good job!"

"Couldn't have done it without you, Number One Assistant." I gave him a tired grin and tapped back.

My cell vibrated in my pants pocket.

"Oh my gosh. I totally forgot about Lydia in all this craziness." I yanked out my phone and flipped it open. "Deborah? How's Lydia?—Oh, hi, Samuel. How's it going? Are you a grandpa yet?" I nodded. "Uh-huh. I hear it can take a long time."

I glanced across at Shane. "Everything's just fine. Don't worry. No, no problems at all. They're eating dinner right now, and I'll be serving dessert in a little while. Now, tell Deborah to stop worrying about me, and the two of you just focus on Lydia and that new grandbaby you're about to meet."

I smiled into the phone. "Everything's smooth sailing over here. Don't worry about a thing. Okay, I'll talk to you later. Give Lydia my love and tell her I said to push."

"No problems at all," Shane mimicked. "Other than having to whip up a whole new main course at the last minute."

"Just call me Wonder Woman." I twirled an imaginary cape. "Guess we'd better start cleaning up now," I said. "Would you check and see if they're done yet, or if they need anything?"

When Shane left, I filled the sink with soapy water and began washing all the pots and pans by hand. I didn't know if such expensive pans could go in the dishwasher, but I wasn't taking any chances. And I've always found there's something soothing about washing dishes. The warm soapy water, the taking something dirty and making it clean, the chance to reflect . . .

I was reflecting on the singles potluck and Simon and what a fun time I'd had when footsteps on the slate floor behind me interrupted my train of thought. "So are the guests all happy campers, Shane?" I murmured.

"Very happy campers, young lady," a deep voice answered.

I whirled around, dripping dishwater onto a pair of Italian leather loafers belonging to bald chicken man.

"I'm so sorry." I grabbed a dishtowel and bent to wipe off his shoes, but he waved me off.

"No, no. I'm the one who should be apologizing for putting you to so much trouble." He gave me a warm smile. "My compliments to the chef. That Tuscan chicken was absolutely delicious." He sent me a hopeful look. "I don't suppose you'd be willing to share the recipe, would you?"

I remembered what Deborah had said at the wedding when asked for her crab puff recipe. "I'm sorry. Company secret." I smiled. "But we'd be happy to make it for you again another time."

"You've got yourself a deal, young lady. Anyone who can roll with the punches as beautifully as you did tonight is someone I want to have on my payroll." He pulled a business card from his pocket and handed it to me. "My name's Phillip Turner, and I'd love to have A Taste of Honey do some catering for my company, beginning next month at a corporate retreat we're having in the foothills."

"Now, Phillip, don't hog the caterer." A buxom redhead strode into the kitchen and sent me a brilliant smile. "My dear, everything was absolutely delicious. I'd love to book you for a tea for my garden-club meeting. Are you free next Thursday?"

Um, was I? Or rather, was Deborah? "I'll need to check with

my partner, but if you give me your name and number, I'll get back to you as soon as possible."

"Phillip, Belinda . . . there you are." Mrs. Harris clicked into the kitchen with Shane on her heels, carrying a stack of plates. "I know what you're up to, but let the poor girl at least serve dessert before you descend on her like a pack of wolves."

"Dessert?" The bald Phillip guy's eyes lit up. "How could we forget dessert? It's something with either strawberries or raspberries, right?"

Shane, who'd set the plates down, retrieved the pink bakery box from the fridge, removing the raspberry-studded Danish-layer cake with a flourish. "Voilà!"

Mrs. Harris suggested to her salivating guests that they return to the dining room where the dessert would be served posthaste. Once the couple was out of earshot, she turned to me with a frown. "This looks like a Jorgensen's cake. Did you buy this from the bakery?"

"No way," Shane interjected before I had a chance to stammer a reply. "Freddie made this cake with her own two hands. She's a fabulous baker." He nodded to the cake, "Would you like us to serve this now?"

"Please. And we'll take our coffee as well." She clicked back through the archway.

"I think I'm going to have to start calling you Shane the spinmeister." I shook my head as I sliced into the cake.

"At your service." He gave a little bow as he filled a silver carafe with the coffee that had just finished brewing. Shane peered closely at the cake top. "I take it this was tomorrow's anniversary cake?"

"You got it."

"Nice cover-up."

"Thanks. Fastest thing I could think of." I sighed. "Now I just need to go back to the bakery tonight and turn Sunday's birthday cake for Anya's friend into tomorrow's anniversary cake."

"At least it's already frosted."

"Iced, remember?" I smiled.

"Oh that's right. Frosting is for housewives." He grinned and filled a serving tray with the cake and coffee. "And I'd better get these housewives and their husbands their cake before they get all desperate."

Mrs. Harris was anything but desperate when she returned to the kitchen at the end of the evening as we were packing up. "Thank you so much," she gushed. "Everything was wonderful. Flawless. Loved the seafood martinis. And that cake was absolutely delicious—much better than Jorgensen's!" She handed me an envelope. "Here's your check and a little something extra for both of you, with my gratitude. Please tell Deborah I'm very impressed and that I'll be calling her soon to schedule my next event."

After we finished packing the gear in the van, I opened the envelope and pulled out two crisp fifty-dollar bills. I handed them both to Shane. "Here you go. Thanks again for bailing me out. I could never have done this without you."

"We make a good team." He pressed one of the fifties back into my palm. "But a deal's a deal." He chugged over to his car. "See ya tomorrow. Maybe I can help you with that third Danish layer cake."

:: *chapter eighteen* ::

I looked at my watch as I clambered into the van. Ten forty-five. Surely Lydia's baby had arrived by now. I punched in Deborah's cell number, but it went straight to voicemail.

"Hey you—are you a grandmother yet? I'm dying to know if Lydia had a boy or a girl! Just finished up at the Harrises' and am heading over to the hospital now, but first I need to make one quick stop. I'll see you soon. Bye."

Back at the dark bakery, I stifled a yawn as I unlocked the back door. My bed was sure looking good to me now. The alarm screeched its ah-oooga melody, and I flipped on the lights as I hurried over to the keypad, where it took me several bleary-eyed tries to punch in the correct code.

Relief. Silence really is golden.

I set my keys down on the island and decided to use the bathroom before I got to work. Afterward, needing a little caffeine fix to make it through the rest of the evening, I rummaged through our employee fridge. Past Nicole's bottled Frappucino, Shane's Calistoga mineral water, and Millie's Kiwi-Strawberry Snapple, I finally found a lone Diet Dr Pepper from the six-pack I'd placed there earlier in the week.

Popping the top, I drained half the can, enjoying the fizzy, cold rush of my favorite soft drink down my parched throat. Then I stretched and popped my back, only now realizing my shoulders had been on stress alert all evening.

Opening the walk-in, I removed the iced cake for Anya's friend and set it on the counter while I rummaged for my favorite writing tip. I attached it to the pastry bag of golden-yellow icing and began to inscribe the cake. I'd just finished the "Ann" in anniversary when I heard a car door slam.

I froze, and my eyes flew to the back door. Had I remembered to lock it when I first arrived? My heart thudded in my chest as I heard heavy footsteps approach. What if it was an ax murderer or a burglar? I gripped the pastry bag in a death grip and looked wildly around for a weapon.

The door flung open, and a rough voice barked out, "Freeze!"

I squeezed the pastry bag so tightly, icing popped out the top like a giant zit.

It was worse than an ax murderer. Anya peeked from behind the two massive cops holding guns on me. "Freddie! What are you doing here?"

The cops lowered their guns. "You know this lady?" one asked.

"Yes, she works for me." Anya, in running shoes and a white velour sweat suit (the jacket unzipped enough to be provocative but still legal) glared at me as she stepped from behind them.

"At this time of night?"

Her eyes flicked from the pastry bag in my trembling hand to the cake in front of me. Ever mindful of the bakery's reputation, the schmooze queen said, "This was a rush order for the morning."

The cops shouldered their weapons. One reported in with his radio while the other gave Anya a stern look that encompassed me. "You'd better train her how to work the alarm."

"Oh I will, Officer. I will. I'm so sorry you had to come out here. Can I get you and your partner something?" She smoothed her hair back. "Maybe some cookies?"

"You got chocolate-chip?" the shorter one asked.

"Of course." She turned to me with a plastic smile. "Freddie, could you get a few chocolate-chip cookies for the officers?"

"Could I have peanut-butter?" the tall one asked.

"Sure." I unlocked the dry storage box, a tall, sealed cabinet where we stored the leftover cookies each day. Using a pastry tissue, I grabbed a few chocolate-chip and peanut-butter ones, which I placed in a small white bakery bag and handed to the shorter officer. "Here you go. Sorry for the false alarm."

He grinned and bit into a chocolate–chip cookie. "Just remember to call the alarm company next time when you have a problem with the code and set it off."

Anya waved as they left. But once the door shut behind them, she whirled on me.

"Now would you please explain to me what in the world you're doing here?"

I picked up the pastry bag and resumed writing. "Just like you said. I'm finishing up this rush order for tomorrow morning for the fiftieth anniversary."

"Really?" Anya's icy stare pierced me. "Well, that's strange, since I saw the Westons' cake finished in the walk-in earlier today."

I set down the pastry bag and did a contrite George Washington. "You're right. An emergency came up, and I needed to use that cake, so I'm now replacing it."

"An emergency? A *cake* emergency?" Anya's heavily shadowed eyes bored into mine. "You've got to be kidding me. What are you playing at? Are you trying to steal from me?"

"No, of course not! I'd never do that. I planned to pay for the cake I used earlier." My fingers clutched the fifty-dollar bill in my pocket, which I pulled out and set on the counter. "See? There you go."

"Like that makes it all right?" Anya said. "If you hadn't been caught, I'd have never seen that money. What makes you think you can come in here anytime you please? Just because you can make stupid little frosting roses and leaf borders doesn't give you carte blanche. I can get anyone off the street to do that. You don't own this bakery, Freddie, *I* do. That's why it's called Jorgensen's. And don't you forget it."

She slapped her hand on the counter, breathing hard. "Why, you wouldn't even have a job if it weren't for me. And if you're not careful, you won't have this one much longer."

I stared at her for a moment. Then something snapped.

Straw. Camel. Back.

And something else—a rush of something that felt strangely like courage.

"You're right, Anya. I won't." I took a deep breath. "I quit."

I picked up my purse and headed to the back door, adding over my shoulder, "Oh, and you might want to find someone off the street to finish decorating those cakes for tomorrow."

. . . .

I walked out with my head high, feeling all confident and powerful at making such a bold move and reveling in the memory of Anya's gaping mouth and stunned expression.

I am not invisible!

Hear me roar!

I drove away with my windows down and the cool night breeze blowing through my hair.

As I drove along the Pacific Coast highway with my Isadora

Duncan scarf blowing in the breeze, I thought about the latest ballet I'd be performing the next day with my troupe of big woman dancers. Unencumbered with a regular nine-to-five job, and living off the trust fund my famous but reclusive mother had left me, I was free at last to unleash my artistic sensibilities and let them take flight. As a result, I was also singing in a girl group and writing poetry in cafés while wearing a black beret and painting in my Monterey art studio overlooking the ocean. My first art exhibit—sculptures of large, joyful, Rubenesque women—would be held that weekend in one of San Francisco's toniest galleries, to which I'd fly in the pilot seat of my own Cessna. Initially, I'd tried my hand at pottery a la Demi Moore in *Ghost*. I'd even had my own Patrick Swayze husband come up behind me at my potting wheel and distract me with romantic kisses while "Unchained Melody" played in the background. But—

A car honked behind me, and I drove through the intersection where the light had long since turned green.

My free-spirited fantasy crumbled about me. What was I *thinking* quitting my job? Yes, Anya was definitely the boss from down below, but at least she'd been a source of gainful employment. And now I was leaving Millie and Shane in the lurch.

I glanced at the digital clock on my dashboard. Ten after eleven—way too late to call Millie and give her a heads-up. She was in bed by nine thirty most nights. But Shane should still be up. As I pulled up to another red light, I punched in his number. "Shane? Have I got news for you . . ."

When I hung up after filling Shane in, I saw that I had one missed call—from Deborah. I listened to the message as I neared the hospital.

"Freddie?" Deborah was alternately crying and laughing. "I'm a grandma! My baby girl had herself a beautiful little boy—

twenty-one inches long, eight pounds, seven ounces. Ten fingers and toes. He looks just like his mama. And he's got a gorgeous full head of soft, curly hair. Thank you, Jesus! Lydia still hasn't quite decided on a name yet, so for now he's just Sweet Baby Boy."

She giggled. "Lydia's sleeping now—she's tuckered out. We all are. This was quite an evening. I wanted to catch you before you drove out to the hospital, but since mother and son are doing fine, Samuel and I are heading home to bed now."

She expelled a tired sigh. "I haven't even asked about the dinner, so you'll have to fill me in tomorrow—we want you to come meet our little grandson as soon as you get off work. Samuel said he checked on you a couple of times tonight, and everything went fine. I knew it would. I had every confidence in you, girl. Thanks again for gettin' my back. I'll see you tomorrow. 'Night."

I did a U-ey in the hospital parking lot and drove back home. I kept it together all the way home. But once I got to my room, the pity dam burst.

I was really happy for Lydia and for Deborah and Samuel— although it was weird to think of Deborah as a grandmother since she was only nine years older than me.

Only nine years older . . . and look at her life. Married to a wonderful man, with terrific children—and now a beautiful grandchild— a beautiful house, a job she loved, and a tight relationship with God. And on top of all that, she was comfortable in her own skin.

And then there was me. What did I have? No husband, no kids, no home, and now not even a job! And my skin was breaking out all over. And I was fat. Who could be comfortable in this skin? I burrowed my head in the pillow and kicked my feet on my futon.

Zsa Zsa nudged me with her wet nose. *You've got me, Mom.*

I cuddled her close and wept. She gave me a kiss on the nose and licked my salty tears.

I cuddled her even closer. Maybe too close. She yelped and jumped off the couch.

Great. Now even my dog doesn't want to be near me.

I glanced at the closed Bible on my nightstand.

And God and I weren't all that tight these days either. I didn't talk to him as often as I should. I hadn't visited him in awhile, so I felt a little funny about just dropping in unannounced and asking for something now. I mean, don't you hate people like that—especially when it's your friends or family? They say they love you, and then you don't hear from them in forever—until they need something. And then they come, hat in hand.

But it was supposed to be different with God, right? He was supposed to be there for you—no matter what. That whole unconditional-love thing. I guess he'd be willing to listen to one of his kids who hadn't called in a while.

So here I was, holding out my hat.

Okay, Lord, what do you want me to do? Can you give me some sort of sign maybe?

Silence.

Let me be more specific: What am I going to do about a job?

More silence.

Then it occurred to me. At least I didn't have to go running to my father—my earthly father, that is—for help.

My ex-fiancé Greg's brother was an investment guru who'd encouraged both of us to buy stock during the dot-com craze. When we broke up, I got rid of every remembrance of Greg—including the stock which sold at a healthy profit. Very healthy. So I stuck half the proceeds in savings and the other half in a mutual fund.

Greg wasn't quite so fortunate. Artist that he was, he never got around to dealing with such petty details. He'd sell the stock one day. But the day he chose was too late. And he lost not quite all, but most of, his investment.

Not that I was gloating or anything. That would be mean. And unchristian.

But was that my answer from God—that I didn't need a job right away?

If I needed to, I could live off my savings for a while. My rent was nominal, my needs were few, and I wasn't a shopaholic. But I really didn't want to use my savings unless it was absolutely necessary. I'd been saving up for the day when I could buy a house. Not just a room of my own like Virginia Woolf recommended, but an entire house of my own—with hardwood floors and a killer kitchen.

Kitchen . . .

I jumped off my bed. Might as well be productive in my misery. Although I'd never given birth, I had stayed overnight in a hospital before. And when I got home, all I wanted was warm comfort food.

Problem was, I wasn't sure if they'd release Lydia in time for breakfast or lunch. To be on the safe side, I decided to make a couple of comfort-food meals to cover all the food bases.

I assembled all the ingredients for a strata—eggs, milk, bread, cheese, and seasonings. I grated cheddar, jack, and parmesan cheese, beat the eggs and milk together, and added in salt, pepper, dry mustard, and a little basil. Then I folded in the cheese and set the eggy mixture aside while I cut the crusts off the bread. I lined the bottom of a greased baking dish with the bread, then poured the eggs-and-cheese mixture over it and placed it in the fridge to chill overnight.

Next, I grabbed some cooked, cubed chicken out of my orange container in the freezer and placed it in the microwave to thaw while I poured rice and water into my rice cooker. While I waited for the rice to cook, I decided to blog.

Friday

So, I lost my job today . . . and I'm not sure how I feel about it. I think I'm running the gamut of emotions, from euphoria to shock, anger, depression, and relief.

It's not like it was the best job in the world . . . definitely not the best boss, that's for sure. But I was good at what I did, and I liked the people I worked with--most of them, anyway.☺ It was comfortable, I knew what to do and what was expected of me. So now I'm feeling curiously adrift and unsure what to do next. Where do I go from here?

Maybe I should run away and join the circus. I always thought I'd like to soar through the air on the flying trapeze, except I don't think the bar would hold me, and I hear they don't use a net. But I hear the fat lady position is open . . .

Can you tell I'm having a bad day? Bet you didn't know you'd have to bring your violins, huh?

I must admit that the day wasn't a total loss, though. I helped a friend out and had fun doing it. A lot of fun, actually. Yeah, it was a little stressful being thrown into an unfamiliar situation and not knowing exactly what I was doing, but it was also kind of exciting. Something completely new and different, not just the same-old, same-old.

So even though I'm a little bummed today, I'm pretty sure things will work out in the long run. I haven't really talked about God much in this blog, but I do believe he knows what he's doing. Now, if I can just remember that when things get weird, all should be well.

Unemployed Betty

I steamed some broccoli and made a cheese sauce from cheddar, Neufchâtel, and milk, then folded in the fresh Portobello mushrooms I'd just sautéed. Yes, Millie's standby cream of mushroom would have been a lot faster, but I preferred to make my sauce from scratch. I stirred in the now-cooked rice and chicken and dumped the whole casserole mixture into a deep Corning-Ware baking dish, which I covered and placed in the fridge next to the mock soufflé, ready to be baked first thing in the morning.

Exhausted but feeling better, I finally fell into bed about two that morning, making sure I set my alarm for seven so I could bring Deborah and family a piping-hot breakfast.

. . . .

At ten minutes after eight the next morning, after a quick detour to Wal-Mart to buy the biggest teddy bear I could find, I pulled into Samuel and Deborah's driveway, where I noticed the Taste of Honey van parked in the same place I'd left it last night.

Gingerly, I balanced the oversized bear on top of the box containing the two comfort-food casseroles and made my way to the front door. I had to set the bear and the box down to knock. Not too loudly, though. I didn't want to wake the baby.

No answer.

I knocked again.

Either they were still asleep, or they'd already left for the hospital to collect Lydia. I fumbled in my pocket for the keys I'd neglected to leave behind last night and, after a couple of tries, found the one for the front door.

I pushed it open gently and called softly. "Deborah? Samuel?" But the house was still. So I stuck both casseroles in the fridge, left a note on the counter beneath the keys, and propped Big Bear on the island with a card saying, "Welcome, Baby." Then I stuck a second card addressed to Grandma and Grandpa in front of Deborah's miniature hot-flash fan.

When I stepped outside, it had begun to rain.

:: *chapter nineteen* ::

The rain lashed my car as I drove home—by a circuitous route so I wouldn't have to pass the bakery. The dark sky and the bad weather fit my mood. I decided it was time to indulge in a little wallowing.

Fortunately Brooke wasn't home, so I could wallow in peace.

I shucked off my wet stretch jeans and T-shirt, pulled my Eeyore nightshirt back on, cranked up my "Music to Listen to When I'm Depressed" CD mix of Alanis Morrisette, Joni Mitchell, and Edith Piaf, and burrowed into my futon, where I inhaled a cheese Danish I'd picked up at the minimart on the way home.

A French exchange student in college had introduced me to Edith Piaf—France's national treasure in the forties and fifties. He'd said listening to "the little sparrow" and drinking absinthe was the first step in getting over an unhappy love affair, and the best music for wallowing.

The absinthe I'd declined, but the Piaf I'd kept.

Nicknamed the little sparrow since she was a diminutive four foot eight, Piaf sang poignant ballads of loneliness and despair and wrote her signature song, "La vie en rose," in the middle of the German occupation of Paris during World War II. And something

211

about her plaintive voice always seemed to echo my own pain while somehow making me feel better.

I pumped up the volume with my remote as I swigged a Dr Pepper and crunched my way through half a bag of Lay's potato chips. And not the baked kind either. There's something about filling the whole room with music, not just listening through ear buds. Which is why I don't own an iPod.

That and the fact that I'm a bit of a technophobe—or at least a slow adapter. Cassettes and CDs work just fine for me . . . so far.

I had my eyes shut and was singing along lustily with Piaf's "Hymn a l'amour"—about the sun tumbling from the sky and the seas suddenly running dry—when someone shook my shoulder.

My eyes flew open to reveal Deborah leaning over me in all her bold red glory—red tunic, red capris, and an elaborately wrapped red turban.

I turned down the volume. "What are you—how'd you get in here?"

"Well," she huffed, "that's a nice welcome. Your roommate let me in."

"Brooke? I thought she was out."

"She was. She pulled into the driveway the same time I did. Said she forgot something." Deborah sat down gingerly on the edge of my futon, facing me. "Will this thing hold me?"

"Sure. It holds me, doesn't it?"

Deborah wrinkled her nose. "What is this you're listening to? Is that French? Sounds depressing."

"That's the point." I clicked off the music. "So, how's Lydia and the baby?" A ray of sunlight filtered through my miniblinds. "Your new *grandchild*? Tell me everything!"

"They're both fine." Deborah beamed. "Tired, but fine. That little boy is the sweetest thing ever. He looks just like Isaiah and

Sam Junior did when they were born. He and Lydia are home now, sleeping. Samuel, too." She chuckled. "Grandpa's all wore out. It's been a long time since we had a baby in the house."

A slow smile spread across her face as she stepped into the hallway and brought in an enormous bouquet of pink Stargazer lilies, which she handed to me. "Thank you, my dear friend—for everything. For last night. And this morning. Mmm, mmm—that egg dish was da bomb. What a blessing to come home and find all that food prepared. Girl, you're the best!"

I buried my nose in the gorgeous bouquet, drinking in the heady scent. "Thank you. These are *beautiful*. I'll just put them in a vase." I jumped up and began rummaging in my closet.

"So this is where you live, huh? Nice big room."

"Sorry it's so messy. I wasn't expecting company." I filled a vase with water, set the flowers on top of my dresser, and cleared a load of clothes from my chair.

"Chill, girl. I'm not the clean police," Deborah said. "I'm the last person to fuss about a messy room, 'specially since you just helped me out." She shifted on the futon and gave me an innocent look. "I was going to call the bakery and thank you, but I remembered you couldn't get personal calls, so I decided to surprise you with a visit there instead." She lifted a single eyebrow in a Mr. Spock sort of way. "Imagine my surprise when the woman out front told me you didn't work there anymore."

"That's right." I moved some clothes and magazines off my chair and sat down. "I quit last night. I'm unemployed."

She sat there for just a minute, looking at me, before responding, "No, you're not."

"Excuse me?"

"You've got a new job working for me. *Partner*." She gave me a sly grin.

My face grew hot. "I can explain about that . . ."

"No need." She waved it off. "Mrs. Harris called this morning and was so impressed with how well my 'partner' and her helper handled everything in my absence." Deborah smiled. "She told me how you whipped together a chicken entrée at the last minute for the guy that was allergic to seafood."

I grinned. "And you know what else?"

"What?"

"That guy happened to be the head of"—I paused for dramatic effect—"*Turner Foods.* And he wants A Taste of Honey to be the caterer at his company's corporate retreat next month!"

Deborah did a Tom Cruise on my futon, pumping her fist and whooping.

And Zsa Zsa, who'd been hiding beneath a corner of the comforter that had puddled onto the floor, streaked out of the room like a flash of white lightning.

Deborah screamed and clutched at her blouse. "What was that?"

"Just Zsa Zsa, my dog."

She backed up to the far side of the futon and flattened herself against the wall. "You have a *dog*? Quick, shut the door, before it comes back."

"Zsa Zsa's not an *it*, she's a she. And she won't hurt you. She's a sweetheart. Poor thing, you probably scared her half to death."

"*Her*? What about me? I almost had a heart attack." Deborah flapped her hand in front of her face.

"I'm sure she did too, poor baby. She's probably cowering under the couch right now."

"Hope she stays there."

I'd never thought Deborah's mocha complexion could look so pale. "I take it you're not a dog person?"

"Whew, you got that right." Deborah slowly blew out a large breath and moved back to the center of the futon.

"Even if the poor little thing has only one eye?"

She crossed her forefingers in the universal sign to ward off vampires and kicked the door shut with her foot. "It was a knee-high devil dog that bit me in my granny's garden in the second grade."

"Zsa Zsa's a sweetheart. She'd never bite anyone. Besides, she's not much bigger than a cat."

"Right. Them little dogs are the worst. Yippin' and yappin' all the time. You never know when they might attack . . ."

"As though she could really hurt you. Besides, Zsa Zsa doesn't yip."

She was off in her own world and hadn't even heard me.

" . . . mindin' my own business, then bam, out from behind the string beans in Granny's garden streaks the neighbor's terrier and latches onto my ankle . . ."

Garden . . .

"Oh, yeah." I reached down and retrieved my black pants from where I'd dropped them on the floor last night, pulling a business card out of the pocket and handing it to Deborah. "This lady wants you to cater some upcoming garden-tea thingy that she said might turn into a regular monthly event."

That pulled her out of her fearful reverie. "See! What'd I tell you? We need to talk about the partner thing. I think it's a match made in heaven. You have to be my partner," Deborah pleaded. "Samuel and I discussed this and prayed about it. And we feel it's what God wants us to do."

"But I've never been a caterer before."

"Yeah, you have. What do you call last night?"

"Helping out a friend."

"And this friend really appreciates it. More than you know." She hugged me. "But you did more than just help, Freddie. You demonstrated you can think on your feet and work well under pressure—a critical catering skill." Deborah grinned. "You're a natural. Remember that day you pitched in at the wedding? You took to catering like a duck to water. That's when I first realized I need some new blood to keep the business fresh."

"So why don't you hire some fresh young thing?"

"Yeah. Like you so old, Miss Not Even Thirty Yet. Besides, I don't want a fresh young thing. I want you! Just like Uncle Sam." She grinned. "Our whole family does. We've had helpers in the past, but nobody we can rely on, other than Lydia. And now that Lydia's a mama, and there's no telling when—or even if—that no-account husband of hers might return, she's going to be pretty busy with the baby." Deborah sighed. "I need somebody I can count on—someone sturdy and dependable."

I looked down at my tree-trunk thighs. "Well, I've got the sturdy part down."

"That's right. You do!" Deborah's eyes flashed. "And there's nothing wrong with being a good, sturdy woman, so you just quit acting like there is. I'm tired of you putting yourself down, girl. And you're going to stop that right now. The Lord made you the woman you are, and you are precious in his sight. *And* in mine. You hear me?"

I nodded.

"Just because some stupid college boy couldn't see what a jewel he had in you, that's no reason to hide yourself away from the world and ride through life at the back of the bus," Deborah thundered. "It's time you did a Rosa Parks, girl, and started living out loud!"

"Woo-hoo! You tell her, Deborah!" Brooke pushed open the slightly ajar door, grinning and clapping loudly. "I've been wanting to tell her that for ages, but I didn't want to invade her personal space."

"I notice that's not stopping you now," I said dryly.

Deborah grunted. "Sometimes you just got to tell it like it is."

"Preach it, sister," Brooke said.

I held up my hands. "I surrender. All right already." I shot a pointed look at Brooke. "Aren't you going to be late for work?"

"I was going to ask you the same thing."

"I quit."

"You what?" Brooke started clapping again. "Well, it's about time. We have to celebrate!" She looked at her watch and grimaced. "But later. Have to run." She flicked a wave as she headed down the hallway.

"Don't you worry none about Freddie not being able to pay rent," Deborah called after her retreating back. "She's already got another job."

After we heard the front door close, she turned to me. "At least I hope she does. If you don't mind my asking, what was your salary at Jorgensen's?"

I told her.

"Oh honey, those were slave wages. You'll make more than that as my partner. Especially now since, thanks to you, we picked up several more steady gigs, which will increase our profits." She gave me a pleased smile. "Mrs. Harris has hired us to do breakfasts *every* Monday for her office staff meetings, and two Wednesdays a month we'll be providing the hors d'oeuvres for her bridge club." She stuck her nose in the air. "La-di-da."

"But in a business partnership, don't I have to buy in or something?" I frowned.

"That's the beauty of owning the business. I can do whatever I want. And I want you to be my partner. *Our* partner," Deborah said. "Samuel and I are a package deal. The rest of it, we can work out with our lawyer and our tax guy."

She picked up my black pants from the floor with her thumb and forefinger and looked at them askance. "One thing, though—the only black clothing allowed on the job will be the *occasional* pair of pants like this. At A Taste of Honey, we like to mix it up with pink, blue, purple, red. Our colors are my signature touch—they set us apart from the pack." She dropped the pants back to the floor.

"Of course," Deborah said, "our food already does that, but I like to add a little pizzazz to the presentation—you know what I'm sayin'?"

I stared at Deborah and then down at my crumpled black pants. Then I steepled my fingers beneath my chin and said slowly, "I'll do the blue and the red and even the purple, but you'll never catch this bottom in a pair of pink pants." I shook my head. "Not gonna happen."

"Does that mean you're saying yes?" Her eyes lit up.

"As long as you don't force me to wear pink."

She whooped and crushed me in a trademark Deborah hug. "Woo-hoo! We are gonna have some fun working together, partner!"

"Sounds fun to me too. I just hope you don't live to regret this."

"Not a chance." Deborah reached into her shoulder-strap purse, which was the size of a small country, and pulled out a red shirt. "And the fun starts right now. We have a wedding to cater this afternoon."

"This afternoon?" I squeaked, staring at the cotton-blend shirt that looked—thank you, God—loose.

"Uh-huh," she said. "I planned to finish the prep work last night after Mrs. Harris's dinner, but, well, you know why that didn't work out. Good thing I'd gotten an early start and done most of it the day before. But there's still a lot to be done, so we'll really need to hustle."

Deborah slapped the futon. "So let's get movin'."

. . . .

Ten minutes later, when we entered her kitchen, we found Samuel and Lydia sniffling and hugging each other tight.

"Dear Lord, what's wrong?" Deborah rushed to them. "The baby's okay, isn't he?"

"The baby's fine, Mama." Lydia turned to us, her face wet with tears. "He's upstairs sleeping." She took a deep breath, and Samuel, whose face was also tear-streaked, put a reassuring hand on her shoulder.

"I called Donnie's mama to tell her she had a grandson, and Donnie answered the phone."

Deborah clenched her fists. "What'd that boy say to you?"

"Sug', take it easy," Samuel warned. He squeezed his daughter's shoulder. "Honey, you go ahead now and tell your mama."

"Thanks, Daddy." Lydia shut her eyes for a moment, and another tear snaked its way down her cheek. She brushed it away and took a deep breath. Then she opened her eyes and fastened them steadily on her mother. "Donnie said he's sending me divorce papers—that he's too young to be tied down with a wife and child. That marrying me was a mistake and he wants his freedom back."

"Oh, baby girl." Deborah enfolded Lydia in her arms and wept. "I'm so sorry, honey. I'm so sorry."

I dug my fingers into my palms and stared down at the floor.

A slight sound made me look up. Deborah was giving Lydia a glass of water. She extended one to me also, but I shook my head no.

"He's planning to move to Miami with some of his posse." Lydia drained the glass and gave her mother a tremulous smile. "So it looks like you and Daddy are going to be stuck with me and little Sam for a while longer."

"Little Sam?"

Lydia lifted her chin. "Yes. My son's name is Samuel James Truedell, III."

Fresh tears cascaded down Deborah's face, and she grabbed her daughter in another fierce embrace. "Oh, honey. Oh, baby girl. You are going to make one fine mama to this precious boy. And your daddy and I will be proud to stick with you and little Sam forever and ever."

"Amen," Samuel said, his arms encircling them both.

I stood there shifting from one foot to another, wanting to back out of the room and leave them to this private family moment.

But Samuel motioned me over. "Please, Freddie. Unless I miss my guess," his eyes gleamed, "you're a part of this family now too. Won't you join us in prayer?"

"Oh yes, please do," Lydia said, extending her hand to me.

So the four of us held hands and bowed our heads as Samuel led us in prayer.

"Lord, we thank you for the precious gift of life and for this beautiful little baby you knit together in his mother's womb. We praise you because Samuel James Truedell is fearfully and won- derfully made. Thank you, Lord, for keeping Lydia and little Samuel safe throughout the birth. And thank you for your love and for watching over us and for carrying us through no matter what. We pray for Donnie too—that you would bring him back to you in spite of his pigheaded selfishness." He caught himself and changed the subject. "We thank you for Freddie also and for bringing her into our lives and for the blessing she already is. Thank you, Lord, for our family."

A loud cry split the air, and we all jumped.

"Sounds like somebody's hungry." Deborah's face split into a wide grin, and she turned toward the stairs. "I'll get little Samuel."

"No, that's okay, sug', I'll get him." Samuel sprinted to the stairs.

Lydia giggled. "Why don't we all get him?" She held her hand out to me shyly. "Freddie, would you like to meet my son?"

"I thought you'd never ask."

. . . .

"This wedding reception's going to be *fun*." Deborah did a little dance as she pulled out her recipe box. "I love this couple. They want a casual reception, not all stuffy and formal. That's 'cause they're older." She grinned. "Once you hit forty, you don't worry as much about impressing everyone—you just want to chill and have a good time." She winked at Samuel. "Ain't that right, baby?"

"I feel that."

"Since their favorite food is Mexican, we're having chicken enchiladas, rice and beans, and a taco bar that my sweet sugar will maintain." She blew a kiss at Samuel, who was shredding lettuce.

He caught her flying kiss and resumed humming "His Eye Is on the Sparrow."

Lydia and the baby were resting upstairs while Samuel, Deborah, and I were power-prepping for the reception in three hours.

She passed me a recipe card. "If you'll work on the enchiladas, I'll go ahead with the taco filling and quesadillas." Deborah nodded to the freezer. "They're already in the baking pans. Just follow the instructions for 'day of' on the card. You should find everything else you need in the fridge."

I shredded cheddar and jack cheese into a bowl. "I just love this kitchen. It's so happy. Mrs. Harris had this great industrial one with all the latest bells and whistles, but it wasn't very warm and inviting."

"That's because she never spends any time in it," Deborah said. "The woman told me she can't cook a lick. All she uses is the microwave and that fancy built-in cappuccino maker."

"I wondered. Those fancy French pans didn't look like they'd ever been used. And there must have been at least twenty of them—all sizes."

Samuel shook his head. "Why you need so many pans if you don't even cook?"

"So you can impress all your rich friends." Deborah's eyes danced. "And your fancy caterer."

. . . .

Two hours later, Deborah and I pulled into the parking lot of the Elks Lodge (Samuel was following in his SUV).

We both saw it at the same time: the Jorgensen's Bakery van pulled up next to the back door.

:: *chapter twenty* ::

O h no," I breathed.

"Maybe it's not Anya," Deborah reassured me. "Didn't you say your friend Shane does the deliveries sometimes?"

I nodded, glued to my seat. "She lets him deliver to small weddings like this."

"Well then. Don't worry about it." She unbuckled her seat belt. "In fact, I hope it is Shane so I can thank him for his help last night as well." She opened her door and eased out of the van. "But if it is your old boss, you just shine it on and be pleasant and cordial . . . Freddie? You hear me?"

"Uh-huh. Pleasant and cordial. Got it." I jumped out and helped her start unloading.

Inside, the reception hall was empty. I blew out a sigh of relief as I followed Deborah and set the enchiladas down on one of the tables.

"Freddie, you start setting up this first food table while I go help Samuel finish unloading the vehicles."

"You sure you don't need some more help outside?"

"Uh-uh." She winked. "This is my chance to steal a quick smooch from my husband before we get all crazy busy." Deborah fluttered her fingers at me and disappeared out the door.

As I set up the four long chafing pans of enchiladas and lit the Sternos beneath them, I noticed the cake table off to one side, holding the chocolate wedding cake I'd baked and never gotten a chance to decorate.

I sneaked over and stole a quick glance at the three small tiers. Perfect—even the tricky-to-master icing roses. I smiled. Shane had done a great job.

"I wondered how long it would take before you came crawling back."

I jumped. Pleasant and cordial.

"Anya." I turned around with a polite smile. "You startled me. I didn't hear you." I glanced down at her feet. Her trademark stilettos had been replaced with soft ballet-slipper flats.

Must have her eye on a short guy.

"It hasn't even been twenty-four hours." Anya gazed at her Rolex with a satisfied smirk. "In fact, I believe it was just over thirteen hours ago when you said you'd had enough and quit. Did you really think you could get back in my good graces by showing up here today and groveling? You'll have to do *much* better than that." She flicked her head at the cake. "As you can see, you're not the only cake decorator in town."

"I realize that. Shane did a wonderful job."

Anya tapped her watch. "I'm waiting. And I don't have all day."

"I'm sorry. Waiting for what?"

"If you think that pathetic excuse for an apology is going to cut it, you're sadly mistaken. Now, hurry up before the guests start arriving." She nodded to the cake-carrying case off to one side. "And grab that while you're at it."

"Freddie?" Deborah glided up behind her. For a big woman, she was surprisingly light on her feet. "You forgot your apron."

"Apron? What apron?" Anya whirled around to glare at

Deborah. "If you'll excuse us, my *employee* and I are trying to have a conversation."

"Actually," Deborah said in a level voice, "Freddie works with me now. And she's not an employee. She's my *partner* and my friend." Deborah handed me my pale yellow apron.

"Thanks." I gave her a grateful smile and slipped it over my head. "I believe you two have never officially met. Deborah Truedell, this is Anya Jorgensen of Jorgensen's Bakery. Anya, this is Deborah Truedell, my friend and new business partner."

Deborah stuck out her hand, but Anya ignored it.

"Figures." Her hard eyes glittered and snaked over Deborah's voluminous red pantsuit and yellow apron. "You two deserve each other."

"We think so." Deborah gave me a side hug. "And the Lord does too."

"Oh, brother!" Anya grabbed the carrying case and huffed away, her ballet slippers slapping against the polished wood floor.

"Thanks for coming to my rescue, partner." We made our way back to the buffet table.

"Honey, you didn't need rescuing. You were doing just fine. I just needed your help with these quesadillas. Isn't that right, Samuel?"

"Uh-huh." He looked up from the taco bar he was setting up and grinned. "My sugar always has trouble with quesadillas."

• • • •

Deborah was right. This was a fun wedding reception. Live music, dancing, even a piñata that rained down Hershey kisses when it was finally cracked open by a nine-year-old guest. The bride and groom—both in their midforties and looking it—were so happy they'd found each other at last that they wanted to share their joy with everyone in a festive, party atmosphere.

And the groom, a balding, bespectacled accountant with a slight paunch, made all the women in the room—including me—cry when he surprised his bride with a heartfelt and shockingly good serenade of Sam Cook's "You Send Me."

"Back off ladies. He's mine," she warned when he finished. Then she grabbed him in a serious lip lock.

Heavy sigh.

.   .   .   .

"Well, that was incredibly romantic," I said to Deborah as we drove away after cleaning up. "Gives me hope."

"You're not even thirty yet." She chuckled. "Plenty of time to get married."

"Tell that to my biological clock," I grumped.

Deborah sent me a look. "His time is not our time. Remember? Better to meet a man who's settled and ready to get married and have a family than some young punk who tells you he loves you and then leaves 'cause he doesn't want to be saddled with a child."

"You're right. I'm sorry." I bit my lip. "How do you think Lydia's going to handle all this? I mean, being a single mom and all."

Deborah sighed. "It won't be easy, Lord knows. Single mothers have one of the hardest jobs around. That's why I'm glad Samuel and I are here to help. I just wish we could help heal her broken heart." She shook her head sadly. "She really loved that boy, you know. Still does. And only Jesus and time can heal that kind of hurt. Although," she added, "that precious little grandson of mine will be a wonderful balm." She gave a proud smile. "Have you ever seen a more beautiful baby? When he looked up at me with those big ol' chocolate-brown eyes of his, I was done for."

"He is pretty cute."

"Cute, nothing! That boy is gorgeous. You tell me when was the last time you saw such a soft set of curls on a child before?"

"I'm not sure I ever ha—"

Deborah's cell rang, which reminded me that I hadn't checked my messages in a while. And a lot had happened in the past twenty-four hours . . .

Oops. One message apiece from Shane and Nicole and three from Millie, who demanded to know what in the world was going on and why hadn't I called her?

While Deborah talked to Samuel, I punched in Millie's home number. She refused to own a cell phone—"too expensive and too intrusive." I got her answering machine. "Hey Millie, it's Freddie. Sorry I missed your calls. I wanted to call you last night after everything went down with Anya, but I knew you were already in bed. And today has simply been crazy—but in a good way. Hope Shane filled you in. I'll call you later and tell you everything."

I flipped my phone shut as Deborah pulled into her driveway.

"Samuel's stopping by the store to get some bread and milk, and he said he'd unload both vehicles when he got home, so we don't need to worry about it," she said as we clambered out of the van. "Which works for me since I'm dying to just get inside and see that sweet grandson of mine." She frowned at the empty driveway and smacked her head. "I can't believe it—I forgot your car's not here. I should have just dropped you off at your house on the way home." Deborah shot a longing look at her front door and then back to the van. "Do you want me to take you now?"

"That's okay—I forgot too. No rush. I'd like to see the little guy again myself. Check out those beautiful curls."

· · · ·

"Hello there, boo." Deborah cradled baby Samuel in her arms and cooed to him. "Did you miss your Grandma today? She sure missed you."

"Look how tiny his little fingers are." I stroked his hand, and he instantly latched onto my forefinger. "Whoa. For someone so small, he's got quite a grip."

"I think he's going to be a third baseman for the Braves," Lydia said.

My purse rang, startling him. Little Sam scrunched up his face and wailed, tightening his grip on my finger.

"I'm sorry. I'm sorry." I nodded to my bag. "Lydia, can you grab that for me? Your son's got me in a death grip."

Deborah jiggled Sam in her arms in a vain attempt to stop his cries while Lydia scrabbled through my purse. The minute she flipped open my cell and said, "Freddie's phone," the baby stopped crying.

I tickled his hand with my finger. "There you go. See. That nasty noise stopped. All gone."

"Freddie? It's your roommate, Brooke," Lydia said. "Here, why don't we switch positions." She handed the phone to me, and I handed Samuel's fist back to her and walked to the far side of the room.

"Hey Brooke, what's up?" I said quietly. And then not so quietly. "Oh my gosh, I totally forgot!"

Deborah gave me a quizzical look as she transferred Samuel to his mother's waiting arms.

"Hal," I mouthed to her. "Hang on a sec, Brooke." I put my hand over the mouthpiece and sent Deborah a beseeching look. "Hal's at my house right now to pick me up for our *date* tonight, which I totally spaced out about."

"So just have him come here to pick you up instead."

I looked down at my salsa-and-cheese-spotted work clothes. "But I haven't even showered. And I'm not dressed."

"You will be. Just tell him to come on over."

"But . . ."

"Go on, now." Deborah nodded. "It'll be fine. Trust me."

And for some reason, I did. I gave Brooke Deborah's address and then followed my friend's beckoning hand down the hall.

Deborah flung her closet doors open to reveal a smorgasbord of colors in every hue of the rainbow. "Mi closet es su closet. You can borrow anything you like. I'm a little bigger than you, but I've got some skinnier clothes too." She pulled out a vivid magenta silk pantsuit shot through with golden threads that shimmered in the light. "What about this?"

"Um, great for you, but way too bright for me."

"How 'bout this?" She held up a flowing lime green and yellow dashiki-style caftan.

"Uh . . ."

"I'm jus' playin'." Deborah grinned. "That's too ethnic for you. I just wanted to see the look on your face."

"Very funny. What about the look on the good doctor's face when he gets here in ten minutes and I'm still in my dirty work clothes?" I sniffed my work sleeve. "And smelling like onions?"

Lydia slipped into the room. "Daddy's back and Sammy's sleeping. Now, Freddie, you go take a quick shower, and I'll help Mama." She nodded toward the hall. "Second door on the right. You'll find everything you need under the sink, including fresh towels. By the time you finish, we'll have the perfect outfit for your date tonight."

. . . .

"There's no way I can wear this." I held up the cobalt blue slip dress. "No sleeves. I told you—I don't do sleeveless."

"I go sleeveless all the time," Deborah said.

"I know. But we've had this discussion before. Remember? Brown fat looks better than white fat."

"Trust me. Just put it on."

I sighed and slipped the dress over my head. It fell in silken folds to my calves, barely skimming my hips and flaring out in a flirty skirt that swayed when I walked.

I have to admit—it felt good. Although I was glad I'd shaved my legs this morning so my stubble didn't snag the silk.

Deborah whistled. "Look out, Marilyn Monroe."

I looked in the master bathroom mirror. "It's very flattering. I look thinner." I held up my arms. "Except for these babies." I pinched the roll of Pillsbury Doughboy fat beneath my left arm.

Lydia tossed me a cream-colored cardigan with pearl buttons down the front. "There you go, Sister Neurotic. Now, what size shoe do you wear?"

"Eight and a half, usually."

Deborah snorted. "Well, I'm a ten, so I can't help you out there, but my baby girl's a nine. Maybe she's got something that'll work. Meanwhile, I'm going to do something with your hair." She pointed to the padded vanity stool in front of the double sinks. "Sit."

Lydia giggled and left on her shoe hunt.

"What's wrong with my hair?"

"It's nice and thick, but it's just hanging there all flat-like."

"I have flat hair. What can I say? There's nothing I can do about it."

"Maybe not, but I can." Deborah reached across me to scoop some white sticky gunk from a jar on top of the vanity. She rubbed the gunk between her hands and then shoved her hands through my hair, lifting it above my head. "This is what I use on Samuel's hair—it's soft like yours."

"Ouch!"

"It hurts to be beautiful. Now, sit still." She pulled my hair up on top of my head, did some kind of swirling, twirling motion, and secured the whole thing with a clip thingy. Deborah stepped back and frowned at my reflection in the mirror. "Too severe." She pulled a few strands loose on either side of my face and a couple at the back of my neck. "There you go. That's better."

And it was.

I stared in the mirror. "My hair's not flat anymore. It's even a little fluffy."

"Uh-huh." Deborah gave me a satisfied smirk. "It's all about product, honey."

"Here you go, Freddie." Lydia returned with three pairs of shoes in her arms that she set on the floor next to me. "I'm sure one of these will work."

"Why do I feel like Cinderella?"

I hummed "A Dream Is a Wish Your Heart Makes" from the Disney film as I tried on the first pair. A sexy, flirty high-heeled pair of taupe sandals that totally swallowed my feet.

"Make that one of the ugly stepsisters."

Deborah held up a pair of cream pumps. "If these are too big, we could stuff tissue in the toes."

I looked at the three-inch heels and shook my head. "No way. I'd fall off and break my leg."

"Only one last glass slipper remaining, ladies and gentlemen," I did my hushed-whisper announcer voice. "Will our Cinderella candidate turn out to be the beautiful princess in disguise? Only the shoes know for sure. May I have a drumroll please?"

I slid my feet into the cute floral flats and took a few tentative steps. "Ladies and gentlemen, we have a winner!" I announced in relief.

Just then the doorbell rang. And Samuel squalled. Again.

"Oops." I clapped my hand over my mouth. "I forgot to have Brooke tell Hal to knock softly."

.   .   .   .

When we descended the stairs into the living room—Deborah first, followed by Lydia, with me bringing up the rear—I could see Hal cooing over little Samuel, whom big Samuel was trying to calm by jiggling him in his arms.

"Hey, Doc, good to see you again." Deborah smiled and made her way to the vet's side. "I see you like children as well as animals."

I knew my face was red. How obvious could she be?

"Oh yeah, I'm looking forward to the day when I have my own." Hal rubbed his thumb gently over Samuel's yellow-bootie-clad foot. "For now I'm just an uncle."

Samuel continued to wail.

"I'll take him, Dad. I think he needs to be fed again." Lydia relieved her father of the baby, introduced herself to Hal, and then hurried off, winking at me as she passed by.

"Hi, Hal," I said. "Sorry about the mix-up."

"That's okay." He turned to face me in his pressed jeans and open-necked navy cotton shirt and did a double take. "Wow. Great dress."

"Thanks. It's Deborah's. And the shoes are Lydia's. We had to do a little clothing triage tonight."

"Well, I'd say the procedure was successful."

"You look lovely, Freddie," Samuel said, moving over to Deborah and slipping his arm around her waist. "I've always liked that dress."

Deborah squeezed Samuel's hand where it rested on her waist. "So, Doc, where y'all going tonight?"

"Oh, there's this great new restaurant downtown I've been wanting to try." He looked at his watch. "But I'm afraid if we don't leave right now, we're going to miss our reservation. Sorry."

. . . .

"How's my patient?" Hal asked as we pulled away from Deborah's. "Did everything come out okay, er, in the end?"

"That's what I hear, although I don't have firsthand knowledge. Poor Brooke's the one who had to clean it up since I was working that night. But I think Zsa Zsa's taking your advice and skipping classic novels—definitive American or not."

"Glad I could be of service."

"You were. Thanks."

The air was heavy with that awkward first-date silence.

Hal broke it first. "So . . . Brooke says you're in the catering business now."

"Yep. As of today." I shook my head. "Amazing how things can change overnight. It's definitely been a whirlwind twenty-four hours."

"I'll say. And you said you weren't spontaneous." He slid me a sideways glance. "Kind of a major decision to make so quickly though, don't you think?"

"Well, it's been coming for a while. Leaving the bakery, that is. A person can only take so much."

"Do you think you'll like working with Deborah? She seems great. Very real."

"She is. And I feel like I've known her forever. Some people you just click with right away, you know?" My smile froze before it had a chance to finish forming. *Oh my gosh. Is he going to take that the wrong way and think I'm coming on to him? Change subject fast.*

"You said you had sisters." I worried the bottom pearl button on Lydia's cardigan. "How many?"

"Four."

"Whoa. A lot of estrogen in that house."

"A lot of testosterone too. I have three brothers."

"Eight kids altogether? Did your dad want his own football team or something?"

"Nope. Just free labor for the family farm. Although we did all play a mean game of football." He looked across the seat at me. "What about you?"

"Hmm?"

"Do you have any brothers and sisters?"

"Nope. Only child."

"That must have been lonely."

"A little." I shifted in my seat. "So what made you move here from Oregon?"

"I got tired of all the wet weather." He drummed his hands on the steering wheel. "It's beautiful country up there—God's country. And I loved all the trees and mountains . . . and, of course, the ocean. But backpacking and hiking in the rain gets old after awhile, so I moved to sunny California."

"Um, I hate to break it to you, but this is *northern* California. We have a lot of rain too."

"Not five days out of seven." He sent me an eager look. "Are you an outdoorsy girl, Freddie?"

"Does reading outside count?"

He laughed. "No. Seriously."

"I am serious."

"Well, I just figured with that whole earth-mother thing you've got going, you'd be the type."

"Earth mother?" I squinted at him. "I think you're confusing me with my roommate. I don't even own a pair of Birkenstocks."

Hal flushed. "Oh look, here we are." He pulled up in front of an English-cottage-style building that looked like a Thomas Kinkade painting, but without the otherworldly light and hidden initial. "Friar Tuck's. I hear the food is fabulous. Apparently the chef is half-English, so it's really authentic."

:: *chapter twenty-one* ::

My heart did jumping jacks as Hal escorted me through the wooden Hobbit-style door of the stone-and-timbered restaurant that reminded me of something out of one of my historical romance novels.

Nice. On a date with one guy and thinking about another. What's up with that? Didn't your mother raise you better?

Oh, gimme a break. What do you expect from someone whose etiquette-challenged mom left without saying good-bye and never even sent a postcard?

"This place is great." Hal's head swiveled from side to side as we made our way through the crush of people in the arched entryway waiting for a table. "Check out the beamed ceiling and huge fireplace."

I was too busy straining to see if a certain chef was on the premises. Although with the size of this crowd, I realized he was probably going crazy slicing and dicing in the kitchen.

"Good evening." An attractive middle-aged woman with a well-modulated English accent and auburn hair shot through with strands of silver greeted us. "Welcome to Friar Tuck's. Do you have reservations?"

"Yes. For two," Hal said. "Baxter?"

"Right." She gave us a warm smile and grabbed two leather-bound menus from the antique side table behind her. "If you'll just come this way, please."

As she led us into the high-ceilinged dining room with hunter-green walls and leaded-glass windows, we passed by a discreet wooden sign that read, "Out of respect for our patrons, no cell phones please." I quickly reached down into my purse to turn mine off.

"Cool place," Hal said to the hostess. "Love the whole English-country vibe thing you've got going on."

"Thank you. I'll be sure to tell my son you like it. He's the owner. And the chef." She offered an impish grin. "So if anything's not to your liking, just let me know, and I'll send him to bed without his dinner."

As we followed Simon's mother across the burnished wood floor, I noticed that she had his same coloring and stocky build—although on her it translated into some big-woman curves beneath her floral skirt and cream-colored blouse. She could have posed for one of those Dove Real Beauty ads.

When Simon told me the name of his restaurant, I'd pictured a brew pub like the ones in college, with TVs blaring out basketball games, sawdust on the floor, and a hundred kinds of beer—not this rich, muted elegance with its dark wood, tapestry, and padded leather upholstery.

Hal pointed to the overhead beams dotted with what looked like round gold or bronze medallions. "What's all the metal stuff?"

"They're called horse brass," she explained. "They were originally decorations for horse saddles. We Brits are a horsy lot, you know."

"So where are all the hunting scenes with the landed gentry

in red coats riding to the hounds?" I glanced at the framed pictures we passed, but they all showed lush rolling green hills dotted with sheep and thatch-roofed cottages. Not a redcoat in sight.

"I'm afraid they're no longer politically correct, my dear," she said with a rueful smile. "The poor fox, you know."

"I always did feel bad for the fox," Hal said.

"Here you are." She ushered us to a small dark-oak table set with Spode. "Your server will be with you in a moment. Enjoy your dinner, and please let me know if there's anything you need. Cheers."

Hal winked. "Tell the chef we're going to hold you to your promise."

"I certainly will." She smiled and glided away, her floral skirt swaying behind her.

"So . . . back to that earth-mother discussion we were having. Whatever made you think that was me?" I narrowed my eyes. "Was it my size?"

"Your size?" He sent me a puzzled look. "No. It just seemed when we met that you weren't really into makeup or fashion. Unlike most women."

"Do I detect a note of bitterness?"

"Hello." A healthy apple-cheeked redhead who resembled Geena Davis with a few extra pounds appeared beside our table. "I'm Henri. I'll be your server this evening."

"Henri?" Hal lifted an eyebrow.

"Short for Henrietta." She sighed. "My mother named me after her favorite aunt, but I prefer Henri. Even though people always think I'm a man."

Hal nodded to me with a smile. "This is Freddie—short for Fredericka."

Her hazel eyes sparked with recognition. "Guess your mum had it in for you as well, huh?"

"My dad." I grimaced.

"Parents." She rolled her eyes. "Could I bring you something from the bar?"

"Just water for me, please."

"Make that two," Hal said. "Thanks."

We opened our menus, and the first thing I saw was Simon's shepherd's pie.

"What?" Hal asked.

"What?"

"You're smiling."

"I am?"

"Definitely some interesting food names, huh?" He stroked his beard. "Bangers and mash, toad in the hole, gammon . . . wonder what they are?"

"I think the bangers and mash is sausage and mashed potatoes, but I'm not sure about the other two. What I'm wondering about is the jugged hare. It's clearly rabbit, but—"

A flash of white caught my eye. I looked up to see Simon— in a white chef's coat and hat like I used to wear at the bakery— beaming and hurrying over.

"Freddie, you came! I'm so glad." He let out a low whistle as he took in my outfit. "Wow. You look really great. That blue is fabulous on you."

I blushed. "Thanks." I nodded to Hal. "Simon, this is my friend Hal. Hal, this is Simon, our chef and the owner of the restaurant."

The two men shook hands, and Hal sent me a thoughtful look. "I didn't know you'd been here before."

"I haven't. This is my first time. I met Simon at our church singles group."

"You're going to try the pâté, right?" Simon asked me. "I

promise you'll like it." He looked over his glasses at Hal. "Freddie and I discovered we're both liver lovers."

Hal shuddered. "I reserve liver for my cats."

"I didn't know you had cats," I said.

"Two Siamese—Yin and Yang."

It was Simon's turn to shudder.

"You big baby," I teased. "I think we need to pray for healing for you."

"Those evil *Lady and the Tramp* cats scarred me for life," Simon explained to Hal with a twinkle in his eye.

"So it *is* the same girl." Henri had returned, a huge smile spreading across her freckled face.

Hal shot her a puzzled look.

"Simon had mentioned a Freddie he met recently, and I wondered if you might be the same person. It's not that common a girl's name." She winked at me in shared boy-name solidarity. "And I'm glad to see you are."

"Me too." Simon ruffled her hair and smiled at me. "And now you've met most of my family. This is my sister, Henri. *Older* sister. Much older."

She punched him in the arm.

"So the whole restaurant's a family affair?" Hal asked. "Cool."

"Right. Simon's got all the talent. Mum and I are just the eye candy." Henri batted her lashes at her brother. "But we all keep an eye out for each other." Her eyes flickered to me with a subtle warning as she pulled out her server pad. "Have you decided what you'd like?"

"Well, I'm starting with the pâté"—I smirked at Simon—"but I'm not quite sure for my main course. I had some good shepherd's pie recently. But I wanted to try something else, and I'm having a hard time deciding between the poached salmon or the roast beef with Yorkshire pudding. What would the chef recommend?"

"Well, if you want the quintessential English dining experience, then I'd go for the beef," Simon said. "I make a lovely gravy for the pudding."

"Gravy and pudding don't sound like they go together. I take it you're not talking tapioca?" Hal cut in, his voice a little sharper than necessary. "You'll have to forgive my ignorance. I'm just a country boy from the Oregon woods."

I gave him a quizzical look. What was it with the country-boy yokel act? I hadn't seen this side of him before.

"No tapioca," Simon said, smiling. "Yorkshire pudding is more like a savory muffin accompaniment, but airy rather than dense—like a popover. You can't have roast beef without it."

"Then roast beef it is." I snapped my menu shut and returned it to Henri.

"And for you, sir?"

Hal frowned. "I don't mean to keep showing my *backwoods* background, but what's gammon?"

Henri flashed him a smile. "Just a fancy word for ham steak."

Hal ordered the poached salmon. I kept waiting for him to pronounce it "sal-mon" like that girl from last year's *American Idol*. But he was an avid fisherman and knew his stuff about swimming upstream. He handed the menus back to Henri. Then, to my surprise and discomfort, he scooted closer and draped an arm over my shoulder.

Simon colored as he looked from Hal to me.

"Right. Shall we be off then and get started on this couple's dinner?" Henri gave her brother a pointed look as she placed a slight emphasis on the "couple."

"Of course." He gave me a stiff smile. "If you'll excuse me, duty calls."

I stared at Hal, giving a pointed glance at his arm around my shoulder. He just smiled at me and leaned closer. So I shrugged my shoulders and kind of wiggled sideways to dislodge the arm.

"Something wrong?" he asked.

"Could we, uh, get to know each other a little better before we start to snuggle?"

I thought I was being firm but diplomatic. Apparently not.

"I see." Hal carefully removed his arm and unfolded his napkin in his lap.

"See what?"

"You have a thing for the chef."

"No, I don't." I could feel the flush creeping up my neck. "I just met him the other night."

He shook his head in mock dismay. "Story of my life. I meet a woman I'm interested in, and she's got the hots for someone else."

"I do not have the hots for him." As soon as the words were out, I realized I was lying. I also realized that Hal had just said he was interested in me. How tacky was that—to be out with one guy and lusting after another? Tacky and unfair. Especially when it was a nice guy like Hal.

I give him my full attention. "You're just trying to distract me from our earlier earth-mother conversation."

"I was hoping you might have forgotten."

"A woman doesn't forget a compliment like that," I said dryly. "So you want to explain that blanket statement you made about 'most women'?"

"All right. I'm sorry. That was definitely a generalization." He held up his hands to ward me off. "And I was thinking mainly of my ex."

"Wife or girlfriend?"

"Wife."

"For how long?"

"We were married two years," he said. "And we broke up two years ago."

I gave him a thoughtful look. "And who wanted the divorce?"

"She did." He sighed. "Remember that young blonde country singer from a few years ago who started out so sweet and home-spun—then, once she got famous, she turned into this diva who wore tons of makeup and skimpy clothes, and her life turned into this club-hopping, shopping-till-you-drop merry-go-round?"

"Jolene Ryan was your *wife*?" I felt my eyes popping out.

"No, no. I'm just saying she started out the same way. When we met, April was this sweet girl-next-door type who lived in jeans and T-shirts and rarely wore makeup. She didn't need to. She had a natural beauty. Like you, except a little too skinny."

Too skinny? My mind boggled. I was beginning to think I was caught up in another of my fantasies.

Watch out what you wish for . . .

Hal stared off into the distance, then gave himself a little shake. "Anyway, long story short, this local modeling agency *discovered* her." He made quote signs with his fingers. "They started sending her on gigs, and within six months she'd turned into someone I barely recognized. Hair extensions, gobs of makeup, false eye-lashes, implants, and more clothes than I've ever seen in my life."

He shook his head. "She became obsessed with her looks—wouldn't even leave the house without a full 'face,' as she called it and just the right outfit." His lips tightened. "Usually something tight and low-cut. Even just to run to the store." He sighed. "But it wasn't just her looks that changed. Everything about her did. All she ever talked about anymore were the latest fashions and her weight. She was terrified she'd gain a few pounds and lose her looks, so she was always dieting. Never allowed any real food in the house."

"No wonder you're looking for an earth woman."

Henri brought our appetizers.

"But enough whining about my ex," Hal said. "That's ancient history. And such a cliché—to spend a date with one woman talking about another."

Simon was right. The pâté was delicious, and so was the beef. The man could definitely cook. Unfortunately, to my disappoint-ment, he didn't emerge again from the kitchen. And when we left the restaurant, his sister and mother bid us a pleasant albeit measured good-bye.

. . . .

Brooke and Jon were snuggled in front of the TV when I opened the front door. She muted it when she saw me. "So? How'd it go? Did you have a good time? Isn't Hal a cool guy? Tell me everything."

"He's very nice, and we did have a good time, but I'm really tired." I sent her an apologetic smile. "It's been a long day, and I need to get to bed . . . can we talk tomorrow?"

In my room, I stepped out of the cute floral flats, carefully removed the borrowed slip dress, and hung it on my corner coat rack.

My answering machine was blinking like crazy, but I was too tired to play my usual imagine game. I just hit play and cuddled with Zsa Zsa.

"Freddie, it's Millie. Are you okay? Where *are* you? What are you doing? What in the world happened last night? Anya said there were cops? Call me ASAP! I've left several messages on your cell, but you must have it turned off."

I punched in her number. "Hi, Millie."

"Freddie! Hang on." I could hear the TV in the background and her murmuring to someone, then a door shutting.

"Sorry about that," Millie said. "Shane and Nicole are here watching the movie, so I had to go in the bedroom to talk."

"Oh, I'm sorry! I totally forgot. I don't want to make you miss it—isn't that movie one of your favorites?"

She snorted. "Yes, but I've been dying to talk to you all day, and I've seen it a zillion times. Now, start at the beginning and tell me everything that happened since I last saw you yesterday afternoon—especially what happened with Anya. She's been spitting mad all day."

I told Millie the whole story, chapter and verse. "I'm just sorry I had to leave you in the lurch like that."

"You don't need to apologize to me. Anya's had this coming." Millie sighed. "Maybe it will be a wake-up call, and she'll realize she can't treat her employees like dirt. Although . . . I'm not sure if a leopard can change its spots. She was coming down pretty hard on Shane today."

"On a happier subject, how's it going with Shane and Nicole tonight?" I asked.

"Well, Shane was a little tongue-tied at first, but once the movie started, he was in his element." Millie giggled. "He was showing off a little, but I thought it was cute. And I think Nicole did too."

We agreed to get together soon to dish more about my new job and the bakery. Then I hung up, thinking about something Millie had said.

Can a leopard change its spots?

I opened my closet doors and looked thoughtfully at a sea of black. I thought of what Hal had said about his wife and how she had changed completely—and not for the better.

Then I glanced over at Deborah's blue dress, which had made Simon's eyes pop. I thought of how my buxom, living-out-loud friend had been encouraging me to come out of my drab cocoon and blossom into a colorful butterfly. I wasn't sure I wanted to be *that* colorful. But maybe I could find a middle ground.

Tired and needing to go to sleep, I decided to check my blog first to see if there were any new comments. Maybe from one of the T-shirt ladies or some other new fans.

I scrolled through, basking in the reflected adulation, until I came to the final comment.

Dear Betty,

I've been reading and enjoying your blog--well, at least most of it. Normally, I'm just a lurker, but I finally decided I had to say something. You know what? It's not just big girls who get the short end of the stick. Small women can also feel overlooked. Especially if they don't live up to the standard idea of beauty. At least you've got a pretty face going for you!

And heavy people can also be thoughtless about excluding people. There's a group of great women at my church, all probably size 14 and over, that I'd really like to get to know. But I don't feel like I can join their group because of my size . . . it makes me feel like an outsider. I've tried a couple of times, but when they talk about their weight issues or struggles, they always say dismissive things to me like, "Not that you can relate . . ."

How do they know? How do you know?

You don't have to be big to feel invisible.

Smaller, but also invisible Sara

:: *chapter twenty-two* ::

Zsa Zsa was panting.

So was I, a little, and my legs still ached from Tuesday's water aerobics. Did I really want to pay this price for a healthier me?

"Come on, baby. If I can do it, you can do it."

I'd gotten up early this morning so I could take Zsa Zsa on a long walk before church. Or a least a longer walk than either of us was used to.

I'd been in the habit of just letting her out in the backyard to do her business, with an occasional excursion down to the corner and back. Lately though, I'd been thinking we could both use a little more exercise. So I'd set my clock, pulled on my tennis shoes, and set out with the princess.

We weren't about to set any land-speed records. But it was nice being out in the cool early morning when no one else was around save another intrepid dog walker or two. And the peaceful rhythm of walking—punctuated by frequent stops for Zsa Zsa to stop and sniff—gave me plenty of time to think and reflect.

I certainly had a lot to think about. Like the response to my blog . . . Was I guilty of doing the same thing I hated the skinny world for doing to me? And was I tarring all smaller women with the same resentful brush? Nicole's beautiful and sweet, friendly face flashed before me.

Okay, major feelings of guilt now. Ready to think about something else.

Like last night's Hal-and-Simon encounter.

After all these years of dating famine—most of my life, really—to have two possible men in my life just felt strange. Who did I think I was—Kim Cattrall?

Not that Simon and I had gone out on a date or anything yet, but I had the feeling I might hear from him really soon. There had been no mistaking the admiration in his eyes when he saw me in the blue dress last night. And, of course, we'd really bonded at the singles potluck.

That man didn't make me feel at all invisible. And after meeting his mother and sister, I could finally believe what he'd told me—that he really wasn't put off by big women the way so many men were.

The more I thought about Simon, in fact, the more I wanted to see him again.

But what about Hal?

Nice guy. Great vet. And he'd made it pretty clear that he liked me, which was flattering. But he clearly had some unresolved issues over his wife leaving him. And the way he'd acted on our date—first with that phony country-bumpkin thing, then getting all possessive—set off alarm bells. Did I really want to go there?

Besides, there was no way in the world I'd ever be an earth mother. I liked my new spiffed-up look, makeup and all. I wasn't about to stop shaving my legs. And the only kind of camping I liked to do was at a B&B.

Were any of those things deal breakers? I couldn't decide. I'd just have to see how things went.

In the meantime, I had my new job to think about—and that definitely needed some pondering. Was Hal right—that I was making a big decision too quickly?

I wasn't naïve. Okay, maybe a little. But I knew no partnership was perfect. No matter how well we got along now, Deborah and I were bound to butt heads now and then.

But even if our partnership failed, wasn't it still worth a—

"Zsa Zsa!"

She'd stopped dead in her tracks, tongue lolling. When I stopped too, she sat back on her haunches, begging to be carried.

I laughed. Once a princess, always a princess.

"Sorry, kiddo—you're on your own. But we're almost home—and we'll get better at this. I promise."

We started out again, not pushing it, but still moving forward.

"Which is what's important anyway," I told my puppy and my already-tired feet.

One thing I'd come to realize—or rather, remember again over the past several weeks—I really enjoyed cooking. I was good at it. And I wasn't going to let any past regrets or present fears stop me from doing it now.

I'd told Simon at the potluck that I rarely cooked because I had no one to cook for. But now I did. And they would be paying me to do it—a definite plus.

But beyond the money, there was something else about the cooking that I liked.

It felt good to be giving. To provide nourishment to people. And as Zsa Zsa pulled me up the steps to the back door, I thought of someone else I could cook for too.

In fact, that was something I could do tonight.

. . . .

I hadn't been to the singles Sunday school in a while, so I decided to pop in that morning. There I noticed that Jared's new flavor of the week was a Teri Hatcher lookalike—only younger.

But that was okay. Now, with two men taking an active interest in me, I could see my Jared fantasies were nothing more than a schoolgirl crush—the wallflower at the dance staring longingly at the popular quarterback who danced by with the giggly, vacuous head cheerleader.

While I was getting a cup of tea and skipping the doughnuts at the coffee cart after class, Jared and his Teri clone approached.

"Hey Frankie, are you losing some weight?" He whistled. "Looking good there. Keep it up." He grabbed a cinnamon twist and gave me a thumbs-up.

Would it be a sin to deck somebody at church?

The thing was, I was pretty sure I hadn't really lost weight. Not much, anyway. But I'd seen this happen before. If a big girl started looking better in any way—new hair, new makeup, even a better attitude—other people interpret it as weight loss. Because they're programmed to think that being skinny is the only way to look good.

Sigh. Another topic for my blog. But this was church, so I decided to just rise above it all and concentrate on what really mattered.

Like getting to the sanctuary before the service started.

I entered the back of the church, swiveling my head to look for Deborah, and bumped into a man leaving the first service. "Oh, excuse me." I turned to apologize and felt my face flame.

"Simon! I didn't expect to see you here."

It had to be a sign.

"I told you I was checking out this church." He sent me that delicious lazy smile that did strange things to my knees. "So did you enjoy your roast beef?"

"Yes. I loved it. In fact, I loved your whole restaurant. Beautiful. It wasn't what I was expecting."

"What, you were thinking maybe peanut shells and dart-boards, perhaps?"

"Something like that. And English sheepdogs serving as bearskin rugs."

"You mean you didn't see old Shep?" He frowned. "We usually trot him out just after he's had a good roll in the muck, but we were so busy last night, guess we forgot. I'll have a talk with Henri and make sure that doesn't happen again."

"Good. I knew there was something missing. I just love the smell of wet sheepdog in the evening."

His laugh was as I remembered it—relaxed and un-self-conscious.

Yes, definitely a sign.

But Deborah chose just that moment to hurry up with Samuel in tow. "Girl, where you been? I'm just *dying* to hear all about your date last night with that good-looking vet . . ."

Simon gave me a tight-lipped smile. "Well, I need to get to work. Lots of prep to do for the lunch crowd."

Guess Simon didn't see the same sign I did. Or maybe he just didn't want to read it.

"Who was that?" Deborah asked as he strode away. "And why did he have that strange look on his face? Did I put my size 10s in it?"

"I'll tell you after the service."

But after the service I had something else on my mind. "Where's Lydia?"

A worried frown puckered Deborah's brow. "At home with the baby."

"Is she okay?"

"Physically, yes. Emotionally, no."

"Do you think it's postpartum depression?"

"No." She sighed. "I think she's grieving the end of her marriage, and she's also more than a little overwhelmed thinking about raising a baby without a daddy."

"That boy going to have a daddy," Samuel grunted. "Nothing wrong with my being both a granddaddy and a daddy, is there?"

"Nothing at all, sug'," Deborah said gently, patting him on the arm. "But it's still going to take time for our girl to heal and adjust."

"You think a visitor might cheer her up?" I bit my lip. "Or do more harm?"

"I think seeing you might do just the trick to take her mind off things." She leaned in with a mischievous smile. "And that way we can both hear the results of our makeover last night."

We walked out to the parking lot together. "I think I know something else that might make my baby girl feel better too," Deborah said.

"What?"

"Some good, old-fashioned fried okra."

"You're kidding! I love okra! I haven't had it in years."

"Then you're in for a treat," Samuel said. "My baby makes the best fried okra in the state of Georgia—or California."

"I think you're a little biased," Deborah said, but she flashed him a pleased smile all the same.

. . . .

"To do okra right, you don't open a can," Deborah explained as I sat at her kitchen island. "You don't even go to the grocery store.

You have to go out and pick the okra from your garden. It has to be fresh." She nodded to the little pile of sliced vegetable in front of her. "Samuel just went and picked this mess of it for me."

"One of our cooks made this for me when I was little," I said, trying to remember how she did it. "Don't you bread with cornmeal?"

Deborah nodded, talking as she worked like one of those chefs on TV. "The best way is to take a little cornmeal, a little butter, slice the okra and roll it in the cornmeal, and pan fry it till it's crispy and brown. Doesn't take long." She transferred a big slotted spoonful from the frying pan onto a paper-towel-covered plate and waved it beneath my nose. "Like so."

We heard Lydia's slow footsteps coming down the stairs.

"Hey, baby girl," Deborah called. "I got a surprise for you."

Lydia shuffled into the kitchen, still in her bathrobe and slippers.

Deborah smiled and held out the plate to her. "Here's you some okra, honey."

"No thanks, Mama. I'm not hungry right now. I just came down to get a bottled water." Lydia opened the fridge and pulled out a Crystal Geyser. "I'm going back to bed now." She nodded at me dully as she shuffled out of the kitchen. "Hey, Freddie."

"See what I mean?" Deborah said. "I'm worried about my girl."

"So am I, sug'," Samuel said, his arms encircling her waist from behind. "Let's take those worries to the Lord."

So the three of us gathered in a circle and prayed for Lydia and her baby and for his love to surround them both.

．．．．

After we prayed, a wacky idea came to me—probably from watching so many *Cosby Show* reruns on cable. I glanced at Deborah's head, covered today in a yellow silk scarf.

"Deborah, I know you don't like to wear wigs, but did you ever buy any just in case?"

She gave me a strange look. "No."

"Oh." So much for my plan.

"But Samuel and Lydia did when my hair first started falling out," she said. "They both went shopping on their own, and each came home with a different wig."

"Did you get rid of them?" I held my breath.

"She kept them," Samuel answered. "She didn't want to hurt our feelings."

"Besides, it's a woman's prerogative to change her mind, and I figured the day might come when I might want to start wearing a wig," Deborah said.

"Great!" I grabbed Deborah's hand and pulled her after me. "Let's go."

"Where? What are you doing, girl?"

"Shh. Just trust me. Isn't that what you always say?" I grinned at Deborah. "Just follow my lead. But be quiet."

Samuel threw us a bemused look as we headed for the stairs.

"Samuel, give us about fifteen minutes," I instructed, "then come on up."

Upstairs, we tiptoed past Lydia's closed door and down the hall. "Is it okay to go in your bedroom?" I whispered.

"Uh-huh. I made my bed this morning, and Samuel always throws his underwear in the hamper." Deborah sent me a puzzled glance. "Why are we whispering?"

"Shh." I beckoned her to follow me. Once inside her room, I softly closed the door and headed straight to her massive walk-in closet. "I didn't want Lydia to hear us." I began rummaging through her clothes. "Knowing you, I'm guessing you've got something with sequins in here."

"Sequins? For you?" Deborah giggled. "I knew you'd see the light someday." She grabbed an armload of glittering clothes and laid them on the bed.

I riffled through them until I found what I was looking for.

"Since you love purple so much, this one's for you." I held out a long evening gown with a slit up the side.

"That's one of my favorite dresses. I wore it at the twentieth-anniversary party the kids threw for us." Deborah held it up in front of her. "But where are we going?"

"We're not going anywhere." I continued to sift through the pile. "There. I think this one will be perfect." I pulled out a long, red glittery gown with a matching jacket and headed to her bathroom. "While I'm getting dressed, can you pull out the wigs, please?"

I changed into the red dress and surveyed my reflection in the mirror. Queen Latifah in *Chicago* had nothing on me.

Except bigger boobs. I tugged at the gaping V-neckline and pulled it up, settling the extra fabric in the back. Deborah's gold lamé belt would fix that right up. And the beaded jacket would hide the looseness.

When I rejoined Deborah, I couldn't believe my eyes. She was a combination of Patti LaBelle and Aretha Franklin, wrapped up in one glittering purple package and topped off with a sleek shoulder-length black wig.

"Wow. You look good with hair."

She preened. "I do, don't I?" She pirouetted in front of the mirror, catching my eyes. "You look pretty fine your own sparkly self. Now, are you gonna tell me what this is all about?"

I told her. Then I scribbled down lyrics at the dressing table while Deborah slicked back my hair and anchored the curly, dark auburn wig over it. "I'll take lead vocals," I suggested, "while you do backup. Okay?" I asked.

"More than okay. I don't want to scare the baby."

Samuel joined us, his eyes wide and beaming as we gave him instructions.

We heard him rap on Lydia's door. "Lydia, honey, can you come to our room for a minute? Your mama and I want to talk to you."

Then he softly raced back to us, and we all got into position.

Lydia knocked on the closed door. "Mama?" she said in a listless voice.

Deborah nodded at Samuel, who hit the play button on the CD player. "Come in, baby girl."

"Baby Love" by Diana Ross and the Supremes filled the air. Deborah and I sang along loudly over the original and with amended lyrics—not about a man who treated his girl bad and left her sad, but about a mother's love for her precious baby and the kisses she'd be showering on him, with a love that would never leave.

Lydia laughed. And cried. And laughed some more.

We made her join us to round out our girl group—in her robe and bunny slippers. Afterward, the three of us collapsed laughing on the bed while Samuel went to tend to his namesake.

"Girl, you can sure sing," Deborah said to me, "but you need a little more soul. You really don't have much rhythm, do you?"

"Nope, but together I think we make the perfect entertainer, bullfrog-voice." My eyes lit up. "I know! I'll sing behind the curtain, while you mouth the words onstage and dance."

"Honey, after this you're not hiding behind no curtains anymore," Deborah declared firmly.

"That's a fact," Lydia agreed. She tugged at my wig. "Freddie, you look good as a redhead. You ever thought about maybe getting some red highlights?"

I hadn't paid much attention last week when Deborah first mentioned it, but now I wasn't so sure. I stole another peek in the mirror. I did look good. Nothing wussy about the reflection that stared back at me.

Lydia turned to her mother. "I'm a little hungry. Maybe I'll have some okra after all."

"About time," I told her. "I've been waiting for mine all afternoon."

Deborah beamed. "I'll fry up some more. That other's gone all soggy by now."

We trooped downstairs and sat around the island, Samuel bringing up the rear with the baby.

"Now, tell us everything about your date last night," Lydia commanded after she'd had her fill of okra. "Did you have a good time?"

"I want to know that too," Deborah said with a smirk. "But first, what about that guy at church today?"

"What guy?" Lydia asked, her eyes widening. "Sounds like someone's getting popular."

So I told them all about Simon and his restaurant and my date with Hal.

"Ooh, this Simon sounds like he's going to give Hal a run for his money," Lydia said. "We need to check him out." She winked at Deborah. "Mama, you've always wanted to try English food, haven't you?"

"Why, yes I have, baby girl. Maybe we can go to Friar Tuck's for dinner tonight." Deborah scratched her head, tilting her wig askew. "Freddie, would you like to join us?"

I shook my head so emphatically my wig slid sideways. "There's no way I'm going back there today—or even this week. He'll think I'm stalking him." I shook my head. "It was bad enough the way Simon and Hal were sizing each other up—like two male dogs sniffing each other."

"Well, now I *know* Lydia and I have to go." Deborah grinned and turned to Samuel. "Darlin', do you mind babysitting?"

:: *chapter twenty-three* ::

That night, while Deborah and Lydia went to scope out Simon and Friar Tuck's, I put my new cooking plan into action. I stopped by Whole Foods on my way for supplies. Then, once home, I set to work cutting up red, yellow, and green bell peppers, zucchini, French-style green beans, and a red onion. I sautéed the veggies in olive oil along with fresh basil, oregano, a couple of cloves of garlic, and a little leftover white wine. I stirred in some Morel and cremini mushrooms, layered sliced plum tomatoes over the top, and sprinkled some shredded mozzarella over the tomatoes to melt.

Brooke walked in the kitchen just as I was pulling a loaf of whole-wheat garlic-herb bread from the oven.

"Mmm." She sniffed appreciatively. "Something for a catering gig?"

Her mouth dropped open when I told her who it was really for.

"Freddie, this is so fabulous," she said later as we finished our Italian stir-fry on angel-hair pasta. "I can't believe you did this for Jon and me. And I had no idea you were this good. I mean, I knew you could bake cakes and all," she added hastily, "and that you're working with Deborah now and everything. But I didn't know you could *cook*."

"Which is probably good." I laughed. "You would have put it in the rental contract."

She fixed me with one of her earnest stares. "But it's so cool—like you have hidden depths or something. Do you realize that in all the time you've lived here, this is the first homemade meal we've all had together?"

"And it's about time!" Jon scarfed down his second helping. "Freddie, will you marry me?"

Brooke threw a piece of garlic bread at him.

After dinner, wanting to give Brooke and Jon a little couple time, I headed to my room with Zsa Zsa. But when I opened my bedroom door, I heard a strange sound coming from the direction of the bathroom. Zsa Zsa sprinted to check out the source of the noise and yelped.

I grabbed my shoe and raced to protect her from whatever creature might have gotten in. Then it was my turn to yelp.

Brooke and Jon came running in. "Freddie? You okay—what the—?"

We all stood staring at the stream of water gushing from the wall behind the sink. "It looks like Niagara Falls in here."

"More like a burst pipe," Jon said, picking his way gingerly through the two inches of water on the bathroom floor. "I better get this water turned off before it does some serious damage." He stopped and looked more closely at the water-soaked wall. "Uh, Freddie, what's on the other side of that wall?"

I shrieked. "My closet!" I squished my way over the soaked bedroom carpet and slid open the closet door to find water pouring inside there as well.

I examined my drenched clothes, some hopelessly ruined,

then gave Brooke a weak smile. "Well, Deborah did say I needed a new wardrobe."

· · · ·

As it turned out, my waterlogged clothes were the least of my worries.

The burst pipe in my bathroom had done extensive damage. According to the insurance claims guy Brooke called and the expert inspectors he brought in to survey the situation, water had been leaking from the old pipe in the wall for some time before it burst. The bathroom floor had buckled, the Sheetrock was ruined, and there was extensive dry rot. But worst of all, mold had invaded both the bathroom and closet floors.

A restoration crew wearing special haz-mat uniforms and helmets were called in to put up plastic sheeting with hazard signs all around the contaminated area—which included my closet and parts of my bedroom. The bathroom would have to be gutted, decontaminated, then completely remodeled. Which meant I'd be homeless for at least a month.

Brooke apologized profusely and offered me the living-room couch and use of her bathroom. But when Deborah heard what happened, she insisted that I come stay in their guest bedroom.

The only kink in that plan was Zsa Zsa.

Deborah was so afraid of dogs that the first night I stayed over, I left Zsa Zsa behind in Brooke's care. It killed me to do so, especially when she gave me that plaintive one-eyed stare of hers. And the next day, when Deborah went with me to get some more of my things, Zsa Zsa launched herself into my arms and lay there quivering.

"She's freaked out by all the chaos," Brooke explained. "And she doesn't understand why she can't go in your room."

I snuggled her to my chest. "Poor baby. I know. It's scary and confusing, huh? I'm sorry, baby. Mama loves you."

Zsa Zsa whimpered.

"Oh, all right! You can bring that dog over," Deborah said. "But you'd better keep it far away from me. And it better not mess up my nice carpet, either."

"Oh, thank you! She'll be good as gold, won't you, baby?" I snuggled my face against Zsa Zsa, who wagged her tail and licked my cheek.

Deborah just shuddered.

But so far, so good. I kept Zsa Zsa with me in the airy pink and green guestroom, with her food and water on a tray in the adjacent guest bath. And every morning and night, she and I took long walks around the quiet neighborhood so she could do her business and both of us could build up our endurance a little.

Lydia and Samuel both fell instantly in love with Zsa Zsa. I even caught Samuel giving her a scrap of meat when his wife wasn't looking.

But Deborah still kept a wary distance. And I understood—well, sort of. I mean, I couldn't see how anyone could be afraid of my little Zsa Zsa. But Deborah couldn't help her feelings. And it was her home, after all, so I just tried to make sure the puppy stayed in my room—which would have been easier if Lydia and Samuel hadn't kept letting her out.

I just kept telling myself to roll with the punches and try to adjust. Which wasn't always easy, because staying with Deborah and her family was a big change for me. A nice one in many ways. But there were still lots of things to get used to.

Like the strong smell of coffee in the morning.

And the crying baby at night.

And so many people all together in one house.

I was pretty used to my solitude. And my own space. And Deborah wasn't really good with the idea of boundaries and personal space.

But in that area, at least, Zsa Zsa turned out to be a big help. She was the only thing that kept Deborah from bouncing into my bedroom every morning and saying, "Wake up, sleepyhead!" like she'd done my first morning there.

Unfortunately, even Zsa Zsa couldn't prevent Deborah's cheery morning *knock* on my bedroom door. "Good morning, sleepyhead. Time for breakfast!"

It's not that I wasn't used to waking up early—I'd done it to report to work at the bakery the past two years. I just wasn't used to so much noise and communication in the morning.

I didn't really mind getting up early. Bakers are used to early hours. But all that human interaction before breakfast was something completely new to me.

. . . .

"Hey sug', you seen my trainers?" Samuel called down the stairs to Deborah my second morning there.

"Did you look in the closet?" she yelled back.

"But I didn't put them in the closet," he called down again.

"Well, maybe somebody else did!"

She rolled her eyes at me. "I've been married to that man twenty-five years, and he still makes me crazy with the way he just drops his shoes and clothes everywhere."

Samuel bounded down the stairs and into the kitchen, scowling at his wife. "Would you please quit moving my things? I can never find anything 'cause you keep moving my stuff from wherever I put it last."

Deborah's eyes snapped. "Well, maybe if you put things where they *belonged*—and not in the way for other people to trip and fall over—it wouldn't be a problem."

"I'm *not* going to have this conversation again," Samuel shouted. "I'm going for a run." And he slammed out the back door.

Deborah stirred her coffee and looked at me. "What's your mouth hanging open for?"

"I've just never seen you and Samuel fight. You're usually so lovey-dovey."

"Shoot. That wasn't a fight. That was just us pickin' at each other." She chuckled. "Our fights can make the walls shake. Isn't that right, baby girl?" she asked Lydia, who'd just entered the kitchen with little Sam.

"Oh yeah. Mama and Daddy can get real loud."

"That's 'cause we're passionate," Deborah said with a wicked gleam in her eye. "Which makes the makin' up all the more fun."

"Okay, okay. I'll take your word for it."

Please, God, don't let them be too passionate while I'm here. Or at least do me a favor and make these walls thick.

I grabbed a yogurt from the fridge. "Moving on . . . I want to thank you again for letting me stay here while the work's going on in my room. I really appreciate it."

"Well, we're happy to have you here, aren't we, Boo?" she cooed to her grandson, whom Lydia had set down on the table in his little portable seat. "Aren't we happy to have Aunt Freddie here?"

I sat down at the table and gazed around the room. "I just love this kitchen. It's so cheery and bright."

"And big," Lydia said.

"That too, but it's perfect for a cook—actually, two cooks."

With the two sinks and the ovens on different sides of the kitchen, Deborah and I didn't trip all over each other preparing for our catering gigs. "It's the perfect setup." I sighed. "Someday I'm going to have a kitchen like this."

Lydia sent me a mischievous smile. "I'll bet Simon the chef has a really big kitchen at his house too . . ."

I stuck out my tongue at her. She and Deborah had been teasing me about Simon ever since their visit to Friar Tuck's Sunday night.

"He has to," Deborah said. "I tell you—I liked that boy."

"He is pretty fine," Lydia said. "And that accent!"

"Mmm-hmm," Deborah agreed. "But what I like is, the boy can *cook*. I always appreciate a man who's good in the—"

The back door opened, and Samuel returned, sweating from his quick jog around the block. "Mornin', everyone," he said.

"Morning, Daddy."

"Good morning, Samuel."

He leaned into Deborah and planted a big kiss on her lips. "Mornin', sug'."

She returned it with enthusiasm. "Mornin', darlin'."

"Oh, get a room, you two," Lydia said.

. . . .

Thursday night I went over to Millie's, where she introduced me to Bette Davis in *Now, Voyager*. Shane couldn't make it because— big news!—he had a date with Nicole. So it was just Millie and me. Which was probably a good thing, because by the end of the movie, we were both blubbering like babies.

After we'd wiped our noses and carried our dishes to the kitchen, Millie filled me in on happenings at the bakery.

"Shane's really doing a good job," she said. "Anya was hesitant about using him at first, but she really didn't have any other choice. I tried to do the decorating, but my hands just don't do what I want them to anymore, and I really messed up the writing. So Anya had to give Shane a shot, and now he's taken your place."

Her eyes widened as she realized what she'd said. "Not that anyone can take your place . . . that's not what I meant."

I waved it off. "It's okay. Really. I'm much happier working with Deborah. It's fun to do something besides cakes."

"One thing you won't believe," Millie said with a mischievous gleam in her eye. "Anya's starting to help with some of the baking now."

"You're kidding."

"Nope. We've been really swamped lately, and Shane and I couldn't keep up with all the orders. So I told her if she didn't want to run the bakery into the ground, she'd either have to hire someone else or put on an apron and help us out." Millie grinned. "Well, you know how tight-fisted she is."

I grinned back. "You mean like that old saying—if she was any tighter she'd squeak?"

"Exactly. So now she works in the back three days a week. She's already learned cookies and muffins, and next week I'm going to start her on the crumb coffee cake."

"Will wonders never cease?"

"Actually, I feel kind of sorry for her," Millie added.

"You do? Why?"

"Well, she doesn't really have friends—"

"There's a reason for that."

"I know. But last week she let down her guard a little," Millie said. "Nicole wasn't working, and Shane was off on a delivery, so it was just the two of us in the back. Her latest guy had given her the slip, and she blurted out, 'I'm forty-four, and I've never been married; my eggs are old, and I'm never going to have a baby!'"

"Whoa. Anya wanting a baby? Who'd have ever guessed?"

"I know. I told her she could adopt—that more and more single women are doing that today. But then Shane returned, and it was back to business as usual."

"Unbelievable," I murmured. And went home that night thinking that people could always surprise you. And the sight I stumbled upon the next day confirmed my observation.

I'd left a tired Deborah napping on the living room couch while I went grocery shopping and ran a few errands. When I returned, Zsa Zsa was nestled in Deborah's lap, and my bareheaded friend was rubbing her tummy and talking baby talk to her.

"Well, well." I crossed my arms over my chest. "What have we here?"

Deborah shifted and tried to paste on an affronted look. "Your dog got loose and came into my living room. She woke me up by licking my head where my scarf had fallen off. Scared me to death."

"I'm so sorry. I'll put her back." Hiding my smile, I strode to the couch and moved to lift Zsa Zsa from Deborah's lap.

Zsa Zsa moved her lone eye from me to Deborah and back again, snuggling deeper into Deborah's lap.

"Well, now that she's here," Deborah said grudgingly, "you might as well let her stay."

The look that little dog gave me was one of pure triumph.

Nobody puts Zsa Zsa in a corner.

Or a guest bedroom.

:: *chapter twenty-four* ::

The retching sound was awful. And unmistakable. And coming from the bathroom stall right next to mine.

"Are you okay?" I called out.

"I'm fine," a thin, reedy voice answered. "I think maybe the shrimp was bad or something."

My heart clutched. Those are not words a caterer wants to hear at an event she's catering. Especially a ritzy, high-end wedding at the poshest country club in town.

Deborah and I had gotten this last-minute gig as a referral from another client, whose prominent-businessman brother needed to put on the ritz to hide the fact that his eighteen-year-old daughter was four months pregnant.

I felt sick—and not from the shrimp. I was going to have to tell Deborah right away. But first I needed to make sure that girl was okay.

I waited for her by the marble sinks. She took forever to come out, and when she finally did, I had to hide my shock.

The Goth-teen with jagged-cut jet-black hair could have been a poster child for anorexia. All jutting bones and sharp angles, she couldn't have weighed more than ninety pounds—dripping wet, in all her clothes and piercings.

She washed her hands, then scooped water from the tap to drink, wiping at her black-rimmed mouth. I tried not to stare at the silver hoops in each corner of her mouth.

"Are you all right?" I asked gently. "Would you like me to get your mother or someone for you?"

"Why?" She pushed her hair away from her sunken, heavily made-up eyes, revealing two more silver hoops in her left eyebrow. Her gaze raked me from head to toe, lingering on my hips and thighs with scorn.

"Because you're sick," I said.

"I told you I'm fine. It was just a piece of bad shrimp or something."

"Well, I hope not, because I'm the caterer. And we got that shrimp fresh from our fish guy just this morning. How many pieces did you eat?"

"What's it to you?" she snarled. "Look, just leave me alone. It's none of your business. I'm free, white, and twenty-one, so give it a rest, fat girl." She glared at me and slammed out the door.

I hurried to ask Deborah if any of the other guests had complained about feeling sick. "Not a one," she said, frowning from behind the buffet table. "What'd this girl look like?"

I nodded to the far corner where the emaciated Goth girl sat drinking and laughing with her friends.

"That's what I thought." Deborah shook her head. "I saw her earlier, gorging herself on a whole bowl of shrimp. The girl ate a whole plateful of meatballs too. She's a binger and purger."

"Isn't there something we can do?"

"Like what?" Deborah said sadly. "She's an adult." As we watched the troubled young girl, a slim, well-dressed middle-aged woman went up to her and laid a hand on her arm. It was obvious she was pleading with her, but the girl just shook off her arm and stormed out of the room.

I sighed and returned to the kitchen with Deborah to replenish the cheese platter while she checked on our fresh-fruit supply. My head was in the fridge when I heard the kitchen door open.

"Excuse me. Would it be possible to get some more fruit for my wife, please?"

A chill ran down my back. I knew that voice.

Slowly I straightened and turned around. "Dad?"

"Fredericka?" Impeccable as always in a gray silk suit that perfectly set off his granite features and silver hair, my father stared at me, his lip curled. "What are *you* doing here?"

"Working. I'm the caterer."

His steely gray eyes zeroed in on my yellow Touch of Honey apron, which was flecked with strawberry juice and a smear from a renegade barbecue meatball that had fallen and slid down my front. He sneered. "I always knew you'd wind up stuffing your face somewhere. First a bakery and now a caterer. What happened? Did you lose your sweet tooth, or did they catch you gorging yourself in a vat of frosting?"

Deborah, whom I'd forgotten was even there, gasped and pulled herself up to her full height. She stood almost shoulder to shoulder with my father. "With all due respect, Mr. Heinz, you've got no call to talk to your daughter like that," she said. "I know the Bible says to honor thy father and mother, but you need to honor your daughter too. Freddie is my partner and my friend, and I'm not going to let you talk to her that way." She wagged a finger in his face. "You should be ashamed of yourself."

His chilly gaze scanned her from the top of her pink-turbaned head down her ample body to her pink pedicured toes in her chunky pink sandals. The same condescending scan he'd turned on me my entire life. "And who are you, Ms. Pepto-Bismol?"

Deborah's eyes snapped. "I'm the woman who's going to kick your sorry butt from here to Georgia if you don't get outta this kitchen right now." Her Southern-flavored words sliced the charged air. "Now, leave."

"I beg your pardon?"

"You heard me." Deborah's chest was heaving. "I said leave!"

"Frederick?" The kitchen door opened again, and Candy, wearing a white linen sheath that showed off her chiseled tanning-bed arms and legs, stepped in cautiously. "Is there a problem?" She saw me and her eyes grew round. "Freddie?"

"Yes, my dear," my father said to his trophy wife. "That's your stepdaughter in all her piggy, food-covered glory. The apple doesn't fall far from the tree, does it? She's wound up just like her fat cow of a mother."

My head snapped up. "What about my mother?"

Deborah hustled over to me. "Come on, girl, you don't need to be casting your pearls before swine."

"Frederick," Candy said nervously, putting her hand on his sleeve. "I don't think this is the time or the place."

He shook her hand off as he would a pesky fly. "Oh, shut up, bubblehead. Since when do you tell me what to do?" He whirled on me. "You've made your bed, and now you can lie in it. I hope you and your porcine friend will be very happy in your little business venture—but don't think you'll get one more penny from me. I've had it. I've done everything I could to make sure you didn't wind up like your mother. I'm not making a habit of bankrolling fatties."

"Bankroll?" I stared at him. "When was the last time you bankrolled *any*thing for me? Yes, you paid for college—and I've been paying ever since. I don't want your money. I don't *need* your money." I was breathing hard now. "And as for your offer to pay for gastric bypass surgery so I can turn into your idea of the acceptable woman—a skinny bimbo with nothing between her ears—you know what you can do with that."

My father made a fist and started to draw it back. He'd never hit me in my life. His abuse was never physical. But I'd never stood up to him before either.

Deborah grabbed a frying pan and rushed between us. "You get out of here right now, Mister Man. Get outta here before I smash you upside the head."

"You heard the lady," said Samuel, who'd just slipped into the kitchen. He spoke in a quiet, measured tone that brooked no refusal. "If I were you, I'd leave. Or that frying pan isn't the only thing that's going to come smashing into your head."

Frederick Wagner Heinz Jr. hesitated and looked from Samuel to Deborah. He shot me a look so full of loathing that it made me step back. Then he stormed out the door, a shamefaced Candy at his heels.

"Well," I said in a shaky voice. "For the main course we had my father. Can't wait to see what we're having for dessert."

And then I began to sob.

"I'm sorry, honey. I'm so sorry." Deborah set down the frying pan and enfolded me in her arms. "There now. It's okay. It's going to be all right. You go on and cry, sweetie." She patted my back and breathed gently into my ear. "Remember, your heavenly Father is not like your earthly one. He'd never do you like that. He loves you, and you are precious in his sight."

My sobs subsided into sniffles, and I accepted the handkerchief Samuel handed me. I didn't even know men used handkerchiefs anymore.

"Go ahead, blow," Deborah told me.

I hesitated, not wanting to dirty the fine, pressed linen handkerchief.

"Go on now," Samuel encouraged me. "You'll feel better."

And he was right. I did.

Deborah tilted my chin up to face her. "Freddie, God created you, and he doesn't make mistakes. He says you are fearfully and wonderfully made. And you are, my sweet friend. Don't you ever forget it. No matter what anyone says."

"I won't." I shook the tears from my eyes and gave her a tremulous smile. "Boy, you were something else. I don't think anyone's ever stood up to my father like that in his life. Certainly not in mine. You were great!"

"You weren't so bad yourself, girl. Good on you!"

"Thanks." I frowned. "But I wish I knew what he meant about my mother."

•　.　•　.

I found out the following week. Candy called when my father was out of town on a business trip and invited me over for lunch—a first for both of us.

Estella, my parents' latest cook and housekeeper, answered my knock. "Ms. Heinz, you look so nice."

"Thanks, Estella." I'd dressed with care for this meeting in the same outfit I'd worn to the Happy Paws open house. Only this time, instead of Deborah polishing my toes, I'd splurged on a pedicure along with my weekly manicure. I'd even bought a cute silver toe ring to highlight my pretty toes.

I was dressed for battle, and I knew I looked good.

I couldn't say the same for my stepmother.

"Hello, Freddie." Candy, clad in one of her old velour J-Lo

sweat suits, flip-flopped her way over to me. Her yellow rubber flip-flops made a jarring noise as they slapped against the gleaming cherrywood floor.

I stared at Candy's feet in amazement. In the first place, she never wore flip-flops except outside by the pool or at the beach. More astonishingly, the polish on her toes was chipped and peeling. And Candy *always* had a fresh pedicure. What was going on?

"You look really nice, Freddie," she said. "That's a pretty color on you."

Say what? My head snapped up. Who was this slovenly, tentative stranger? And what had she done with my wicked, not-a-hair-out-of-place stepmother?

Close up I could see that Candy's face was scrubbed clean. Without her usual expensive makeup, she looked old and vulnerable.

"Shall we go into the conserva—" She stopped herself. "To the *sunroom* for our lunch?"

"Uh, sure." I followed her to the far end of the muted beige living room and through the French doors to the octagonal glassed-in sunroom my father had installed last year. He always insisted on calling it a conservatory, as if he was lord of an English country estate.

Whatever its name, it was a pretty room. Furnished in airy wicker, with a plantation-style ceiling fan, it offered a panoramic view of their pristine backyard and orderly garden. Candy sat in one of the floral-cushioned wicker chairs on one side of the glass-topped round table, and I sat down opposite her, in front of the other Staffordshire place setting.

She shifted in her chair awkwardly. "Would you like some water?"

No. What I'd really like is for you to quit being all Emily Gilmore-ish and just tell me about my mother so I can get out of here.

"Okay," I said.

She poured water from the Waterford pitcher into our crystal goblets.

"Thanks. Now, about my mother—"

"Oh, Estella, there you are," she said, relief evident in her voice, as the cook-cum-housekeeper arrived with a crystal salad bowl. "Estella's made her lovely salmon salad for us. I remember how much you like it." Candy placed her linen napkin on her lap and started to fill my plate. "Just say when."

I snorted. "Well, that's a first. You sure you don't want to measure out my portion?"

Candy flushed and returned the serving spoon to the bowl. "I guess I deserve that."

"Ya think?" I sat up straighter in my chair. "I'm really not hungry, Candy. I know—those are words you would have killed to hear while I was growing up. Well, I'm saying them now, so can we just cut to the chase, please? What is it you want?"

Her hand trembled, and she took a sip of water. "I'm sorry for what your father said about your mother, Freddie, especially while you were working. That wasn't the time or the place."

I longed to throttle her not-so-taut throat. (Looked like someone was due for another chin tuck.) "Just tell me about my mother," I said, my stomach lurching at the possibility of finally meeting her after all these years. "Do you know where she is?"

Candy sent me a look of compassion—a look I'd never seen on her face before.

And I knew.

"I'm afraid your mother's dead, Freddie. She died more than fifteen years ago."

I sucked in my breath.

Then she told me the whole story.

Candy sighed. "Your father met your mother at one of those Renaissance Faire things in Napa Valley. Her name was Susie Kowalski, and she was from Fresno, but your father didn't know that when they met. He only knew her as Fauna."

"Fauna?"

She nodded. "That's what she rechristened herself. It was the seventies, and she was a free-spirited type who worked all the Renaissance Faires throughout California and the Pacific Northwest—usually playing the role of a lusty tavern wench who served mead and grog." Her fingers tightened on the stem of her goblet. "Your father let some friends drag him to the Faire. Unlikely as it seems, he and Fauna had a little too much grog and ended up spending a drunken weekend together." Candy reached out tentatively to touch my hand. "And eight months later, Fauna showed up on your father's doorstep—enormously pregnant and demanding money."

I yanked my hand back. "Are you telling me I'm the product of a drunken one-night stand?"

She gave me a sad smile. "Well, not exactly. They did spend the entire weekend together."

"And that makes me feel so much better," I said. "A two-night stand, instead." My mouth felt like the dusty Iraqi Army had marched through it. I took a long drink of water. "Go on."

Candy hesitated.

"Tell me everything. The whole story. I deserve that, don't you think?"

She nodded. "I've always thought so, and I've wanted to tell you several times over the years, but your father wouldn't hear of it." She fiddled with her wine glass. "And you know how your father can be."

"You mean Dad the control freak? The man who's never wrong

and whose word is law?" I quirked a bitter smile. "I thought it was just me he controlled."

"Oh no. Not by a long shot. He was just more demanding of you because you were, after all, the only product of his loins." She gave a little snort. "That's exactly how he always put it."

"But is he sure about that? I mean, if my mo—this Fauna person—had a wild weekend with him, who's to say there weren't others?"

"That's exactly what your father thought," Candy said. "He was tempted to laugh in her face and just send her away. Especially since"—she shrugged an apology—"she was so . . . large. She'd put on a *lot* of weight during her pregnancy, and it definitely wasn't all baby. Frederick was disgusted by the sight of her, and he was disgusted with himself for having ever touched her." She hurried on. "Although, of course, she hadn't been that big when he met her. Or he'd never have given her a second glance, no matter how drunk he was. You know how he is . . ."

Yeah. Just a little.

"Anyway, your father did figure he wasn't the only one. If she'd slept with him so readily, then she'd probably slept with others. But . . . your father also desperately wanted an heir.

"You see, he'd contracted a virulent case of chicken pox that rendered him sterile. His doctor told him he'd never be able to father a child." She looked off into the distance, a sad smile tugging at her lips. "And he never did—again. So if there was even the possibility that this child was his, he wanted it. He wanted you," she said gently.

"No, he wanted a boy, someone to carry on the family name. I've always known that."

Candy sighed. "Your father decided to take Fauna in for the final month of her pregnancy so he could keep an eye on her and also keep her out of sight from everyone. The moment she had the baby, he'd have a paternity test run to find out if it was his or not," she said. "If it was, he'd keep the baby, pay her off, and send her on her way. If not, then he'd just send her on her way with her baby and not a penny."

Candy twisted her wedding ring. "Your father and I had started dating by then, so I was spending time at the house and I saw a lot of your mo—Fauna. Confinement wasn't good for her." Candy sighed. "She developed an insatiable appetite and continued to eat and eat, gaining an extra twenty-three pounds in the final month of her pregnancy."

"Which I'm sure thrilled Dad to no end," I said dryly.

"He didn't have much contact with her," Candy said. "He preferred to keep his distance."

"Interesting how some things never change."

She gave me a reflective look. "Yes . . . isn't it? Anyway, after you were born, the paternity test proved you were his child. Your father, true to his word, paid Fauna off, and she left town. Eagerly."

"Eagerly?"

Candy gave me another sad smile. "I'm afraid she wasn't really the motherly type. She admitted as much."

"So good to know that neither of my parents wanted me."

"Oh no," Candy protested. "Your father wanted you very much. He paid her, didn't he? More than once."

"What do you mean, 'more than once'?"

She looked down at her plate. "I'm afraid Fauna contacted Frederick twice more demanding money. Once when you were seven, and again four years later."

"So my father kept her from seeing me?"

"She never wanted to see you," Candy whispered, shooting me a look of regret. "And after that last time, we never heard from her again. Two years later, we read in the *Chronicle* that she'd died of a heart attack. She was still working those Renaissance Faires when she died."

"But she must have cared a little," I said in a small voice. "You said she wanted to name me Angelica. You don't give a name like that to a baby you don't want."

A tear escaped Candy's eye and found its way down a barely visible laugh line. "I'm so sorry, Freddie. I made that up to . . . to make you feel better."

She sniffed and paused, as if debating whether to tell me something else. And finally she did. "*Angelica* was the name I'd always wanted to name a little girl if I ever had one. Which I didn't. And I guess I wasn't much of a mother to you, either." She gave me a sad smile.

No you weren't. But then how could you be when you were married to my father? I saw it all so clearly now. Candy was in the same situation as I'd been in all those years—longing for and wanting Frederick Heinz's love and approval, but never getting it.

"What's your real name, Candy?" I asked her softly.

"Real name?" She gave me a puzzled look.

"Your real name isn't Candy, is it?"

"Of course."

"Oh. I thought it might be short for Candice or something."

"Oh no." She giggled. "My Mama and Daddy said I was the sweetest little thing they ever did see—sweet as candy, so that's what they named me." She gave me a girlish smile that quickly faded.

"Speaking of candy, I have a confession to make, Freddie. Your daddy's the one who ordered me to search your room for candy bars. And he had me put the lock on the refrigerator door." Candy released a defeated sigh. "He did everything he could to prevent you from turning out like her . . . and I went along with him because I was crazy in love.

"And," she lowered her head, "he introduced me to so many nice things—he *bought* me so many nice things."

She lifted her head, her eyes imploring me to understand. "I wasn't used to that. I didn't have much growing up, and your father gave me so many things I'd never have had otherwise." Her eyes flashed. "But I've been trying for years to think of how to leave him and get out from under his cruel thumb. And seeing what you've done—the changes you've made in your life—has given me courage to be more independent."

Whoa. My prestige-conscious stepmother leaving her privileged society position as Mrs. Frederick Heinz Jr.? I must be in an alternate universe.

Candy took a deep breath and rushed on. "I was thinking . . . maybe I could join you and your friend in your catering business?" She gave me a pleading look. "I have some great connections and could get you sooo much business."

What? Not only leaving my father, but wanting a job? And not only that, but with me—her imperfect, plus-sized stepdaughter?

Now I know I'm in an alternate universe.

I felt a sudden rush of sympathy for Candy. My lifelong enemy. And something else, too. Not mother-daughter bonding—I didn't see that ever happening—but maybe, just maybe, something like the tentative beginnings of a possible friendship?

"I'll talk to Deborah and see what she says." I gave Candy a reassuring smile. "I'm not sure if she'd be ready for another partner at the moment, but we always need someone dependable to help. How soon could you start?"

Candy's makeup-free eyes widened. "Oh I couldn't leave just yet. I have some minor surgery I need to get taken care of first."

Well, of course you do. What was I thinking?

. . . .

"So apparently I didn't break my mother's pelvis when I was born after all," I said to Deborah that night when I recounted the whole Fauna saga—except for Candy's wild and flighty idea of wanting to work with us . . . someday. That part I left out.

Deborah shook her head. "Honey, that sure is some story. Sounds like something from *Days of Our Lives*. How come your stepmother never told you all this before? I mean, after all these years?"

"My father swore her to secrecy—and everyone else too."

"How do you know that?"

"I called a woman who cooked for us when I was young—her name's Priscilla. She confirmed everything."

"Oh." Deborah's eyes brimmed. "I'm so sorry, Freddie."

"Me too, but it sure explains a lot."

. . . .

The Rubenesque beauty with porcelain skin and flowing auburn locks was the belle of the Renaissance Faire in her green velvet gown. Every man wanted to dance with her. Every man wanted to claim her as his bride.

But my mother said no to all of them because there was only one who had a claim on her heart.

She held out her soft white hand to me with its square-cut costume-jewelry emerald winking in the sunshine.

I placed my small, childish hand in hers, and together we ran and frolicked over the grounds.

That night, even though it was a warm summer evening, I couldn't stop shivering.

. . . .

I couldn't sleep. Instead, I alternately paced and wept and held a squirming Zsa Zsa close as my mind replayed the events of the day—the revelation that confirmed what I'd always somehow known about my mother. And my father.

The cold reality that neither one had ever loved me the way a child needs to be loved.

Finally, as dawn filtered through my window blinds, I did what I should have done when I first went to bed. I prayed. And prayed.

Spent and weary, but with a measure of peace, I padded down to the kitchen for a cup of Earl Grey.

"Deborah! What are you doing up so early?"

"I needed me a little time in the Word." She took a sip from her favorite fat yellow mug, which bore the same scripture as the entrance to her house: "Taste and see that the Lord is good." Then she grimaced. "This coffee's gone cold. Would you mind dumping it and getting me some fresh?" She extended the mug to me over her open Bible.

After filling the teakettle with water, I crossed over to the coffeemaker to pour Deborah a fresh cup.

I was adding the cream and sweetener she liked when her rich, deep voice—albeit softer than normal—gently punctured the morning air.

"Here's what I was reading this morning," she said. "Listen. It's Jesus talking." Then she read aloud from Matthew: "'Who is my mother, and who are my brothers?' Pointing to his disciples he said, 'Here are my mother and my brothers. For whoever does the will of my Father in heaven is my brother and sister and mother.'"

    She didn't say anything else.

    She didn't have to.

    I set the coffee mug down with shaky hands and turned misty eyes to my friend . . . my sister . . . my mother.

:: *chapter twenty-five* ::

It was time to make some changes. And Deborah's love and kindness—basically God with skin on—gave me the courage I needed to make them. I started with an appointment to get my hair cut and weaved at a pricey salon. Normally I just went to SpeedyCuts and paid twelve bucks for a trim every two months, but this one time I decided to shell out the big bucks.

When I looked in the mirror, I knew the result was worth every penny. My hair fell in a blunt cut that flattered my face, and the subtle red and gold streaks looked natural and "kissed by the sun" as the stylist said. What's more, my eyes popped. Always my best feature, they now took center stage on my face.

When they told me the price, I decided that although I was still worth it, from here on out I'd go for the weave-in-a-box instead.

I also started using tan-in-a-bottle, but only on my legs, so I wouldn't blind the women in my water aerobics class with all my pasty whiteness. After my first try, which left me with orange streaks for a week, I got the knack of applying it—a definite improvement. And the legs themselves were getting a little firmer, thanks to the aerobics.

And my daily walks with Zsa Zsa.

And my swimming—which I'd begun doing at the same club where we did aerobics. I figured since I had the bathing suit, I might as well use it. And I loved the feeling of weightlessness and the velvety feel of the water on my skin. I also enjoyed how graceful, strong, and powerful my swim workouts made me feel.

I even suspected I was losing weight, though I hadn't actually had time to weigh myself. And when Deborah and I went to Payne Tryon to find replacements for some of the clothes that had been ruined in the bathroom flood, I found the same sizes looked a little more hip and hung better on me.

I bought a few pairs of cute capris, a couple of camisoles and sundresses, and even a white tank. Plus some nice black slacks, a slinky black skirt and top, and a black scoop-necked tunic.

"Nuh-uh, you ain't gettin' any more black," Deborah said when she saw my selections. "This is your new start, and you need to celebrate with color."

"I am, but I want some black too."

"I don't think so—other than maybe this one pair of black dress pants. Every woman needs one good pair of black pants," she acknowledged as she picked up my other choices and headed for the racks.

"Stop right there."

"Say what?"

"I told you that I want some black, Deborah. I *like* black. You've got to stop trying to make me over into what you think I should be. It's *my* body and *my* life, and if I want to wear black from head to toe, that's *my* choice!"

Deborah stared at me.

"I'm sorry." I was instantly contrite. "I didn't mean to yell at you."

But Deborah's mouth curved into a pleased smile. "Well, it's about time."

"What?"

She began to applaud. "You finally stood up for yourself, girl. Good for you." Deborah grinned. "I know I was taking this fairy-godmother a little too far, but I knew that sooner or later you'd give me what for. I just didn't know it'd take you so long." She handed me back the hangers of black. "I especially like this one shirt with the scooped neck."

. . . .

Isaiah Truedell came out from Georgia for a visit a few weeks later, after I'd returned to Brooke's and my beautiful, newly remodeled bathroom and closet.

I was impressed. This was one good-looking young man. But too young for me, of course. Besides, he brought a surprise with him—a fiancée named Beth.

"*That* I wasn't expecting," Deborah huffed on the phone when she called to tell me. "Isaiah's completely gone, and so is she. But she seems real nice and sweet, and she's a Christian, so that's good. And she's asked me if I'll teach her some of Isaiah's favorite recipes. So tonight we're making pecan pie."

"Hey," I protested. "You won't even give me your pecan pie recipe."

"Honey," she said, "I didn't say I was going to teach her *everything.*"

. . . .

I joined the weight-loss class at church, not for the weight-loss aspect so much as the fellowship. And the Bible study—my leather-bound NIV got a daily workout as a result.

At home, I cooked for Brooke and Jon once a week—if my schedule allowed. And I got rid of my orange food containers that used to hide my food, replacing them with see-through ones instead.

I also blogged for the last time.

To All My Friends in the Blogosphere:

In America, we always seem to think bigger is better. Except when it comes to people.

I started this blog because I'm a big girl, or rather woman, and I was fed up with the way the world treated me. There were, and still are, those who were mean or thoughtless, and there were many others who looked right through me as if I were invisible. To them I was invisible, because I didn't fit the accepted standard of womanly beauty. I was big, so I didn't really count.

And for years I went along with that. I walked around with my head low and my shoulders hunched over, trying not to call attention to myself. To hide away from the world because I wasn't thin enough, pretty enough, worthy enough.

But not any longer. This big girl is changing her tune.

I don't think I'll ever be thin enough to fit into society's skewed view of the ideal woman. I'm just not built that way. But I've realized it's not society's view that matters. It's mine. And, more importantly, God's.

Who loves me just the way I am.

Remember that great old Billy Joel song from the seventies? "Just the Way You Are"? That's my mantra these days.

I was going to sign off there, because that's a great

killer ending, don't you think? All strong and confident and cool and together. In writing, you always want to leave 'em with a killer ending.

But I'm not a writer. I'm a caterer. A baker-turned-caterer actually. And I have a confession to make. A *mea culpa*.

A while back someone wrote to call me on my--and other big women's--exclusion of women who weren't in the Big Girl Club. And I realized I've been doing the same thing I accused the rest of the world at large of doing . . . excluding someone because of their size.

Pot. Kettle. Black.

It also made me face the hard fact that I'd done the same thing to a former coworker of mine who just happens to be slim and drop-dead gorgeous. I was judging N. by her appearance rather than by who she is: a sweet, fun, and generous young woman who has never been anything but kind and friendly to me.

And for that I apologize. And promise to try and be better in the future. I'm working on it. I'm working on a lot of things. I've decided that even though God and I love me just the way I am, that doesn't mean I can't put a little effort into becoming a little better.

Not for society's sake. Not for my family or friends' sake. But for my sake, and God's.

What I won't be working on anymore is this blog. Today is my last post. I don't feel the need to rant anymore, and I really don't have the time either.

Life is full. Life is good. I'm a happy girl.

So thanks for listening and for sharing. I wish you all *big* happiness.

Ciao, Betty

．．．．

I was cleaning out the fridge one afternoon, wearing old jeans and a ratty T-shirt when (naturally) I heard a knock on the back door.

When I opened it, there stood Simon.

The same Simon who'd been studiously avoiding me at church ever since the Hal date-night debacle. I'd tried to approach him once or twice to talk, but he always hurried away before I could reach him. I'd even consented to visit Friar Tuck's with the Truedells, but while his mom and sister were guardedly cordial, Simon never made an appearance.

Finally, regretfully, I'd written him off.

But now, here he stood with a determined look in his eye. And a hand behind his back.

"Simon." My heart fluttered, and I pushed a stray hair behind my ear, conscious of my disheveled appearance. "What a surprise. Would you like to come in?"

"No, thank you," he said in that delicious accent that made me want to jump into his arms. "I just came to say something."

His words tumbled out in a rush. "I know that you're seeing that vet, but I've been thinking about you and thinking about you. And I finally had to come tell you that I thought we had a really great connection, something special that night we met. Something I haven't had with anyone else, and I don't want to lose that."

He stuck out his chin. "I just came to serve notice that I plan to fight for you. So tell your vet friend to be prepared to do battle."

He pulled his hand from behind his back and thrust a bunch of wildflowers at me. "Oh, and these are for you." He started to turn and walk away.

"Uh, Simon?"

"Yes?"

"I'm not dating Hal. We haven't been out again since that night in your restaurant."

He just stood there on the step, still half turned away. Then that delicious slow smile suddenly spread across his face.

"Oh. Well, in that case . . ."

· · · ·

The doorbell rang a few nights later when I was putting on my mascara. Knowing Simon's goofy Siamese cat phobia, I hurried to finish so he wouldn't have to encounter Eliza on our first date. But in my haste, I smeared mascara on my cheek and had to start again.

By the time I joined Brooke and Simon in the living room, Simon was sitting uncertainly on the couch with a purring Eliza in his lap.

"Nice kitty," he said, awkwardly patting her back.

Zsa Zsa jumped on the couch in rescue mode and fixed her lone eye on Eliza as if to say, "Back off. My mom likes this guy. And besides, he can bring us fresh meat."

At the upscale seafood restaurant where one of Simon's friends was the chef, we continued the résumé game we'd begun at our first meeting.

"Favorite books?" I asked him over a yummy meal of fresh cracked crab, green salad, and sourdough bread.

"The Bible, the Terry Brooks Shannara series, and anything by Bill Bryson."

"I love Bill Bryson's travel books—sooo funny! Favorite sports and leisure activity?"

"Sailing or riding my Hog." His eyes lit up. "I want to take you for a ride."

"Not in this universe."

"Aw c'mon. I've got an extra black leather jacket you can borrow."

"And I've got a pink tutu that would look really nice on you."

"Okay, okay. Point taken. Favorite bo—"

"Freddie! How are you? It's been a while." Zsa Zsa's shaggy vet beamed at me.

"Hi, Hal. How are you?" I nodded across the table. "You remember Simon, don't you?"

"How could I forget?" Hal reached down to shake Simon's hand. "The chef from our one and only date. I knew I didn't stand a chance when I saw the sparks flying between you guys."

I blushed as Simon shook Hal's hand with a pleased smile. "Good to see you again, Doc. How's the vet business?"

"Going well"—he sent me a teasing look—"especially since I haven't had any dogs in lately with a taste for *War and Peace* or *A Tale of Two Cities*. So how's my favorite one-eyed dog doing these days? Brooke told me she'd recovered nicely from her dietary indiscretion."

"Zsa Zsa's doing great." I grinned. "She's lost her taste for literature and is going after Brooke's tofu now instead."

Hal barked out a laugh. "Well, someone has to like it." He touched my shoulder. "Well, I'll let you two get back to your dinner. Nice seeing you again." He ambled off.

Simon adjusted his glasses. "So, as I was saying . . . what are your favorite books?"

"Aside from the Bible, *Anne of Green Gables*, *Little Women*, and most English mysteries."

"Okay. Favorite sports and leisure activity?"

"Walking, swimming, water aerobics, and cooking."

"We've got to do that!" His lips curved upward in a pleased smile.

"What? You're excited about the water aerobics? Sorry, bucko. For women only."

"No, I mean the cooking. We should cook together sometime."

I shook my head. "You'd cook rings around me, Chef Man."

"I don't think so. I still remember that superb potato salad you made the first night we met."

"And how could I forget that yummy shepherd's pie?" I fluttered my lashes at him.

"See! Wouldn't you like to learn to make shepherd's pie?" He sent me an innocent look, then waggled his eyebrows. "I'll share my recipe if you'll share yours."

When he pulled into my driveway at the end of the evening, Simon said, "Oh, by the way, one of the things I left off my résumé . . . I'm addicted to blogs. There's a few travel and cooking blogs I read regularly, and a few months ago I started on this new cooking blog by a female chef I especially like. And it was linked to another blog called *The Rantings of Betty Bigg.*"

I sucked in my breath.

He continued as if he hadn't heard. "You know, I really liked Betty. She started up this dialogue between people about how big women are treated differently and how the world looks upon them and everything. She made a lot of good points, and I liked what she had to say. But . . ."

"But?" I shifted in my seat.

He turned and fixed his hazel eyes gently on me. "But I always detected a lot of anger beneath her calls to equality. Until recently, that is."

"Oh?"

"Yes. In her final blog it sounded as if she'd made peace with some of her demons. Sounded like the anger was gone."

He locked his eyes on mine. "Is it gone? The anger?"

I nodded. "Got a better outlet for my energies."

"Good." He leaned over and captured my mouth in a kiss.

A kiss that left college-boy Greg, the former love of my life, in the dust.

:: *chapter twenty-six* ::

A month later, Deborah, Millie, and Simon threw me a birthday party for my thirtieth birthday.

I wore my favorite pair of dressy black pants and a red silk
tank with a sheer red overblouse. My pedicured feet gleamed fire-
engine red—my new ruby toe ring, a gift from Deborah and
Lydia, winking up at me—but I stuck to clear polish on my
French-manicured hands.

Deborah and Simon did all the cooking—a sumptuous array
of Southern and British foods (ribs, roast beef, fish and chips . . .)
with enough vegetarian offerings to accommodate Brooke and
Jon. And Millie and Shane contributed the cake, a tall, dense,
chocolate-orange torte with thick fudge frosting that wasn't even
on Jorgensen's list of offerings.

"Mmm, this cake is da bomb," Deborah said. "I do have a
weakness for chocolate."

"You sure do, sug'." Simon draped an arm around her neck
and pulled her close. "Me too."

Hal came and brought his new girlfriend—Shauna, the
marathon runner, who enjoyed hiking and backpacking with him.

Even Anya stopped by and managed to spend an entire

evening without reverting to her usual snarky self. She spent a lot of time with Lydia and baby Samuel, holding him and making faces to try and get him to laugh. After a few awkward moments, she also discovered that while she wasn't exactly a dog lover, she was definitely a Zsa Zsa lover.

Who could blame her? My dog seemed under the distinct impression that the party was for her. She went from person to person, greeting her fans, and even outschmoozing my former boss.

The only person not on the guest list was my biological father. That's how I thought of him now. But Candy surprised me by showing up—and, to my delight, bringing along our old cook, Priscilla.

"Thank you, Candy." We hugged tentatively.

Simon was in the midst of telling Deborah and me his recipe for Scotch eggs when Deborah's cell rang.

She grimaced. "Sorry. I meant to turn this thing off." She glanced at the number and frowned. "It's an Atlanta area code, but I don't recognize the number. Maybe it's Isaiah's fiancée." She flipped open her phone. "Hi. This is Deborah."

Her face went gray, and she clenched the phone tight. "What? When? Oh dear Jesus. Oh dear Jesus." She started rocking back and forth.

And then she sat down hard.

Samuel hurried over. "Sug', what is it?"

"It's Isaiah," she answered numbly.

Samuel took the phone from her. "Who is this? What's happened?" His eyes filled with tears as he listened, and he gathered Deborah in his arms as she began to wail.

"Mama, Daddy." Lydia sounded frantic. "What's wrong?"

Samuel swallowed hard. "Your brother fell and hit his head. That was Beth. He's . . . he hasn't come to yet. They think he might be in a coma."

"No!" Lydia whispered.

Apparently, Isaiah and Beth had been having a picnic in the bleachers at the baseball field on campus. Isaiah had been goofing around, running up and down the bleachers to show off his physical dexterity. But he'd caught a foot on the edge of one of the bleachers and fallen, hitting his head on the concrete.

He was still unconscious, and the prognosis didn't look good.

I booked the entire family on the next available flight to Atlanta, and Simon and I drove them to the airport.

. . . .

For the next three weeks, Deborah, Samuel, Lydia, and Beth kept vigil by Isaiah's bedside.

Back in California, I prayed and prayed while I continued to run A Touch of Honey, calling in Shane and Nicole for backup as needed. Simon even pinch-hit a time or two—an incredible sacrifice of time since he worked such long hours at his restaurant.

Finally, late one night, my phone rang, and I dreaded the thought of what I might hear.

"Freddie?" It was Deborah, and she was crying. But they were tears of joy. "My baby's going to be all right. He's going to be all right. He's out of the coma, thank you, Jesus!"

Thank you, indeed.

. . . .

Even though Isaiah was out of the woods, his recovery was still going to be a long, hard road.

Deborah gave me all the details when she flew back to Lantana the following week. Samuel, Lydia, and the baby stayed in Decatur with Isaiah. "The doctors say it will be months of rehabilitation and hard work before Isaiah's back to his old self,"

Deborah said. "And even then, he may never be exactly as he was before." She lifted her chin. "But we're praying and trusting the Lord for the outcome, whatever that may be. We're just happy he's still here with us." She gave me a tired smile.

Isaiah's accident had taken its toll on Deborah. She'd dropped some weight and developed new lines around her eyes and mouth. And when she removed her scarf, I saw she was now completely bald.

She rubbed her smooth head. "How do you like my eightball?"

"Very nice." I reached out and patted it. "So smooth."

"Just like a baby's behind," Deborah said. It felt good to laugh together.

Deborah rubbed her eyes and sighed. "Freddie, there's something I need to tell you, and I'm not sure how."

My throat clenched. "Is it Isaiah—something else the doctors said?"

"No, no. Like I said, he's going to be fine. It's just going to take some time." She took a deep breath. "And we're going to need to spend a lot more time with him."

"Well, that's okay. I can handle things at this end." I patted her hand. "You take all the time you need."

"That's the thing." She took another deep breath. "While we were back home with Isaiah, it was as if we'd never left. All our family and church friends jumped in and enveloped us in this warm cocoon of love and prayer, and the Lord showed us he wanted us to come back to Georgia. That that's where we belong, where we need to be—especially now. Our place is by Isaiah's side."

She stole a look at me. "So, we're going to be moving back home to Decatur. All of us."

I gulped. "Even Lydia?"

Deborah nodded. "She realized she only has one brother left, and she didn't want to be that far away from him again. She wants little Samuel to grow up with his Uncle Isaiah." Deborah swallowed. "Freddie. Say something."

I swallowed too. "Well, of course you should move. There's no question. Family is what's most important."

"So you're not upset?"

I smiled over the knot in my stomach. "Well, maybe a little sad, because I'm really going to miss you. But not upset. Not really. I understand."

"Even about the business?"

"What do you mean, the business?"

"Well . . . we'll have to sell it," she nodded her head at the kitchen, "and this house too, of course."

"Sell the business? *Our* business? A Taste of Honey?"

Deborah gulped. "Uh-huh."

"But why?"

"Because we won't be here to run it anymore."

"But I will."

"I know, honey, but we can't afford to keep the business while we're living in Georgia. We have to sell everything so we can start again back home."

"Everything?"

She nodded.

I looked around the kitchen—the big, beautiful killer kitchen that I loved. The place where I'd spent so many happy hours.

And a wild and crazy idea began to take form.

Or maybe not so wild and crazy. Why should I keep renting a room? I'd always dreamed of owning my own home, and I even had money set aside for the day when I was ready to buy.

Could that day be now?

"Deborah . . . what would you think if . . ."

. . . .

We met with an accountant and a Realtor and a lawyer and all sorts of other professionals. And it turned out I *could* afford to buy both the house and the business from Deborah and Samuel. All that money I'd squirreled away over the years was finally going to come in handy.

But I decided I didn't want to buy Samuel and Deborah out completely. Who knew? They might change their minds and move back to California someday. Besides, Deborah would always be A Taste of Honey to me. So they would still be silent partners and have a small stake in the catering business. But I would be the main owner.

Me. Invisible Freddie owning her own house and business.

I made some changes once the transaction was complete— adding some more California cuisine to the menu, including calamari, lettuce wraps, sushi, fondue, my seafood martinis, veggie pizzas, and fresh, interesting salads including one with organic baby greens, bosc pears, candied walnuts, gorgonzola, and balsamic vinaigrette that quickly became a favorite. And while I was at it, I also added a line of gourmet dog biscuits to the catering line, using Zsa Zsa as my official taster.

And while I was making all these changes, I decided there was another important one I wanted to make as well.

. . . .

Two and a half months later, I threw a huge pool party at my new house to celebrate my new home and business. I was now a full-fledged duck to water and had even put in a backyard pool (good thing I had that investment money) so I could swim laps anytime I wanted. Simon and I spent all morning in the kitchen cooking together (I finally relented and gave him my German potato salad recipe) to prepare a sumptuous feast.

He'd just fed me a plump, juicy strawberry from the gorgeous flower-bedecked fruit and vegetable sculpture, and a little of the juice started to trickle down my chin. But he captured it with his mouth, and we were kissing and giggling together.

"Now, that's what I'm talkin' about!"

"Deborah!" We sprang apart, and I hurried over to hug my grinning friend. "I thought you weren't going to be able to make it."

"When have you ever known me to miss a party?" She gave us a knowing look. "Looks like I got here just in time." Deborah sat down on the yellow bar stool, adjusting her lime green pantsuit. "Pass me one of those strawberries, would you, Simon?"

"Anything for you."

She inhaled the strawberry. "Mmm, mmm. That is one thing I have missed about California—all this wonderful fruit."

"How is everyone?" I asked. "Isaiah? Lydia? Little Samuel?"

"They're all fine. Isaiah's getting stronger every day, and the doctor says he's making great progress. And little Sammy—oh, I wish you could see him. Cute as the dickens—looks just like Samuel Junior when he was little." She motioned for me to lean forward, and she gave me a loud smack on the cheek. "And that's from Samuel and Lydia. They said to say hey."

She glanced around the kitchen, taking in the framed travel posters of Paris, London, and Munich. "I like the changes you've made."

"Thanks. I decided to put some of my dreams on the wall so that I can see them every day while I cook."

"But they're not just dreams," Simon said.

Deborah's eyes darted from him to me. "Is there something

you haven't told me?" Her eyes gleamed. "Maybe some big announcement you're planning to make at the party?"

"No." I frowned at Simon. "We're just talking about some future plans—some trips down the road someday . . ."

"Talkin's good." Deborah popped another strawberry in her mouth. "Doin's better."

"I always knew I liked you, Deborah," Simon said. "A woman after my own heart."

I pouted. "I thought *I* was that woman."

Simon grabbed me and planted a big kiss on my lips. "That you are, baby. You've got my heart and so much more."

But Deborah was right. I was planning to make an announcement at the party.

Just not the one she thought.

· · · ·

"Watch out babe," Simon yelled. "Brooke's going to spike it!"

"Got it!" I jumped high out of the water and slapped the volleyball over the net we'd stretched across the pool.

Nicole, on the opposing team, made a valiant reach for the ball, but failed and fell backward with a splash.

"That's game!" Simon crowed. He swept me into his arms and planted a wet kiss on my lips in front of God and everyone. Then he whispered into my ear, "Did I tell you how good you look in that green bathing suit? It matches your beautiful eyes."

His mother glided over in a peach one-piece with a skirted bottom. "Right then, you two, break it up," she said with an affectionate smile. "I think your guests are hungry. I know *I* am."

Simon laughed as we pulled ourselves from the pool. "Caterer's work is never done, right, babe?"

After toweling off, I tied my Hawaiian print sarong around

my suit and joined Nicole, Shane, and Deborah at the buffet table where Deborah was handing Millie an appetizer of miniature crab cakes with tropical fruit salsa.

"Hey Deborah, you're a guest. You're not supposed to be serving."

She filled another plate. "I'm not serving, I was just giving some food to a friend." She winked at Millie and dipped a crab cake into her fruit salsa, then popped it into her mouth. "Mmm, girl, this is *good*! You're gonna have to give me the recipe."

I matched her mischievous grin. "Absolutely. When you give me the rest of your crab puff recipe."

"Well . . . maybe we can work something out. But listen, I got an idea for later."

. . . .

"Freddie, sing louder," Millie urged, glancing at Deborah and putting her hands to her ears.

Deborah stuck her tongue out at Millie and swung her hips faster to "Stop! In the Name of Love." She'd talked me into resurrecting our old Supremes routine—minus the wigs, which she'd left in Georgia.

"You go, Deborah," Shane and Nicole yelled.

"Sing out, sweetie," Simon urged.

And I did sing. And dance. Until I swung my hips just a tad too hard, shifted my weight to catch myself, and brought both Deborah and me collapsing to the floor. And laughing until we were breathless.

"It's all right, girl," she wheezed as we started to help each other up. "Song was tellin' us to stop, right?"

. . . .

"Freddie," Anya said to me with a grin, "Diana Ross has got nothing on you."

"Right," I shot back. "That woman never did get the dance routines down. No rhythm at all."

Anya's face got a little red as she glanced over at Deborah, obviously worrying if she would be offended. My former employer had softened quite a bit in the dragon-lady department over the past months, but she was still pretty high-strung.

Deborah just laughed and put a hand on Anya's bony shoulder. "I've been meaning to tell you, girl—that cake is beautiful."

Anya had helped Shane decorate the sheet cake for the party, complete with "Congratulations" and a tipped-over jar of honey spelling out the words, "A Taste of Honey."

"Very creative," I added to my old boss. "Couldn't have done better myself."

Anya beamed. And I didn't make my big announcement until everybody had a piece of cake.

· · · ·

After everyone had left, and Simon and I were alone cleaning up, he came up behind me while I was washing dishes and nuzzled my neck. "I like your new name, babe. It suits you."

That was my announcement.

A whole new me.

With a brand-new name. One I liked.

Freddie didn't fit. Besides, I'd always hated it. And I'd certainly never been a Fredericka—no matter how hard my biological father tried to force me to be. I had no desire to be a Fauna. And Betty Bigg didn't fit anymore either.

Instead, from now on, I would simply be Kate—although Simon could call me his Katie. Which he could now do in public.

He turned on the stereo and tugged me away from the sink. "Katie, love, I think we should have another party soon so you can let everyone know about your *other* name change."

Simon gave me that delicious slow smile that warmed me all over. And then he slow-danced me around the room to Billy Joel's "Just the Way You Are."

:: *And for dessert . . .* ::

Anya fell in love with the art of baking and sold half-interest in the bakery to Shane and Nicole, whose joyous wedding was catered by A Taste of Honey and featured a first-ever hamster groom's cake. Anya, meanwhile, went back to culinary school. Two years later, she married her teacher, dropped out of school, and had a beautiful little boy she named Emeril.

Millie retired and bought a condo in a seniors complex in Florida, close to her kids and grandkids, where she's teaching community college courses on film and cake decorating, taking salsa dance lessons, and juggling three admirers.

Brooke and Jon got married in a sprouts and tofu ceremony catered by A Taste of Honey. Henry and Eliza were the ring bearers. Trouble is, not even Brooke could manage to get cats to take orders. The couple is blissful, but they still haven't found the rings.

Hal, the vet, and Shauna, the marathon runner, entered the Boston Marathon and placed in the Top Twenty. Now they're hoping to squeeze the Ironman Triathlon and the National Dog Agility trials into the same month.

Deborah and Samuel returned to Africa as missionaries, where she lost thirteen pounds and became an authority on native dance.

She and Samuel are now proud parents of a little adopted African boy they named Simon. Deborah tells me he looks just like Samuel, but I'm taking that with a grain of salt.

Deborah's son Isaiah recovered fully from his injuries and married his fiancée, Beth, whose pecan pie now rivals his mama's. Beth and Isaiah took over the family catering business. Meanwhile, Lydia married Isaiah's physical therapist, and baby Samuel—who talks up a storm—is soon going to have twin sisters.

The culinary team of Simon and Kate (née Freddie) Shattuck are famous in the Lantana/Sacramento region for their flagship restaurant, Friar Tuck's, their Taste of Honey catering services, their line of gourmet dog biscuits, and their innovative motorcycle-based food-delivery service (brilliantly managed by Simon's sister, Henri). And for living their lives in the biggest, boldest way possible.

After suffering a broken heart from the boxer down the street, Zsa Zsa fell in love with a chow/terrier mix. They had a passel of pups that came out looking like the Tribbles from that old *Star Trek* episode. She's now retired from the puppy business and content to take care of the house—especially baby Deborah Kate.

And everyone, of course, lived happily every after.

:: Acknowledgments ::

Without these people lending their help and expertise behind the scenes, *Miss Invisible* would have had to be retitled *Miss Not There Yet*. So heartfelt thanks to:

Becky Danek and the hardworking staff at Danek's Bakery in Carmichael for answering my myriad bakery questions and for all the yummy treats! With special thanks to Tammy Salcedo, cake artist extraordinaire, who took the time to demonstrate the art of cake decorating and to answer further questions.

Debbie Rothermel, my sweet sister-in-law, for all her cake-decorating tips and the beautiful gift of our wedding cake, which was the inspiration for some of the wedding cakes Freddie created. Also for the great eating-cake-from-the-van story!

Michelle Fails, for the down-home Southern cooking tips, Betty Curtis, for all the pet help and for giving me the idea for one-eyed Zsa Zsa. Also Laura Cowan for the childbirth breathing tips; Sharon Hetland for her Danish-layer-cake recipe inspiration; Florbela Souza for all the catering hints; Jennie Damron for all the scoop on twins and babies; foodie Anne Peterson for myriad delightful menu suggestions (including the seafood martinis idea); and Pat McLatchey, who *really* invented the dish I call

Tuscan chicken. And finally, Lana and Michael Yarbrough for my Elk Grove writing getaway and Chef Michael for all those delicious dinners. (Thanks for the defined biceps too, Lana.)

Kelli Standish, for the Gap mirror conversation and for always cheering me on. If I looked up *encouragement* in the dictionary, it would say: "Kelli Standish."

Mary Griffith, who loosely (but not as largely) inspired Deborah and who vetted her language in early chapters. And Toni Terrell for the dance music tips.

Renee Reed, Ami's "fluffy" friend, for her first-reader response and for the great "hail damage" cellulite description.

Gracie, our lovable canine daughter, whose spirit inspired propeller-tail Zsa Zsa (but who has both eyes and no penchant for paperbacks).

Editors Ami McConnell and Anne Christian Buchanan, who work invisibly behind the scenes to help make my writing sing. You rock!

Ditto Beth Jusino, my agent, who always cracks me up.

Special thanks to my dear friend Annette Smith, for reading early chapters and liking them, really liking them. Also for reading later chapters at the last minute and offering much-needed encouragement—and pot-liquor answers—when I was ready to call the men in the white coats.

Finally, to my beloved and longsuffering husband, Michael . . . thank you for everything, honey. There must be a special place in heaven reserved for the husbands of neurotic authors.

:: *Reading Group Guide* ::

1. *Miss Invisible* begins with the line, "One size does not fit all." In our looks-obsessed society, could you relate to that comment?

2. It's been said that fat is the last acceptable prejudice. Would you agree? And why do you think that is?

3. Have you ever felt invisible because of your size? And was it men or women who made you feel that way?

4. Have you ever hidden from the world—made yourself invisible by how you dress and act—to prevent yourself from getting hurt or disappointed?

5. In Freddie's fantasy world—and in her Betty Bigg blog— she's always saying or doing things that she doesn't have the courage to do in real life. Are you guilty of doing the same thing? Or do you have the courage to stand up for yourself to others—politely and diplomatically?

6. Who was your favorite female character in the book and why?

7. Freddie's friendship with the plus-size, outgoing, content-in-her-own-skin Deborah, helps her to blossom and grow

into the woman God wants her to be. Do you have a
Deborah in your life that has helped you do the same?

8. Were Freddie's problems and insecurities due to her bigness?
Or did they stem from the fact that she was abused (mainly
from her perfectionist father) and was attracted to other
abusers? Or maybe both?

9. Do you ever find yourself judging large people in restaurants
when you see them eating dessert and think, "Well, no
wonder she's so big! She's stuffing her face with cheesecake!"
Now that you've grown to know Freddie and Deborah, will
you still react this way?

10. Who was your favorite male character in the book? Hal,
Simon, Samuel, or Shane, the intern?

11. As women, we all have issues with our bodies. Did you
like the fact that by the end of the book Freddie became
comfortable enough in her own skin to not only wear a
bathing suit in mixed company, but to also relax and have
fun in a co-ed volleyball game in the pool? Would you have
been able to do that?

12. How did you feel about Freddie changing her name to Kate
at the end of the book? Did you agree with her decision?

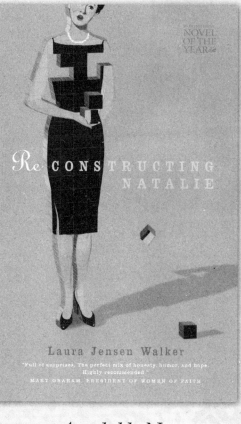

Enjoy these other books by

Laura Jensen Walker

THOMAS NELSON, INC.
Since 1798